The Man Who
Lost Himself

The Man
Who Lost Himself

by
OSBERT SITWELL

Published in New York by
COWARD-McCANN, INC.
IN THE YEAR 1930

Printed in the U. S. A.

FOR

MARGARET GREVILLE

IN ALL AFFECTION
AND
BECAUSE SHE IS SO
CONSTANT A FRIEND

Caution to Readers

The author begs humbly to point out that all the characters in this book, including himself, are entirely fictitious.   He can no more now take the responsibility for his own views in the future, should there be one, than for those of the other persons he has created.

Preface

IN this book the author has essayed to carry further a method, which, for all his humility, he claims to have originated in " Before the Bombardment." Convinced that movement is not in itself enough, that no particular action or sequence of actions is in itself of sufficient concern to dare lay claim to the intelligent attention of the reader, that adventures of the mind and soul are more interesting, because more mysterious, than those of the body, and yet that, on the other hand, the essence does not reside to any much greater degree in the tangle of reason, unreason and previous history, in which each action, event and thought is founded, but is to be discovered, rather, in that balance, so difficult to achieve, which lies between them, he has attempted to write a book which might best be described as a Novel of Reasoned Action.

This book has not been easy to write. He modestly hopes it may be less difficult to read—for, alas, so many authors write novels which, it appears to the reader, must have been easier to write than they are to read.

The difficulties persisted to the end. Though he had finished it, he still fretted over the various stages of the story he had unfolded. And one night, even, the Deity appeared to the author in a dream (absit Dr. Freud!) and pronounced his opinion. He was a good, old-fashioned god, with flashing eyes and a long, piebald beard—" not in the least like a clergyman," as the author remembers having rather inconse-

quently reflected in his dream—and issued in a considerable measure of appropriate glory out of a large, white cloud. "If you had only paid a little attention to the way I wanted the book written," he said, " it might—nay, it would—have been a very different production. All the time you were at work, I was putting out suggestions to you. Especially I wished for a different ending. You gave no heed to me. But now the harm is done, and I must positively refuse to take any responsibility in the matter."

It seems only fair, therefore, to give this disclaimer, damping as it was, full publicity. Any blame there is—at any rate if it concerns the end of the story—must attach to the author rather than his Creator.

But this was not all. The very moment the book was finished, and to be called, as the writer had long planned, " The Man Who Found Himself," it was discovered that a novel of identical name was announced by the publishers as ready for publication in the following week. This was, of course, quite accidental, for ideas hang about in the air over our heads in much the same way that fish glide and linger in a pool, and one author is as likely to hook a title as another. It was none the less disheartening, for the name so well fitted this book which now sees the light. However, after mature reflection, the help of a few friends—and one, in particular, to whom the writer now makes his grateful acknowledgments—it suddenly became plain that if a Man has Found, he must also have Lost, Himself. Accordingly the book is so entitled.

ALGECIRAS,   O. S.

August, 1929.

The Man Who
Lost Himself

WITH the years that pass, the background of the mind, increasingly enriched, grows ever more absorbing in its interest. The solution of many a thing, that at the time constituted a mystery, is revealed in the light of those occurrences which preceded and followed it. Old people, then, do not so much live in their recollections as in the unlooked-for relationship between them. The various threads—whether an event, or the action of a person—of which memory is composed form themselves into a tapestry, manifest a design that was not visible in earlier years : a design which—and this for the elderly is a tragedy—can never be seen complete in one lifetime, however long its span ; must always be left behind one with the threads hanging and broken.

Yet there are but few things belonging to the personal and more or less immediate past which do not explain themselves in terms of the general pattern, and it is possible that by examining, in connection with those earlier events which he confided to me, the known facts of Tristram Orlander's death, and by giving these the direction implicit in the former—by, as it were, attempting to bring out and finish the design—we may reach a just conclusion as to that which took place. Whether my conjecture, however fantastic it may appear, is an accurate reconstruction of his end, no one can ever definitely pronounce. Indeed, the fear of being dismissed as a superstitious and credulous simpleton would have prevented me from making these facts, and the subsequent deduced fictions, public, did I not feel so certain that, since the whole affair belongs to literary history, they should be recorded. I have therefore decided to add to that part of my narrative, in itself difficult to believe, but which I heard from his own lips, those perhaps grotesque inferences that fit on to the first and in with the later actual events, such as they are—leaving the whole among my papers in the form of a tale. It must be remembered that though in his second, more prosperous if less notable period, we drifted apart, yet for many years we were intimate friends, and I could rely absolutely on, at any rate, his own belief in the things he told me : while for the earlier part of my story, referring to our travels together —during which the atmosphere that should have prepared him for some culmination, could already be seen ominously piling itself up—I am able to consult the journal which I kept at the time.

Many, perhaps, will refuse to place credence in my words, because in their sanguine refusal to consider history, they will urge that death can never assume so strange and awful a garb. Such things, they will say, do not happen. But, if it must be allowed that a spiritual and romantic magnificence, a tragic radiance, illumines the end of Shelley, until in his case it seems almost as though God, deciding to follow the precedent which he had set with Elijah, had resolved to take unto Himself his prophet, calling all mankind to be witness of his fiery ascent; if it be conceded that a certain fitting quality of grandeur, yet with enough of renunciation in it to proclaim that the poet has triumphed over the dandy and man-of-the-world, pertains to the closing scenes of Byron's life, when almost in sight of a terrestrial kingdom—the first one ever conquered by a poet—he dies amid all the sordid details of a camp life that must have been repellent to him, thereby gaining another and more permanent dominion; if it be admitted that there is, too, something splendid in the final action of Marcel Proust, who in that supreme forgetfulness of himself in his art that had always characterised him, was prompted by his intense spirit of scientific inquiry to say, as he lay dying, that since he had always known that, owing to want of experience, the approach of death was a thing he had never understood, he had accordingly left blank the pages of the death scene in the last volume of *A la Recherche du Temps Perdu,* but that he would now dictate them, and exhausted and in torment as he was, to continue for three hours to do so, until suddenly he stopped, lay down, and was in a moment dead; yet who can pretend that the deaths of great writers are for the most part other than ugly or horrible?

This question we will shortly consider. First let us examine their nervous equipment. We know, through the correspondence of Gustave Flaubert that when, in order afterwards to write of it in *Madame Bovary*, he was studying the effect of poison upon the person who takes it, himself developed its symptoms and had to be treated for them medically. Susceptibility of this kind may, of course, have its compensations, for, similarly, though he had long been a victim to insomnia, when engaged before starting *Bouvard et Pecuchet* in observing the peaceful if stupid life of his country neighbours, he began of a sudden to sleep fourteen hours a night, and continued in this welcome state for several months. But because, as we see proved in these two instances, the nerves of imaginative writers must be more subtle and delicate, more highly attuned to every tone and vibration than those of banker or ploughman, it is possible that they are also to this greater degree frightened of illness and death. To suggest this is in no way to insinuate that such artists are invariably morbid and morose, but only to imply that at a certain moment there comes on them a fit of rebellion, equivalent to that which, we are told, at times seized the more materially-minded Queen Elizabeth, making her kick, scream and rend her ruff with her jewelled claws, till tears of terror furrowed the paint down her raddled old cheeks. But may it not even be that these identical moods are in part responsible for the attempt of the artist to gain immortality by other than physical means ?

Indeed it appears as though famous men of letters and imagination are apt to meet with an end as exceptional as themselves, whilst, in addition, when alive being liable much more than the ordinary person to a morbid prescience of it. Furthermore, it is precisely the author in the highest degree capable of appreciating and describing the tones and shades of bodily suffering and mental horror, who is seemingly the most certain to realise them himself in his own last moments. Thus Edgar Allen Poë, an artist more concerned with death, its attendant terrors and mysteries, than any other writer in the English language, was finally overwhelmed by a death more dumbly and ludicrously horrible than any which he had invented and described. One winter's morning he left his home, telling his wife that he was going to Richmond for a consultation with his lawyer and would be back the next day. He arrived there in a blinding snowstorm, to find that an election was in progress. What exactly occurred is uncertain : we do not know whether on his own initiative he had consumed drink or drugs, and was, perhaps, already so dazed as to render it difficult for him to protest or put up a fight. But of this much we are certain : that American politics were then in an exceedingly corrupt state, and that, as a consequence, this man of genius was kidnapped at Richmond station, drugged, and dragged round by political bullies from one polling-booth to another, there to register a shaky and guided signature, a non-existent vote, on behalf of a candidate of whom he had never heard. All day long he was plied with drink and drugs and carried along by his persecutors, until he had visited between forty and fifty of these voting-places : then he was forsaken by them, to be found dead next morning in the brown, trampled snow of a deserted street. What can have been the thoughts of this poet, in his few but doubtless recurring moments of full consciousness and sobriety, as like a dumb automaton, he was driven and bludgeoned round, or lay there helpless, a martyr gagged by his own vices and lashed to his own sense of horror ? How farcical —with that touch of farce which only himself had known how to use in order to deepen the grotesque and tragic tenor of his tales—must have been to him, the first ·American artist, the thought of his peculiar and exquisite talent obliterated for ever in order to aid the triumph of some dull, wooden-witted candidate of the saloon-bar in a local election.

Then, to take another example, there is that passage which no reader of the de Goncourt Journal will ever forget, describing a dinner given in honour of Tourgeneff. At this feast to the great Russian author, then on a triumphal visit to Paris, were present, in addition to the de Goncourt brothers, Alphonse Daudet, Zola, Flaubert and de Maupassant. It was an occasion to which all these celebrated authors had most eagerly looked forward, because it was expected that the conversation would be of an inimitable brilliance and gaiety. Almost at once, however, after they had sat down, Daudet gave the talk an unlooked-for direction by relating how, as a young and apparently healthy man, he had one morning awoken, feeling quite well, to discover his pillow stained with blood, for him the first token of the consumption which was to ruin his life. And now each in turn described his symptoms and his fears. Zola expatiated on his peculiar dread of death by suffocation—though this was a decade or two before his servant called him one morning to find his rigid, asphyxiated corpse clutching the window, still battling for air after the manner of those Roman slaves, whose contorted skeletons—eked out with plaster till round them has formed once more the authentic outlines of the face and figure—can to this day be seen in the Museum of Pompeii, eternally fighting in their attitude the red-hot rain of ashes that once smothered them. Maupassant, too, came to an end that surpassed in horror any he ever invented, a mad giant battling for months with furniture and inanimate objects as though they were demons. And how many authors, before and since, had they been alive or in Paris at the time, would have been justified in taking part in the conversation of that morbid banquet : the excommunicated Tolstoy, a second Lear, though one not driven out by his devoted daughter, but instead by his own love of mankind, his own soul that had been the field of so many cruel conflicts, knowing that he was to die, leaving his home at the age of eighty-two, to try to end his life in the great Optina Monastery willing to perform the lowliest of tasks there on condition that he was not required to enter the church, sitting up all one night, to write an essay on the process of death, and setting out, no one knows when or why, to die at the station-master's house at Astapovo, a wayside station amid the snowy steppes ; Baudelaire, that exquisite poet of the shadows and true diviner of art, who, like de Maupassant, died mad ; and the Abbé Prévost, who after a false death came to himself, his eyes slowly opening with a supreme look of terror as he realised that in truth he was being vivisected.

It is with such an order of horror, but one further intensified by the presence of facts which can never entirely be elucidated, that this story must be classed.

Certainly Tristram Orlander was the gayest and most brilliant of companions in his youth : but that a person of his temperament, and with nerves somewhat disordered from the strain he was in the habit of placing upon them, was frightened of anything so remorseless and inevitable as death, goes without saying. His very unpunctuality, notorious among his friends, must certainly have made him dread the only occasion in life for which it was impossible to be late. Further, the mere possession of such a sensitiveness seems, as we have noticed to attract events of the very kind to impress it.

The intrinsic interest of my narrative, in that it concerns a famous author, should assure it of publication after my death. Here, then, are the facts, woven in together with my surmises, and just as no one can question, so, too, need no one believe me unless the tale carries its own conviction. But, because in my anxiety to keep as close as possible to the events of which I am certain in the first part of the narrative, I have almost followed in places the actual text of my diary, it may be that the suppositional reader of this document will be willing to pardon the no doubt numerous discrepancies in style, outlook, and, even, in humour : for then I was young, opinionated and headstrong, but now, as with aching eyes I read over this manuscript which is at last finished and put together, I am an old, tired, and perhaps disappointed man.

The identity and works of Tristram Orlander are, I suppose, among the few things of which it is needless to inform the present generation : while to the next one, for which, possibly, I am writing, it may be that these syllables will carry a yet greater weight of glory. He belonged, essentially, to that queer, comparatively modern sect—Voltaire is one of its earliest and most conspicuous leaders—the members of which can be detected by the phenomenon that the fullness of their fame a little precedes a widespread knowledge of their work ; their names, percolating through a small and discriminative audience, are familiar to a wide public ignorant of their writings. It is as though some blind instinct as to the quality of these authors guides the crowd from the first moment to recognise them with its hatred and coarse abuse. While still almost a boy, Tristram Orlander had found himself famous—and this although his first book was a volume of poems, a medium that will never attract a horde of readers—but famous in the sense that his views and sayings were bandied about and repeated, quoted and printed, till the sound of his name beat like a nearing drum within the consciousness of the mob. Yet, apart from this hatred without reason, his celebrity was deservedly great with those who loved literature, and had he died at the age of twenty-eight—by which time, for he was always a prolific author, the best books that he was ever to write had already been issued or were just appearing ("March on Babel" and "Ring Down," in my judgment by far the finest, were published in 1923 and 1924 respectively)—his name would have been secure without any artificial heightening of its interest. The wit, beauty and erudition so clearly manifested in these and other works of his early period had, then, assured him fame at the time, and the respect and attention of posterity, long before the enigma of his end had come to make everything connected with him into a focus of morbid curiosity. But, as it was, his reputation as a writer was to pass through the most curious processes of revaluation.

Considering how widely read he is again at the moment, how much talk, and how much genuine excitement, his work and himself have aroused latterly, it is remarkable that there have appeared so few records of his early days. And, since it is necessary, in order to reach the full meaning of the eventual tragedy, to understand the trend of his mind, life and character, and, because of all his friends I enjoyed over a long period the best opportunities of observing them, together with the corrosion to which time and circumstance, as much as their own nature, made them liable, it seems better to attempt here some slight account of his career.

Originally we met at our first school. It already required no great discernment to recognise in Tristram the budding of a rare and poetic intelligence. After the manner of most interesting children, he was at the same time both backward in some ways and unexpectedly advanced in others. His character was even then clear-cut, and he read with a surprising quickness all books—except school-books—that were within reach. Many clever boys are prigs, but fortunately he was not "clever" in this sense, nor a prig, for he lacked that particular and spectacled precocity, so quickly diagnosed at school—and labelled under the term "giglamps"—nor was he one of those stooping, scholarly, curatical boys with protruding teeth, who so distinguish themselves in their studies at this early age that they constitute for a time, before they leave, the hope of the future, and then disappear for ever, except for an occasional, enthusiastic, if spotty, emergence at an "Old Boys' Dinner" or "'Varsity Match."

Albeit Tristram's unusual mind and temperament had at first made him rather disliked by his schoolfellows, nevertheless over this suspicion engendered because he did not quite fit the standard mould, and over the natural antipathy entertained by lower for higher types of life, he was soon able to triumph by means of the happy combination of charm, vitality and courage that was his. Yet, in spite of the flow and leaping of high spirits, which throughout his life made of him an ideal companion, he was a nervous, queer child, and his character presented an infinite number of contradictions. Often as shy and reserved as at other times he was self-possessed and forthcoming, diffidence would suddenly obscure him at his most confident, in the middle of one of his gusts of laughter. He suffered violent revulsions of feeling, moods of depression unusual in one so young, and hours, even, of an exaggerated pious fervour, during which the simple tenets of the English Church would be examined, tested and lauded with alarming vigour.

This recurrent fanaticism was entirely the unconscious achievement of his parents, who, priding themselves on being " modern "—a word which in that distant era signified a much more definite position and set of ideas than it does now—had purposelessly forbidden their son any religious instruction. When, therefore, the child was old enough to detect the existence of such things as systems of faith, these often influencing millions of people, and on occasion so strongly that it would drive these hordes on to the most wild and hysterical outbursts of feelings—the discovery came as an overwhelming shock, making him concentrate his whole intelligence upon it. This intensity, moreover, made itself felt in many other directions, though the main effect of his personality was one of extreme buoyancy.

In any case, now that he was at school, no religious fervour, however heart-felt, could in a sensible boy long survive a few sermons—so full of allusions to youth and Sir Galahad, coupled with intriguing, mysterious insinuations as to the miseries of after-school life " where temptations be-set a-mun," so imbued withal, with a kindly, twinkling comprehension that " boys will be boys," so crammed with little illustrative fables, allegories and parables of a cleanlily-tender order— delivered by child-fancying-clergymen in the chapel. The phase passed, therefore, leaving in its wake a small residue of mystical feeling, native to his temperament, and which, though it may not have been apparent, perhaps never deserted him entirely, even in his most materialistic years.

As a child he was superstitious, and, indeed, long afterward continued to be so. I can still, for example, recall with amusement his ludicrous but quite genuine misery whenever a Friday happened to fall on a thirteenth. And if it had been any other boy, he would have earned my contempt, for I had been taught to regard such failings as " tapping wood " and bowing to the new moon, as so many signs of weak intellect or, worse still, of affectation.

Nevertheless, it must be admitted that many boys

are superstitious. The reason for this probably is, that since it is their fate to pass through every phase discarded by man in his long journey toward civilisation, it is at about the age of nine or ten that they halt, for a year or more, at the fetish and augury stage of the savage. In this particular case, however, Tristram's credulity was heightened by his possessing, at this period of development, an indubitable and curious power of intuition—or perhaps one should say, rather, of being aware of small happenings that would shortly take place without the necessity of being informed of them beforehand. Such an attribute is, I think, much more common among children than is generally supposed, but leaves them for ever when they attain the fullness of their mental stature and grosser senses. That one considers such a faculty surprising in Tristram, then, is not because it is so rare, but because one does not expect to find it in a child of so lively and active an intelligence : for it is usually the child with the fewest mental processes to impede his receptivity who exhibits it in the highest degree.

This ability to foretell applied itself more often to small things than to important ones, and acted with them more surely : the more trivial the event, the more easy and accurate the divination. A typical instance of his minute but singular gift in this direction was that, with an unfailing exactness, he could predict, though only a few hours beforehand, the visits to him at school of friends and relations, without having received from them any ordinary announcement of their intention. Very seldom would this power direct itself toward matters of greater consequence : but there were exceptions, and certainly, many hours before he was informed of it, he became aware of his mother's sudden and tragic death, though from her latest letters she had appeared to be in good health and happy.

It may well be that a faculty of this kind is capable of rational explanation, and that, indeed, if properly tested and examined, it might help to make clear to us the solution of various mysteries. Who knows, even, that it would not yield a clue to the nature of time ? This is a subject, it may be, for scientists, rather than for an old poet, to discuss. Yet, if for a moment we may assume that such is the case, it is evident that at a later stage in his life, we must recall that at one time Tristram had possessed a strange gift, for this identical power may not have been altogether unconnected with the mysterious incidents that took place in Spain in after years.

From the first, Tristram Orlander and I had entered into one of those immediate friendships of childhood. Now that both his parents were dead, it became the custom for him to spend with us a considerable part of the holidays. My parents were soon as much devoted to him as was myself, while, not only over them, but over most elderly people, he exercised that subtle spell which the vital, and occasionally noisy, ever cast upon the quiet and sad, and which bestowed upon him an absolute impunity.

Together we passed to Eton, where, too, everyone seemed disposed to allow him a certain latitude. Often when we should have been engaged in pursuing a ball —whichever ball was ordained by tradition and the inscrutable government of such things as appropriate to the season—or in applauding ecstatically those who aided its muddy, noisy and illogical career through space, instead we would wander round the large, grey courts and robust towers of the flinty, Victorian-eyed castle which piled itself so splendidly over us—that castle which is the only one to capture on the grand scale all the hard charm, neatness and mechanical precision of a toy fort—or else we would stroll up and down the Long Terrace, just above the spires, green domes and turrets of the tree-tops that now sounded out their most transient music, as the birds darted and leapt about them, or dropped suddenly down under them to their deep-hidden nests. Tristram Orlander had already decided to be a poet ; more than that, indeed, a great and famous one. His head, his room, his pockets, all were crammed with verse. And it was in these ideal surroundings that we surveyed the future— thus framed-in, what an enchanted vista it seemed, boundless and golden as the plain before us. As we slouched along in the correct manner (for to that extent we must conform), displaying those out-of-date raven-winged clothes and hats which bring in so rich a revenue to the school-tradesmen, we could see, far away over the cumulus grey clouds of the nearer trees, beyond the flow and eddy of the minute streets of Windsor, with their clean, prim curves, their trim brickwork and dapper paint, their miniature people on bicycles or in cars, beyond the rusty toy-drums of the gas-works and the festering, black scars cut by the railways—that No Man's Land which supplies life and light—beyond, again, the river, flashing and rippling its body along under the sunshine like a serpent, to that more distant, disciplinary world of clergymen converted into bats by their wide-winged, black robes and angular, pointed mortar-boards, and of boys dressed as though for some funeral which had all this long time been in preparation. The pleasant, green oases and cloistered courts of this separate dominion, the twisted, red columnar chimneys and lusty, rugged trees, were all rather unexpectedly dominated by the fleecy bulk of the old chapel, its sweet chimes sounding among them as though, with a bell attached to its neck, a gigantic but kindly sheep had turned shepherd. Beyond, again, stretched the playing fields, now speckled with a network of white ants, chasing or crawling across them, though the daft clamour of levied enthusiasm that must accompany the superseding of one of these dull and ritual rhythmic antics by an ever more meaningless momentary turbulence was lost to us among the sounds of the nearer town, and by the church-like cawing of the rooks flapping up toward us.

It was clear that the whole of this wasteful, antiquated, rather beautiful machine, under charge of its mouldering but venerable guide, was working toward the celebration of this same funeral—a funeral for which it had already been in mourning a century before the event materialised—with ever increasing speed : so many boys turned out from it each year, standardised and to type, amused by the same jokes, in arms at the same challenges, with no intellectual zeal that could be knocked—or rather, bored—out of them, with no ideas, and few ideals save a valuable if restricted sense of duty, together with a natural love of pleasure, which they had never been taught to differentiate from happiness.

However, the effect of this engine where it failed—albeit very seldom—to standardise was, instead, to make more emphatic a boy's idiosyncrasies. And Tristram's natural love of the arts could not be crushed out of him, though he may have learnt to dissimulate it. No doubt this constant need of disguise bred a habit, left its permanent mark upon his character, even though this was not to become noticeable for very many years. Another result of the system under which he laboured was, perhaps, to increase his natural extravagance : while it may have been, too, among those sharp-toothed towers, across those metallic-green lawns against the knife-like edges of which you felt that you might cut your finger, and down those avenues of painted tin trees, that both of us acquired that love of sight-seeing, most amiable and effective of drugs, a passion which never left us and is to play a certain part in this story.

Soon after we had left Eton, the funeral that both of us had detected as the object of so much endeavour, but of which we had not been able to understand the exact nature or foretell the precise date, was performed on a gigantic scale and quite regardless of expense. At first it was calculated by those most likely to know that the obsequies would extend over only ten days : then that they might be prolonged for as much as three months, but in the end it was not until four years had passed that the affair was concluded. And by this time most of the young creatures whom we had seen from the terrace above as small white ants scurrying across diminutive, flat green spaces, learning the team spirit, the need of blind obedience to a hallowed stupidity, had been sent to be butchered—displaying during the process an unquestioning and unquestioned gallantry born of this system—in the repulsive, but reminiscent mud-flats of France and Flanders.

Tristram Orlander escaped the massacre of the innocents, for, in accordance with that queer code which then governed the military world, he had been rejected for the army—not on account of his clearly exceptional talents, but because he was adjudged not strong enough to be slaughtered. Thus the warfare of our youth manifested, together with an unexpected adoption of

Christian tenets, an absolute disregard for the principles of evolution, and allowed only the old, the weak, the lunatic and the criminal to survive. Indeed, had Tristram's gifts been recognised, doubtless he would not have been spared. Fortunately, however, they were ignored, and he was given an appointment in his native country, Ireland : one, too, which at any rate allowed him to make his own use of evening and night-time. Thus, when he and I met again, after five years, it seemed to me that, though in the interval he had already built up for himself a considerable reputation as a poet, he had not, apart from his increased knowledge and range of observation, changed much in mind or character.

His appearance, though, had altered beyond expectation. As a child and through adolescence, he had remained rather unattractive, an effect greatly enhanced by his carelessness as to how he looked. But evidently at the age of about twenty, as so often happens, he had sloughed his old skin, fluttering out of the discarded chrysalis into a development of good looks that had been quite unpredictable. Actually of Irish origin, Tristram looked unmistakably English—but then that is the unfailing stamp of the Irish gentleman, unless he belongs, instead, to the long-upper-lipped, thick-eyebrowed peasant-type variety which is its other manifestation. English he undoubtedly looked then, but English of an older day.

His tall, slim, but wide-shouldered figure had drawn

itself up : the face had sculptured for itself out of the youthful, rounded contours, a firmness of line and a look of purpose which had hitherto been lacking. His long head, with its high-bridged, narrow-nostrilled nose, the eyes and eyebrows uplifted toward the temple, his forehead rather high but with the hair descending to a helmet-like peak in the centre, until in itself it suggested something of the arrogance of a golden plume, all showed the refinement of the gothic type, now every day becoming more rare—and yet not so rare, for it can be seen effigied in stone, marble or alabaster on hundreds of decaying and mildewed tombs spread over France and England. But when flesh and blood come to soften, and breathing to animate it, one of these stiff images springs to life with a surprising vigour and proud grace. In a sense, though, it would be correct to assert that such a type was inappropriate to modern life, more at home on tourney ground, or with a hooded falcon on its long wrist, than in office, in rotary-club or on the golf-course, and to affirm that this exterior, distinguished though it might be, was scarcely the most suitable vase for the flower that it sheltered and, indeed, somewhat obscured. It was a rather too impersonal convention, a mould handed on from one generation to another. It would be impossible, in spite of any unconscious efforts to escape such classification on the part of the being imprisoned within, not at once to identify the species of his shell or the place which he occupied in evolution. Indeed, it was as though he had been endowed with an aspect and stature calculated by Nature more for the harbouring of an executant than of an original talent, except that the somewhat set quality was made to count for little by an unusual sensitiveness of expression, and was, further, almost annihilated by the flame of life that flickered through him with an intensity that kindled his every gesture just as it lighted his every phrase. Of this vitality, the vividness of eye and hair was outward token : his hair, it seemed, had so much life in it that it had assumed two shades of gold instead of one, and his eye transmitted that which, once seen, can never be mistaken, the authentic flash of genius.

The general outline was in its essence medieval. Nevertheless the sensitiveness of the face, the curiously pinched-in, and slightly distending nostrils, the almost ascetic intensity and pallor which at times one would notice in it, perpetually conflicted with another, most contrary expression, for his head often exhibited a quality that more resembled the animal-look of a young satyr as conceived by a Renaissance painter, with very much of the formalised wildness of this creation of the antique world. Such an affinity was further enhanced by the carelessness and untidiness that had assumed, had grown into and was permeated by, his attribute of a curious and personal elegance.

Most artists have something of the dandy in them, and had he been rich, a dandy, one suspected, he would have been. His family had in centuries past wielded considerable political influence, had produced celebrated soldiers—though never before a poet—but was now extinct save for this last bearer of an uncommon and perhaps rather beautiful name. Coming of this ancient family, of an order already perishing, he was poor, though to this origin, surely, he owed his exuberance, charm, obstinacy, and, above all, pride. And in his pride we find rooted the reason for the natural, careless foppishness of his clothes : for the idea, probably even unformulated to himself, was the old aristocratic one that anything he did must be correct, anything he wore, a mode in itself. And by so thinking he made it one. Yet I see him as standing rather apart from the generation to which he belonged, and when I reflect upon the past, it seems strange to me that the young Tristram Orlander, who in so many respects, as much in his outward form, then appeared singularly untypical of his time, should now have come to represent it for the young so much more than those jazz-bishops, bird-fancying poets, stern, preaching journalists and big-business, after-dinner speakers, who, though all the time they were in reality drumming and trumpeting themselves into oblivion, then seemed the very quintessence of the age.

In any effort, therefore, to sum up his appearance, to present him as he then was—for though the reader must have seen portraits of him, usually he will have been represented as an older man—it is upon the altogether unusual refinement of that young face, and the constant changes of mood it registered so finely, that one must dwell : a refinement, moreover, which was later to leave it, and seemed all the more exceptional in a man of such marked and distinctive features. A face entirely governed by the soul, one would have pronounced it, until one had observed the slow, animal warmth of his smile, that rare, double smile of eye and mouth.

Much more than in looks, though, had he developed in conversation. Now this, of all arts, is the least fruitful, the one most seldom found in conjunction with a gift for writing. On the contrary, it is often some hindrance to speaking freely that helps to encourage and bring out a gift for written expression, and it may well be true that a gift for talking is really injurious to an author, inasmuch as he may be inclined to waste in it both time and ideas. Moreover, since the popularity of the Russian novel among English authors—a cult very strong at that moment—and the ensuing transplanted worship of the Holy Idiot, writers no longer even wanted to talk. It had become unusual, almost " bad form." An easy but meaning mumness now marked the formerly glib literary figures. The voice, when forced by circumstance to sound, was high, tired though emphatic, its stress always falling on that syllable which was least prepared to receive it. Tristram, then, had flowered into almost the only real conversationalist of his epoch : and, just as his looks proclaimed him a born leader, so through the medium of talk as much as of writing, the transmutation of this leadership from a physical to a mental one, made itself felt.

Not the least infliction of old age is that if you have counted among your friends those who have enjoyed great renown as talkers, you are continually being asked by the young, who hope to draw out of you a full account of him, whether this or that celebrated man was really such a wonderful conversationalist as people say. To my regret I remember how as a boy myself plagued old gentlemen about Whistler and Wilde in the very same manner. But the answer to such ingenuous inquiries—though in almost every instance they can be countered with a decided negative—must invariably be either "yes" or "no" without qualification. For how are you to paint a flower that dies in flowering, a parasitic bloom, furthermore, that has its deep yet intangible roots fast embedded in the talk of others—for no monologist can ever become a great talker? This is the ultimate vanity, a supreme illustration of dust to dust, since to convey its beauty and interest it is necessary to explain the context, which died also in being born, to outline the character of each person talking, or joining in, and to imitate, even, the quality, texture and rhythm of each voice. Then one must describe in detail each pass and counterpass, the dexterity of each thrust and feint, as it were, and make clear the reference in each inflection, with every suspicion that was latent in it of parody or pathos. Thus, to convey the special attributes of the conversation of an artist in that medium is one of the most difficult feats of virtuosity imaginable, difficult enough, withal, through the spoken word : while for a writer adequately to conjure them up, he would be compelled to develop the highly specialized technique of the football or boxing correspondent of an English daily newspaper, or that of the bull-fight reporter to a Spanish journal— languages so complicated and peculiar that to learn the writing of them takes a lifetime, while only those who understand nothing else, can comprehend them when written. But here, alas ! we are forced to attempt the impossible.

In an earlier paragraph it has been suggested that as a boy Tristram had been noisy : but now the energy which had been responsible for this sound and fury had been harnessed and made to produce wit, just as a torrent may be transmuted into light. Never did he screech or howl hyena-like in conversation ; in this unlike a few of his contemporary talkers—for those clever persons of the period who did not remain slavonically mute, were inclined, perhaps in reaction against the formality of antecedent Victorianism, to bellow. With all true wits, he was silenced by the racket, hubbub and hullabaloo of a large party.

Yet for him it was never necessary to join in loud but squalid competition. When scarce raised, his voice would subtly, and in spite of itself, call others to a willing silence. In a day, when, as part of the trend toward uniformity, people had lost their personal tones and were apt to speak with a group voice—so that at once, if introduced to a stranger, you could distinguish the various throat-and-nose symptoms of Bloomsbury, Chelsea or Mayfair, decide which were his friends, assign him to one or another coterie of fashion, or to such and such a literary gang—Tristram, almost alone of his generation, spoke with his own and unmistakable accents. In no review of the gifts that he brought to life, as separate from those he brought to art, can one ever omit the singular charm of voice that was his, a voice that level and unobtrusive in its pitch, had yet concealed in it a fascinating and indefinable music. And, indeed, as I look back on my young days, on the years that followed 1918, I find—and how many of my friends have attested the same thing—that this quiet music haunts the background of it to an extent one would hardly have deemed possible.

Though much has been said and written of his brilliance in the art of conversation, I have as yet seen or heard no mention of the most singular talent that he manifested in it. With Tristram in the room some delicate, intangible element of flattery surrounded each person with a nimbus of satisfaction. Some of the superfluity of the energy that caused him so easily to outshine, he had been able to convert into that rarest of social faculties ; one which enabled him to extract from others a contribution of the same degree of excellence as his own, to invest them temporarily with his genius. Was not this evasive, evocative talent, one wondered, connected with the mysterious power of hypnotism : were we not in reality under a spell ? For in his company, not merely was I often the witness of my own scintillation, but was privileged to observe the most uninspired of our friends blaze out all at once with an unparalleled effulgence. Yet not only could he induce them to show their powers at a level to which they were, except in his presence, incapable of attaining, but also to exhibit them at their most typical ; a much more subtle miracle, in that a bore would become amusing, illuminating, yet remain withal radiantly himself, every variety of ennui still latent in every sentence that he uttered. " How like him ! " one would echo momentarily, with a new admiration—till suddenly one would realise how unlike him it was.

This almost supernatural endowment—for when submitted to analysis, such it must appear—far from making people jealous of Orlander's gifts, forced them, if only out of self-conceit, to love him. Though not for an instant did they recognise the magnitude of his contribution, they would, nevertheless, feel grateful— but condescendingly grateful : here at last, they were convinced, was one who could appraise their wit and worth with the same critical but appreciative eye as themselves in their best, their truest moments. There were others, they knew, not so understanding. This gift, then, was perhaps the secret mainspring of a popularity that, though ever so limited in extent, was of an undoubted force.

As for his friends, it is true that the greater part of them he had selected from among those who amused or interested him. These were artists and writers bound to him by community of tastes : he lived in their company, and they formed a group of which he was the acknowledged leader. If some of them flattered him, as his enemies alleged, this flattery was unusually born of genuine admiration, rendered to him as tribute, a just due which he had worked hard to earn. Further he could not—doubtless a weak point in his character—live and work without constant praise and incense from those in whose judgment he trusted, and if also he was only too willing to believe in the judgment of those who adulated him, at least he was fully aware of it. Flattery was a necessity for him, soothed his nerves, oiled the machine of his mind, enabled it to work longer hours, and better, and caused him to open out in the society of those who applied it. But the very existence of a group of this sort was naturally an annoyance and irritation to many who found no place in it. Most of its members were boring, it was said. But Tristram maintained that these bores, if boring, were his own, ones whom he had chosen for some definite virtue : and who, therefore, were not fatiguing to him, whereas the quiddity of a bore is to be vampiric.

It must also be made clear that his friends were by no means confined to the admiring members of this band, for he numbered among them every sort of person, some as much out of keeping as out of sympathy with him. There were, for example, old school friends, or those who had known his parents or had been kind to him as a child. These wondered why he had deserted such respectable family traditions as politics or the army in order to write books, of which they were resolute in their refusal to understand one word, yet were so kind, so affectionate, even devoted, that he could not find the necessary hardness of heart to throw them off. Possibly he had not even the inclination, for he was a loyal friend, it seemed. But never for a moment would these " old friends " (friends who traded on their " oldness ") allow their fondness for him to debar them from goading him, or tiring him out. Nevertheless distressing as are these grey spectres of past friendships and of affections that are outgrown, ghosts that must haunt the life of every intelligent man, because so much friendship in early life is merely unconscious experimentation, ghosts who so often, alas ! recognise their own insubstantial and phantasmal nature, yet insist on still moving enviously among the living, is there not, perhaps, a quality peculiarly touching in this love of theirs, that is, after all, so disinterested and sincere ? For they gain nothing by it. Not in the least degree addicted to artistic or literary snobbishness, each success that crowns the efforts of him they have elected to haunt, is to them merely one more reward of his sin, for they would rather consider any unsuccessful soldier or incompetent politician than the most interesting and distinguished sculptor or musician.

On the contrary they must invent for him in their own minds some claim on their esteem. Thus, if their chosen victim is, let us say, a famous painter, they will, while never making the slightest reference to his art, while absolutely ignoring his works which lie piled-up round them and hanging on the walls, at the same time make a point of inquiring constantly whether he " still keeps up his music "—stressing the " his " as though in some way it was at the same time both an idiosyncrasy and a peculiarly unique personal possession—by this signifying their knowledge of him in some distant period, which he is now striving to forget, during which he may have attempted, very badly, to play the flute or guitar. And, however often they may be dealt with on this point, they will thereafter constantly allude to it, again deplore his failure to have " kept it up," for since to these ghosts every remark is lost, the point of every joke, of every reference, obscure—so infinitely far are they now in mind from him they haunt and persecute—their friendship must ever be sought for back through the miasmas of the past. Even the energy, of which it is their curious power and privilege to drain the creative mind, gives them nothing in return, is wanted for no purpose, utterly wasted, unless it is this that enables them so frequently to materialise : and yet such is their affection for the living that they cannot help but cling and linger. Nor for an instant was even Tristram able, as he was with a living bore, to lend them his own brilliance.

Alas ! such did not constitute the only kind of spectre :
there was, too, for him another species of temporary,
and perhaps still more pitiful ghost—more pitiful because in the case of these phantoms, men, however
kind, need not admit of any claim. But then in this
identical lack of title is the whole essence and secret
of their pathos, for they have, perhaps, never been real
people at all, never to anyone, never flesh, blood and
brain, but are those who can only be embodied out of
others, only exist for the moment in the glow of fame
that emanates from those with whom it is thus necessary
for them, in obedience to the natural law of their creation, to make friends. These phantoms, then, resemble
the salamanders which the people of the Middle Ages
conceived could only live within the momentary tinsel
flicker of the fire, are like those transparent, ribbon-like
fish that can be seen gracefully undulating into life (for
only their movements differentiate them from the substance of the liquid round them) as the waters of a
glass-walled aquarium are for a second illumined for
our instruction, or, again, can be compared to those
planets that we see glittering so brightly in the night-
sky, seeming to give out so much radiance of their own,
and yet which, we are told, in reality only reflect and
borrow the majestic glory of the sun. In fact, from
their conversation, it is to be doubted whether they can
exist except in relation to famous people, for all that
you learn from them of their lives concerns the mighty,
and as though treated with luminous paint, they still to

a slight extent retain the impression of the light that has passed or failed. After the example of Melchizedek, they are apparently without father, without mother, and without descent, need give out no ectoplasm in return to other ghosts, need suffer no Aunt Mabel or Uncle Henry of their own, for whom, like ordinary mortals, they must during all their span from time to time immolate themselves in the cause of duty. Conscious, perhaps, of their so tenuous hold upon life, these ghosts wilt, fade out, disappear at the first breath of hostile criticism upon the work of him they haunt : nor is this to be considered a fault or in any way as condemning them, for since the fame and success of others is the very blood in their veins, their life itself, they are once more but obeying the natural, if primitive law of their existence, the law of self-preservation ; which fact, again, may be responsible for the phenomenal lack of embarrassment they display at their own behaviour.

Though such spectres must with any artist aid the process of exhaustion, many will say that he who incurs such friendships deserves them : but how is he, his mind always engaged underneath with other things, and though continually to be deceived in life, never disillusioned about it, to judge between these ghosts and the real people that they often so ably mimic ? And Tristram, sociable by nature, underwent all the rather amusing indignities to which the artist who enjoys seeing people must submit ; and chief of these is this sudden taking up by ghosts of those they deem promising

—a process only equalled in swiftness, dexterity and enthusiasm by the subsequent putting of them down. Indeed, Tristram was particularly a subject for such treatment, because in addition to the fact that seeing fresh people always interested him, his literary reputation was of a kind that caused his books to be very well received one week by some section of the press, while the next week, and from another quarter, the criticism would be adverse and, often, abusive : so that he would burn the fingers of those who took him up almost as they first grasped him.

For the admiration he received as a writer was in proportion to that which obtained for him as a man. It was vehement, though as yet narrow, united to a wider fame born of aversion : an aversion prompted not so much by his arrogance as by a dandiacal grace that consciously a little parodied it, and found vent, when he wished, in an insolence that for all its effectiveness was assuredly nervous in origin. Indeed, a gift for over-sharp sayings in any man is usually the sign that it has been forced upon him, a token of nervous exacerbation caused by constant, wilful and vituperative misunderstanding.

Chief of the ransoms extorted from Tristram Orlander by Nature, in return for the numerous advantages she had bestowed upon him, was a very highly-strung system, the delicacy of which others were as much apt to overlook as was himself. But that which appeared to be an abundance of vitality was doubtless in great part due to the extravagant way in which he lived upon the capital of his nerves. Just so might a man who spent all he possessed seem rich to those friends who knew nothing of his financial condition. And as far back as these early days there were several symptoms of the prostration that must ultimately come. Sometimes in the midst of one of his most daring and lofty flights, when the talk would be lifted, soaring on its own wings, his old shyness would return to overwhelm him, and he would be struck silent : and many were the times when he would sit for hours, crouched up, listless and despairing, though for no reason. Then it was as though the flame had passed out of him. His eyes lost their fire, his face its colouring, so much did his health, the very quality of his looks, depend upon the nerves. There were, too, even at this stage, long, black tunnels of sleeplessness through which, every now and then, he must crawl all night : but, being young, these occasions were soon dismissed from his mind.

The contradictions in his character were still manifold. One would have expected that to be late for every appointment would make a shy man still more shy. But he could never be punctual. Timid as he was, even of entering a room, yet with a curious perversity his worn nerves demanded the stimulation of people and parties. Great, of necessity, was the effort they imposed upon him compared with others, who thought less, gave less and did not so much enjoy excitement : for it is precisely he that in reality the whole time works and gives out when in a gathering, who appears to us others to be the most naturally talented at such things, the least awkward and most amusing member of it.　But on him, actually, is levied a toll out of all relation to so trivial an eminence.

In money matters, also, he united comparative poverty to an extravagance, perhaps inherited, but which certainly aggravated it further and was totally unjustified by his means.　Had he, even in those days, been willing to write for money and popularity, he could soon have achieved his object.　But, as yet, he possessed all the integrity of his gift and years, in spite of a new sense of worldliness which I thought it was possible to detect creeping over him—a development oddly at variance with his natural carelessness, as well as with his former religious and mystic leanings, and which I, for one, was inclined to regret.　And his extravagance, if continued, must force from him sooner or later, it was clear, some sacrifice of the principles of his art.　So great, however, was the influence he wielded over his friends, that not one of us dared to warn him of his folly.

Just as the prodigality with which he lavished his nerves in the cause of his friends was also to be observed in his treatment of money, so did a passion for excitement, connected with this same trait of generosity, deliver him into a hundred love affairs in which he squandered the treasures of his affection.　Each, as it followed swiftly upon another—all the more swiftly because his looks and quick, unusual temperament, his rare combination of young animal and pale ascetic, of voluptuary and austere thinker, made him attractive to many women—was to be for him a matter of lifelong devotion : yet it would leave him with an abruptness equal to that with which it had seized upon him. But, as long as it endured, he pursued it with that vehemence which was in this period the distinguishing mark of everything he did, said, or thought, and by means of his own intensity, raised it from the level of a common, often squalid, intrigue—even though this was accomplished through some process of self-deception—on to a far higher plane.

From this account of Tristram Orlander it will be seen that he was a person liable to sudden moods, violent changes of feeling, and one who made for himself perpetual struggles. But although he had already been battling under a self-imposed strain for some years ; writing, talking, staying up till all hours, living at the outward rate of a dozen ordinary people, while at the same time carrying within him a load of inward lives, and treating everything except his money affairs, however important, with seriousness, none of this was to be read in his looks. Now, at last, his financial state began to worry him. This had long been inevitable, for such troubles are cumulative. Yet, in spite of all these things, at the age of twenty-eight or nine, he still appeared to be twenty. But, albeit he looked so young, his collapse was surely much more connected with the age at which he found himself than with any special difficulty.

It is often stated that men change their entire bodies every seven years ; that is to say that in a healthy body every part is renewed and made good within that period. But how much more does this apply to the mind, and to the mysterious, intangible force which both works and shapes it. The sad chain of memories —all the more poignant in proportion as the things recalled are happy and distant—contain the only links that unite the succession of strangers which is each one of us. Certain ages, too, are obviously more cruel, more critical than others, and thus one is continually surprised at how little attention is paid by those interested in crimes and tragedies to the age of the people implicated, when therein often resides the whole explanation and responsibility. Looking back over the long stretch that divides me from those days, I understand that Tristram had reached a crucial period. The deposit of melancholy which during each year has been precipitated upon the memory so slowly, so gently as to have been indiscernible at the time, now first becomes noticeable, and we begin as well to review that which hitherto has scarcely existed for us, the past. Up till this age the future has heavily outweighed it, but the two scales become equal, and then soon the balance shifts. We are inflicted with a desire to make the most of life, before it sinks into a deadened middle age. The very fact that the vital forces are in reality only approaching their full power—though, since the elasticity and leaping vigour of early youth have dwindled, this truth is disguised from us—only enables us to feel the agony more sharply, and we are left with indefinable sensations of haste, expectancy and discontent. He who is ambitious sees the future, from this platform to which he has now ascended, dexterously foreshortened : the span is already ending, it seems. Moreover, there are, of course, instances in which the severity of this climacterical fever is in part capable of individual explanation. Thus it may be that the distracting sense of unrest from which Tristram was now to suffer was the result of heredity : for at his age all his ancestors for many generations had been married, settled against a traditional background, and either had provided themselves with a routine of hunting, shooting and the like to dull their perceptions and anæsthetise such achings, or else had found set before them a very definite and recognisable plan of achievement.

When all these things are said, however, it is plain that the breakdown which was now to crush him, would never have occurred had he not been the victim of an unhappy love affair. For him, a despot in such things, this was a new and terrible experience. In a competition, the most serious for which he had ever entered, he had been beaten. And, since his competitive sense was very strong, this failure destroyed his confidence. Many things had come to him so easily—fame, friendship and, on other occasions, love—that this first, most bitter defeat prostrated him.

*   *   *   *   *   *

To his friends Tristram's love for Ursula Rypton seemed inexplicable. It may, of course, be urged in reply to this, that such is always their position ; the only falling in love for which they can ever allow adequate reason is their own. Further, it must be admitted that there were many of them—one cannot say whom she disliked, for too definite an impression would be conveyed by this word—but of whose existence she continued steadfastly to be unaware, her lovely, blank blue gaze fixed on them unseeingly. And then, in this instance there assuredly was some justification for bewildered surprise. Not for a moment must it be assumed that I am hinting that it would have been singular for anyone else to fall in love with her : but in Tristram's case it had seemed most unlikely. The fact which had altogether removed it for us from the realm of probable complications for him—and with Tristram we had realised only too well that all possible ones were probable—was that he had been an intimate friend of hers for several years, during which period he had never stopped indulging in a hundred dreary, and often sordid, love affairs with women not to be compared with her in any respect. Naturally one had concluded that had he been going to do so, he would have fallen in love with her long ago. And then, too, it had seemed unlikely that two types of a perfection so nearly akin should attract each other in this particular way.

Lady Ursula was a celebrated figure of her time, her fame dependent on a particular union, ever growing more rare, of beauty, distinction, youth and brains. But what added interest to these gifts, was that, with the exception of her youth, they were so largely self-made. From her earliest years, her character had been strong enough, her dramatic sense sufficiently developed, to enable her to design herself for a part of her own choosing, while her vitality, abundant and unbounded as that of a whole shipload from the New World, had furnished her with the energy requisite for the carrying out of her intention and for that continual struggle with her parents which it enforced upon her. For Lord and Lady St. Donat, much as they loved their daughter, would rather—or thought they would rather —have had a pretty, less lovely, more conventional daughter, "more like other girls," and fought against this chiselling and modelling of herself as much as against the clothes which she adopted for the setting of them. Indeed, during many years, until Ursula became old enough to prevent it, Lady St. Donat could seldom see her daughter without tugging—or as she called it "arranging"—her hair, and pulling and dragging her clothes in a paroxysm of motherly affection until the poor child looked as though she had been unexpectedly exposed to a hurricane.

But these days were over. It was conceivable that

her parents had, in a sense, been right in their view ; that Nature had not intended her for a great beauty, or, at any rate, not for one of that period into which it had compelled her to be born. In the early twenties of the century, as in all transitional times, it may have been easier for an ugly woman, through some process of emphasis and stylisation to achieve the renown—and actually the effect—of beauty, than it was for one whose loveliness clearly belonged to an earlier and more aristocratic age to adapt her type to that admired at the moment. But Ursula had known how to extort this gift, also, from Nature, and excelled in the art of transformation ; one essentially modern and feminine, so that in accordance with each fashion—albeit she always made it her own—her shape and appearance, though ever controlled by the same intense personality, were entirely altered. Thus, if you looked at a photograph of her at the age of twenty, and then at the age of twenty-five, during which short time dress would have undergone a complete revolution, it would be difficult at first, to imagine that both of them represented the same individual. She had determined from childhood to be a great beauty of her own day, and, accordingly, she became one : though her face and figure had always about them, I think, a suavity very much at variance with the hard and broken rhythms that characterised the period. She struck, in fact, a full and harmonious chord in an age given over to quarter-tones. The deep, unemphatic, at times almost harsh, music of her voice, that yet in its coldness was more emotional in effect than the warmest cadences, and invested every word she spoke with a greater significance than it contained, so that the most trivial utterance became almost delphic in implication, issued from lips that matched the wide, shadowy gaze of her eyes. Glamour, so much easier to find in the distant past than in the present, was in the air round her : everything about her, while essentially of her own time, alluded to some remote, partly known, partly imagined, land : but her eyes in their deep sockets, and with their calm, almost cruel steadiness of focus, helped one to the correct attribution : that of a gold and ivory effigy, left over, young and unmutilated, from the antique world. Even her gestures, the very lines that her clothes, however much in the fashion, tended to assume as she walked, had about them some lingering breath of the distant, blue and classic winds that have tried to lift so many sculptured robes. In fact, during a century which was both mock-heroic and anti-heroic, something still clung to her of the spirit of the Heroic Age : but it was never enough to hinder her movements or get in the way of other people.

For this statue, notwithstanding, was inhabited by a spirit, swift, witty, elusive, and, above all, contemporary : for she was, as we have suggested, a figure of her own chiselling. The very patina that bloomed over her, she had helped to fashion : for this glamour in which she was steeped, though in some degree nat-

ural, was also, in part, of her own industrious creation
—and, now that it had been brought into being, was
indestructible. Not in her most chaotic moods could she
efface it. Her personality, irresistibly attractive, imparted to every inheritance its own tone, often triumphed
against itself : while her innate elegance was so evident
that she could join in the blatant vulgarities of an age
which knew and admitted it was vulgar, and thereby
not only fail to soil herself, but lend to them a certain,
most unexpected distinction. Similarly, when on occasion she indulged a deliberate rudeness, she was often
as apt to make a friend as the enemy she desired, because in any personal encounter she must allure,
whether or not she wished it.

Yet that in many respects her character and disposition fitted the exquisite beauty of their shell must
as much have added to her own enjoyment as to that
of her friends. To participate in this knowledge was
almost as though one had been allowed to share in a
curious and very delightful secret ; for the profusion
of her gifts, both, as it were, from Nature and from
herself, had very early in life—almost before she had
left the schoolroom—made of her no less an object of
envy and malice than of curiosity. Although most of
the things alleged against her were fantastic inventions,
there was, of course, a reverse side to so much beauty
both of form and content. When it was said that she was
very selfish, rather careless of others—faults allied to
the extreme determination we have noticed in her—

there was doubtless a great deal of truth in these statements. She belonged to a generation that had blossomed during the long years of the first European War
—days during which, in the name of fine qualities such
as altruism and love of one's country, the most appalling crimes and follies had been enacted, culminating
in a sense of loss and futility and in a general misery
that were to last for several decades. Thus, in comparison with such hypocrisy and its results, a little
selfishness, as long as it was frank, had come to be
regarded by the young as almost a virtue. Moreover,
it must not be forgotten that she regarded herself and
her life as a work of art, and to the perfection of their
design she had sacrificed many things and must sacrifice
many more.

With an intellect altogether uncommon, and of an
unusual kind in her sex, she had chosen a little to
neglect it, except in as far as it helped her to enjoy
life and to minister to her vanity by a show of knowledge and memory. Thus it was usually displayed in
practical channels, in such things, for example, as those
countless paper-games that were then the fashion. Similarly, with a natural discrimination in matters of art,
she had never studied it for its own sake. To her, art
and literature were only means to an end ; this end
being to crush out of every year of life its fullest, finest,
ultimate aroma. She liked, with so many other intelligent persons, to steal a deeper, more vivid and biting,
impression of things, people and events than she could

otherwise obtain, through the use of an easy plagiarism.
Yet here, her logic was in error, for while her intention
was the sensual one of extracting pleasure through this
method, the greatest pleasure, on the other hand, can
only be gained through individual observation. Unable in reality, I apprehend, to forge for herself a true
and personal vision, she would not attempt it, but preferred instead to borrow the senses more acute than
her own, of poets, painters and novelists. Poussin and
Turner supplied her with wooded landscapes and
golden mists, Marvell with gardens, Constable with
mills and streams, the Italian painters with an approach,
first to religion (which, otherwise, might have wearied
her) and then to the theatre. She realised, in addition,
that she must do something to make the fashionable
world—though she had no thought for any other—
interesting : she must be able at one moment to see it
whole with the eyes of Balzac, at another to snatch from
Proust that microscope which could reveal so many
worlds within the one of which she was aware. And
this very aptitude, or perhaps necessity, for plagiarism
may also have been largely responsible originally for
her friendship with Tristram : for he, too, could give
new eyes for old. At first, also, it pleased her that he
should often be seen in her society, because, since he
was a personage of his time, this was one of the things
which she felt she had the right to demand for herself.
In the course of several years, however, there had
grown up between them a relationship, based on real

affection and admiration, and one which she genuinely prized. But the fever, intolerable in its burning, was now swiftly, fatally to descend upon him. It threatened to break up entirely this valued and familiar companionship. And this, Lady Ursula realised, would be for her a catastrophe : she had chosen the few intimate friends, as apart from a horde of acquaintances, that she wanted : and their company was a continual necessity to her. Moreover, as an artist in her own medium, she comprehended that in certain developments of friendship, in that quickness of allusion and understanding, in that identity of outlook and humour which can only grow out of a long association of this order, was, perhaps, to be found the principal joy of modern existence.

If, therefore, one is forced later to assign to her some of the blame for Tristram's breakdown, it cannot first be too strongly emphasised that at the outset she displayed real wisdom and courage, and that his temperament transformed Tristram into an impossible suitor, just as the conditions of his life would have made of him, at any rate for her, a disastrous husband. That she had grown to consider their friendship as a thing so precious, aggravated the position still further, and made her liable to lose her judgment, in the same way that if we are moving any fragile object which we particularly treasure, we are all the more likely to drop it. The perpetual scenes to which he now subjected her, were all the more painful, in that in this one instance

she really cared too much to wish in any way to drama-
tise the position for her own amusement. In the place
of a faithful, understanding, witty and brilliant com-
rade there was now substituted, as though through
some transcendent feat of prestidigitation, a sensual,
impetuous, obstinate, gloomy, and even stupid, lover.

She did not wish to lose him out of her life, she
told him, but he ought to have known that marriage
between them was impossible, since she did not love
him. How could he, penniless and extravagant, for a
moment think that she would marry him : or did he,
perhaps, expect her to live with him ? She had often
in the past rated him for his adoration of low types,
of women whose lives were shoddy and lacked shape :
had his constant affairs with them blinded him to the
fact that there were others more fastidious ? It was all
very well, she said, for him to storm at her, proclaim-
ing that the bending of life toward one purpose was
selfish, but if only he, too, would remember that life
had a pattern, it might have saved him from these short
snatches of ugly design. Moreover, to fall in love with
her now made them both look ridiculous. His sense
of humour, if nothing else, should have kept him from
it. With her, she protested, it must always be love at
first sight or not at all. Indeed, his proposals, so late
in the day, were almost insulting. She refused to be
treated as one who " improves on acquaintance."

Thus, with a true instinct as to the only possible
means of averting catastrophe, she attempted to prevent

him from reaching a level of tragedy, endeavoured to laugh away his protestations and the tempestuous scenes that ensued. And this required an effort, for they hurt her. Further, in order to lessen the pain her words might inflict upon him, she constantly urged him to remember that he must have known that she would never accept him. She had always made clear her determination to marry a rich man, for herself had been brought up, and lived still, in an atmosphere, altogether peculiar and difficult, of poverty combined with and set among great possessions. This indigence, as her parents considered it, though comparative, and scarcely perhaps so grim a spectre as they pretended, had yet almost attained the dignity of a family skeleton, except that far from being hidden away, and bolted in a cupboard, they were apt to brandish it aloft in the open with a certain pride. But her existence was, nevertheless, restricted by a lack of money, which at the same time was often rendered worse by wanton flights of luxury that would end as suddenly as they had begun. When she married she was determined, therefore, that her life should alter in this respect. Every possible splendour of background must then still be afforded her; but she must be able, too, to offer every luxurious detail in the foreground. Nor, in fact, was Ursula's attitude entirely mercenary. It was, again, the sculptor's instinct. That she should be rich was in the interest of the whole world, for she knew that she was capable of an amplitude and beauty of life which few could achieve. Was she, then, to shatter her own creation, already taking shape, for the sake of marrying a man she did not love?

Little by little, however, and to her consternation, this attitude began to alter. She grew impressed, in spite of herself, by this imploring, bullying whirlwind of a lover, by the fury that consumed him like a flame, by his energy, as he denounced her selfishness and want of heart, by his arrogance as he told her that, through her refusal to marry him, she was losing the opportunity of her lifetime. She was touched by the appealing quality of his looks, as remorse for the things he had said once more overtook him, by his timidity, new to her, though it was as natural as his pride. But more than by anything else was she moved by the simple, universal signs of being in love which he manifested— strange to observe in so old a friend—symptoms unexpected in one who had been so often a lover; by the pathetic efforts, for example, that he now made to overcome the natural carelessness of his appearance, by the trouble so obviously expended on brushing his hair into a shape more like that adopted by other people, and by the fact, however irritating, that he would, when he was in London, walk for hours in the darkness outside Rypton House, under the illusion that he could not be seen. Further, the perpetual revolutions of passion through which he passed were beginning to increase his physical fascination for her. Spontaneous and artless as were these moods which alternated so violently, mistaken as they appeared, even to him on subsequent reflection, they yet began to carry for Ursula an emotional force together with a burden of pathos, that no system of tactics, however skilfully devised, could possibly have borne. And at this moment, which might have been so favourable for him ; at this moment when she discerned that all at once she had mysteriously grown to love him, and that her strength of will, the one thing in life of which she had been certain, was no longer to be relied upon, she became unnerved. And it is only now, in fact, that any blame can be attached to her for her treatment of him. Hitherto, though she had been true to her own mind, and frank with the frankness of which she alone among women was capable, she had been generous. But she had become frightened, and fright made her cruel.

Tristram soon realised that some profound change had taken place in her, in her feelings for him ; that there was something she was hiding from him. And suddenly he guessed its nature. From the first, both experience and his own sensitiveness had warned him that nothing in the world was more improbable than that this companion, whom he had known so intimately for several years, should fall in love with him. But if, as many of his friends thought, one of the reasons that he loved Ursula with such intensity was the consciousness, so new to him, that this passion was not returned ; if it were true that he had at last incurred the fate of the sensualist, snared by that which he could not obtain, yet now that the marvel had taken place, his emotion was inexpressibly heightened. A wild elation—not only because his love was requited, but also because his will had at least conquered—took possession of him. Alas, he could not foresee that this miracle was to bring him nothing but sorrow and disaster.

Love of this burning order was for Ursula a new experience : but now that it had woken in her, her instinct at once made her realise that it was as firmly rooted in her nature as in Tristram's. She must not let it capture her. The only thing, therefore, was, in as far as possible, to avoid him : and this would be painful enough for both of them, since it had long been their habit to meet constantly, to visit picture-galleries and concerts, to lunch and dine and go to dances together.

But she was compelled, she thought, to take a far more sad and serious decision. Circumstances forced her, she believed, to look round quickly for a husband, rich and distinguished : otherwise the plan of her life might come to disaster. She must hurry on the day which up to now she had been inclined to allow to drift towards her.

In this resolve, she had for once been confident of support from her parents. The life of her father was governed by an innate and profound distaste for any manifestation of intelligence, except when it occurred in those animals on whom he could visit it with death.

He would wile away hours by relating stories which
would describe, in minute detail, the remarkable mental
powers he had observed in fox, stag or otter as he
drove it to its fate. But in men, cleverness was different ; and toward the creative mind, that peculiarly human development, he bore a grudge that was all the
more ferocious in that he could give it no vent. A man
of action, there was, alas, nothing he could do to prevent books being written or pictures painted. Even tar
and feathers were forbidden to this degenerate age.
And in any case, as he used to say, " feathers are too
good for such folk " ; for, like many other enemies to
human intelligence, he had been driven to find comfort
in the sagacity of birds. All intelligent, bless 'em, and
without any airs or graces. Indeed, as though inspired
by the very spirit of contradiction, himself was not without literary pretensions, and would despatch, every
week or so, a letter to the *Scrutator* on this subject—
letters which, after a judicious polishing up of their
grammar by the office-boy, were published in those
august columns.

Lady St. Donat, on the other hand—a haggard,
rather beautiful old harridan, who seemed to levitate
like a medium among countless veils and draperies,
and was full of the most irritating, antiquated mannerisms, left over from the esthetic period—prided herself
on a peculiar love of literature. This she displayed by
an unthinking hatred and vehement denunciation of
everything written since 1872, an *annus mirabilis*,

when, at four years of age, she had been kissed on the same afternoon by George Meredith, Carlyle, Ruskin and Lord Tennyson. The permanent state of arrested mental development that had apparently ensued on so precocious an experiment had won for her a great reputation, all her life, for being " artistic " : a condition she further emphasised by each year turning out a great number of highly-coloured and much-varnished oil-paintings. These evinced an unmistakable personal style, and usually portrayed idealised varieties of well-known earthly scenes : cities in which, jumbled together, St. Peter's at—or rather from—Rome, the Parthenon, the Great Mosque at Cairo, Hampton Court, the Pyramids, the garden at Villa d'Este, York Minster, the Taj Mahal, Isola Bella, St. Paul's Cathedral, the Palazzo Vecchio of Florence, the Sphinx, Genoa Harbour, the Alhambra and Milan Cathedral, all set in a perpetual sunset glory of picture-postcard lakes and date-palms, among which fluttered, according as your taste might translate it, a homely sea-gull or an exotic white ibis, vied with one another rather surprisingly. When in particularly high esthetic spirits, the painter, to add human interest, would suspend an angel with a flaming sword in mid-air above the mingled spires, domes and minarets or throw into the foreground any of her favourite characters from history, Joan of Arc, Alfred the Great, Queen Elizabeth, King Arthur, Mary Queen of Scots, Lorenzo the Magnificent, Lord Byron, Jenghiz Khan (the influence of the Russian Ballet was here to be detected), the Black Prince, Saladin, or Ellen Terry. The machicolated bulk of Rypton Castle was full of such *macédoines*, and some had even found their way, it was stated by the servants who showed visitors round the staterooms, into American picture-galleries.

Added, then, to Lord St. Donat's ineradicable hatred of literature, and to his wife's conviction that all writers should, as it were, be born dead, there was, equally strong in each of them, a distrust—in relation to their daughter's male friends—of all who were not rich. Ursula had been on their hands now for some years. She was not an easy daughter. "You never knew what she would take it into her head to do next." And her parents showed a great anxiety to see her settled and conventionalised. But to their child's surprise, she now found that they had made of Tristram an exception, and actually regarded him with favour as a prospective son-in-law. Indeed, they genuinely liked him, and merely hated his poetry. He would probably " grow out of it," they felt. His name was a good one. Further, they realised that there was " something in the boy "—by which was signified their belief that, were he willing to sell his talents and abandon his silly ideals, he would make money and a career. And surely now, if only for Ursula's sake—not to mention their sakes, for they would be very kind to him—he would become, as they put it, " sensible." Her father, indeed, resolutely refused to believe that he was a poet. He did not look like one. His manners and appearance def-

initely removed him from that detestable, if comic,
category ; a class of which Lord St. Donat's conception
had been built up by perpetual attendance over a long
stretch of years at all the correct musical-comedies and
revues, in which a poet was inevitably either the butt
of the funny man or, sometimes, the funny man himself.
Then, too, there were the modern dramas of Bohemian
life, of which the poet was hero, but owing to the
silliness of the play, fared even worse. Such entertain-
ments are now fortunately extinct, but to Ursula's father
they had been very useful, for they had taught him
to distinguish a poet at a glance. Lady St. Donat, with
her infant reminiscence of hirsute giants, agreed with
her husband that Tristram did not in the least " look
it," was merely unusual, and " original "—nothing
worse. Indeed they would now often discuss between
themselves, the possibility of Ursula's marriage to
Tristram, and the career that would be open to him,
were he only to be guided by their advice. Nor need
he, Lady St. Donat thought, give up literature at once.
A best-seller (she would tell all her literary friends
about the book, and, of course, " recommend it "),
politics, and then, perhaps, a colonial governorship.
Things had altered, and Lord St. Donat said that the
Party *wanted* brains now. Thus, when it transpired
that their daughter was trying to avoid Tristram, they
at first did everything in their power to aid his cause.

To her consternation, Ursula found that her parents
were almost trying to force upon her a marriage with

him. For months the battle proceeded. The St. Donats were even sufficiently gracious to intrigue with their rich friends—without ever telling Ursula or Tristram of it—to obtain for him posts which he was invariably obliged to refuse. These usually consisted in such things as "unpaid secretaryships" (always unpaid, though one day, it was said, they would lead to SOME-THING) of a tedium that would have triumphantly prevented his accomplishing any work of his own.

Soon, however, owing to his incessant spurning of these opportunities, the feelings of Lord and Lady St. Donat for the young man underwent a change. From liking, they passed to disapproval : disapproval deepened into hatred. They began to comprehend that he was not only poor, but stubborn ; determined to remain poor with all the obstinacy at his command. Indeed, so frenetic was Ursula's father, that he was reported to have described Tristram to a group in the bay-window of his club as " a fellow who lives on his WITS —what ! "—a label which, harmless as it may sound to foreign ears, unused to the subtleties of our tongue, nevertheless in England always imputes dishonesty and attaches to a man a weight of moral condemnation. But not only were the parents angry. Tristram had long been fretting and pestering his friends with this hopeless love affair, and all of them who were not themselves writers or painters, every practical person, even my own father and mother, who had known and been devoted to him since he was a child, were enraged at his rejection of these pieces of problematic good-luck. But even had he been willing to take one of the positions found for him through the influence of Lord St. Donat, even had he been sure of founding a great fortune, this would not in the least have caused Ursula to change her mind. For, if she would not marry him because he was poor, still more firmly, to do her justice, would she, at this time, have declined to accept him were he to give up, against her wishes though for her sake, his chief claim to consideration : that of being a writer of more than talent.

While, however, refusing to chase these material if elusive will-o'-the-wisps, which Lord and Lady St. Donat, to borrow a sporting simile, " put up " for him, he at the same time declined to relinquish his pursuit of their daughter. Now rushing to the other extreme, they forbade her to see him, a move which nearly turned the scale in his favour. For it was as though she had lost two friends : first her charming, intimate, amusing, clever companion, and then the passionate, bad-tempered, attractively-animal, scene-making lover into which he had been transmuted. All her instincts, all her sympathies were on his side, and her parents were now as much disconcerted at the vigour with which she defended him in any argument as they had previously been pained and puzzled at her coldness. But being certain that if she were to run away with him she would ruin both his life and her own, she found the strength to desist. Moreover, she had chosen ; had decided that she must marry Lord Drayling, a young, very rich, rather ordinary but clever and ambitious man, who had long been in love with her. If her parents had conceived that this match was possible, they would never for an instant have lent Tristram their support. But upon this subject Ursula had shown herself so steadfast that they had altogether abandoned hope.

Though I do not think that he as yet suspected the likelihood of this marriage, Tristram was furiously jealous, and, as result of the tortures he suffered—an aching that seldom left him by day or night—became restless beyond measure, and grew to look exceedingly ill.

When people say that jealousy is a " primitive " emotion, they should add to this dictum, that it is one which obviously attacks equally, and with its greatest virulence, the highest as much as the lowest type of man, though the actual resulting frenzy may be different in kind. At these two extremes it appears to aim—perhaps because they comprise the most emotional of men —in just the same manner that a few rare physical diseases, such as hæmophilia, assail only the most powerful and the most miserable in circumstance, the royal-families and the slum-dwellers. When jealousy attacks the higher type, judgment and intellect can to a certain degree control, though never defeat, it. Reason prevails, but an intense vein of suspicion underlies it; while the very restraint causes the agony, unrelieved by physical action, to be more prolonged and acute. But when this terrible scourge assaults the lowest, most primitive type, it leads to violence.

Properly speaking, jealousy is not an emotion at all, but an abrupt chemical change in the blood, that takes the form of a series of recurrent fevers. It leaves the victim, as suddenly as it sprang upon him, exhausted, but apparently cured and free of poison : then, all at once, it swoops down upon him again without warning. Like Prometheus, the struggling prey cannot defend himself against this vulture that consumes his vitals. The delirium induced may be absolute, and last only for a minute, in which case murder most probably results, or may be partial and continue for a day or two at a time. And when, during a trial for murder, the prisoner pleads that " something came over him," that for a moment he " saw red," this statement is a true description of the process that was at work within him. It was, as he says, a physical sensation. The tide and surge of blood overwhelmed him, and he killed.

With Tristram the fever would endure for two or three days at a time, during which periods he would become a person transformed. Jealousy with him was as the wand of a wizard which turns all it touches into something base, striking all loved objects into the likeness of toads, and things of night. Silent save for unreasonable bursts of rage with his best friends, he would be for ever wondering—though not a word would escape him of it—with whom Ursula was talking, with whom dancing. If she was not in London he was always now in movement, eagerly rushing down to the south of France or up to the north of Scotland, to Rypton Castle or to Venice. These journeys he would undertake on the merest chance of seeing her, for he was not always informed of her whereabouts : and unless he deceived himself, as is the custom of those in love, he must have known that, even if he found her, no very warm welcome would await him, at any rate from her parents. For though he continually forced Ursula to see him—and she was fully conscious that it was better for both their sakes that they should not meet—latterly she had shown great forbearance, treated him gently and kindly in spite of his turbulence. This she did, not only out of opposition to her mother and father, who, she considered, had interfered at every possible juncture, but because she was on the verge of taking a step which must, she knew, inflict on him the greatest anguish : nor must she allow him to observe that she suffered equally, was really as wretched as himself. But at this period it was useless to attempt to be nice to Tristram. Once he had arrived where she was staying, it was as though a tornado had descended.

After creating a furious and pointless scene, he would scurry miserably back to London : and, as he writhed in the train, would vow to himself that his passion was now over, perished, burnt out. There would follow the usual swing-back of regret, remorse and affection, while his wounds were envenomed anew through fear of the effect on Ursula of what he had said or done—which, such had been his temper at the time, he could now scarce recall. In atonement, he would overwhelm her with letters, telegrams and presents.

In London, he would never be still for a moment. His own work was either totally neglected for a long period, or if he wrote at all, he took to it as though it were a drug, by means of which he might find oblivion in a world of his own creation. Only thus, and in seeing people, could he lose himself. Further, such a life of trains and crowds told more than ever on his purse, and this, in turn, upon his health. He was now heavily in debt. His existence was increasingly one that consisted in devious, even dubious, devices to elude and pacify creditors—hardly the sort of life, surely, which he could have expected Ursula to share. But so much was he in love that he had lost all sense of reality.

It was when he was in this rather morbid state of mind and soul that, as he lay peacefully in bed one morning, he opened the paper quite casually, to read in it the announcement of the engagement of Lord Drayling to Lady Ursula Rypton. (Incidentally, I remember, the day on which it was made public was the thirteenth of the month, a date of which Tristram, despite the possession of a fine and logical mind, still entertained his old, childish distrust.) Though for some weeks it ought to have been obvious to him that this union was on its way, his first sensation was one of surprise. He had blinded himself to the nearness of it. And then Ursula had never mentioned to him the possibility of such a thing. Here, for the second time, she had been cruel : and once more the cruelty had arisen from mingled love and fright. She loved him enough to be unable, absolutely unable, to break the news herself to him ; she was afraid of his response, and of its effect upon her.

And now he made a discovery : for his next emotion, he found, beneath that of surprise, was one of relief—and even in this state, he was amazed at it. But amazement, too, was hard, for he had moved so far away, was released, bereft of feeling. He could not feel, for nothing mattered and he was far away. He was, it seemed to him, calm and ever so distant, as though his essential self had withdrawn itself into some secret and invisible fastness within the body—a fastness of the existence of which, even, he had been ignorant until now, and out of which it might never again emerge. And it was curious that this hiding-place was within, not without.

That morning and afternoon he spent walking about in a numbed and dazed condition, though through the mists, everywhere he could see the photographs of her, the posters on which the news was written, so that her image haunted him, even in this inner retreat, albeit nothing could reach nor hurt him in it.

The breakdown, to which this had been the prelude, was serious enough in itself : but the doctors, informed of his family history, regarded it much more gravely.

His father had died young, as the consequence of a mental malady—though its nature had always been disguised from the son. And as the days, and then the weeks went by, his progress was far from reassuring. Sleep had left him almost entirely, and could only be induced by drugs. He was forbidden to receive his friends—with the exception of myself, who helped to look after him—and this deprivation of the very thing in which he found his chief pleasure still further aggravated his misery.

At this period when members of the medical profession were in doubt as to the correct treatment of the patient, it was their invariable rule to recommend that he must move far away from them : nor did they ever allow consideration of his financial state to deter them from such a decision. And Tristram's affairs were now as involved and ailing as his health. Owing what were for him large sums, at the same time his illness debarred him from earning even the usual meagre additions to his small income. But the doctors insisted that he must go abroad—and for a considerable period—as soon as he was well enough to travel. Furthermore, he must give up all work for a year. He needed " taking out of himself "—sight-seeing, for example, though he must not be allowed to tire himself or become excited. And at first it would not do for him to travel alone. He must have a companion.

In fact, Tristram's prostration threatened to be almost as much of a disaster for his friends as for himself.

The money, which many of them could ill spare, had to be found for his travels. Nevertheless, they were not inclined to grudge it.

At last, and slowly, very slowly, he began to mend. And now myself was chosen to accompany him on his journey. It was in that moment a responsibility which I rather dreaded, though at any other time it would have been a pleasure. But I was very busy just then. It was awkward to have to leave London, for a new book of mine was appearing, and I was not sure that my own nervous system was so robust as to encourage me in nursing cases of this kind for long periods. We had often travelled together before, it was true, but then he had been answerable for himself. And now even the burden of his unpunctuality would be laid upon me. It was most distressing, withal, to see a friend in this sad condition. However, go we must. Italy we had often visited together and knew well. So on this occasion we decided to explore Spain, a country of which Tristram had long felt the appeal, though he had never, hitherto, been able to go there.

The doctors were pleased with our choice of country, as it would provide, they thought, a very complete change. It must be remembered that this tour, on which we were soon to set out, took place nearly a decade after the close of the first " World War," or " Little World War," as they now call it. There was acknowledged to be about the Spain of those days—as, no doubt, there is of these—a quality all her own, that

to some was as refreshing as to others it was obnoxious.
She had always stood a little aside from that movement
toward a general and monotonous uniformity which
had been gaining strength in Europe for a century or
more—a movement aided by the establishment in so
many countries of burgess-republics and conscription,
and supported by the Big-Business interests both here
and, above all, in America.   An aristocratic nation,
Spain had ever refused to descend into the market-place
and join in the brawl, in the scrum and scrimmage of
industrialism and war, that twin-headed, Siamese ogre.
Indeed, if she must have one, Spain has ever preferred
a war of her own, if possible with herself, so that each
soldier knows that he will find in his opponent a
caballero or *hidalgo* whom it will not disgrace him to
fight ; for it is as easy to judge a man by his enemies as
by his friends, and they should surely be picked as
carefully.   But failing the attainment of such a model
campaign, it must at least be near home or on Spanish
territory.   The result of such, at any rate partial, an
abstention from the fashionable crazes of the day, was
that Spanish poverty, denounced by democrats as the
worst in Europe, proclaimed itself as still of a medieval,
and not an industrial, order.   Food, no doubt, may
have been scarce, but there was untainted air and pure
sunshine.   If there were here few pleasure-machines
and silk stockings, there was at least none of the foggy,
muddy, polluted gin-palace-Saturday-night squalor, only
enlivened by two or three maimed soldiers playing

phono-fiddles, that was to be found at this time in the northern countries. The music to be heard in Spain, too, was of a different kind. It was true that there were plenty of halt and maimed to be seen, but as a consequence of Nature's infamy rather than of man's. And there still existed in this " backward " land, we were told, a sombre indifference to fate, together with a strange gaiety and love of dancing, and, above all, a belief and comfort in religion not to be discovered in other places where education and science had already selfishly withdrawn from the poor this prop for their self-esteem. Thus it was hoped by his friends that in the life of this country, so different, as everyone agreed, from that to be observed elsewhere, Tristram might find an anodyne.

Since it was now the early spring, we were advised to go first to the south of Spain, for the north moves straight, and often in the space of a day or two, from an iron cold to a red heat, and at present it would be frozen. It was difficult to know how to reach the south, for this was long before the inauguration of air-liners : air-planes were too expensive, too perilous then, be-sides, to be comfortable for a nerve-patient : while to travel by rail would be far too tiring for him. We decided, therefore, to embark in an English boat that called at Gibraltar on its way out to India.

Looked back on as part of our whole travels, the voyage to that port appears to occupy a space of time entirely out of scale with its actual duration, though physically we were as comfortable as is ever possible upon the ocean. If the sea is rough, all men are equal before the steward, and the fiercest dragon of a chutney-fed colonel becomes as a little child again. But it remainded surprisingly smooth, and thus we were privileged to see to perfection a new world. The fine weather drew out of their various caverns the most improbable menagerie of sea-borne mammalia, encouraged them to pace the decks as though these were a series of floating Mappin-terraces. Isolated after this manner, high up and against a background of palest blue, toned down in its turn by layer after layer of white, cotton-wool-like mist, one was positively obliged to pay attention to their tricks, for there was no other object in view to distract the mind, except when, very occasionally, a loud hooting proclaimed that another series of floating-platforms was nearing us, and our performers would all flock to one side of the deck, there to survey the rival troop with the feverish, though gaping, curiosity of the animal world. They would pass each other, but not without some suspicion and jealousy, manifested by growling, shouting and waving, and then would swiftly settle down again to their various tricks and devices.

Many of them, indeed, appeared to be very skilled and highly-trained, and exhibited the most diverting, intricate antics, such, for example, as throwing rings on to wooden pegs. With a delicious touch of fantasy, too, the authorities had below installed for their benefit a special mechanical circus, full of electric camels, horses and elephants upon which, should they be in the necessary high spirits, they could disport themselves for hours. Then, in addition, there were bicycles, the pedals of which could be worked with an alarming rapidity, and, apart from the fact that these machines were in reality stationary, thereby adding one more jot to the uproarious fun, recalled that rapid, dwarf machine for the riding of which the lamented "Consul" used to gain so much applause.* Moreover, one reflected, that in no other respect were they his inferiors in cleverness, for doubtless, like him, they had many of them drawn out and signed their own cheques for the journey.

However, the performers, one supposed, were like all their kind delicate. Such a life, which must need constant practice thus always to be at the highest point of achievement, was, of course, exhausting and could evidently only be supported by the aid of enormous meals, and, in between the shows (obviously it was all done by kindness), of cups of soup, tea and coffee, piles of sandwiches and cakes, offered them every half-hour or so by their attendants to the sound of bells, gongs and bugles. Or might, again, the reverse

* "Consul" was by far the most distinguished ape on the music-hall stage of my youth. He rode his own specially designed bicycle, and drew on his own banking account. It was stated at the time of his death, some fifty years ago, that he had in his own handwriting petitioned the bank authorities to allow him an overdraft, and that as a result of this request being refused, "Consul" had died of a broken heart.

proposition be the correct one—that such a guzzle-régime could only be survived through constant, frantic, and pointless over-exertion ?

Paralysed after their orgies of food and exercise, the redder-faced men would descend to the smoking-room, to remain prone on sofas, limp in armchairs, panting as would stertorous sea-monsters, their purple veins swelling visibly, and covered with twinkling beads of sweat as though still fresh and moist from the depths of ocean. The low room was decorated with palm-trees, and was very overheated, so that it resembled to a certain extent the tropical reptile den at the Zoo-logical Gardens. The sham, old-oak beams, too, sug-gested that crocodiles or alligators had climbed up on to the ceiling, there to remain motionless until suddenly a beam would move, and there would be a cruel, smil-ing snap of the white teeth. But no such morbid imagery suggested itself to our circus, and here its members paused comfortably, just as a railway-engine halts in order to take in water after a long, non-stop run, to fill up with whisky-and-soda. For the first few minutes, save for the restful plashing of the siphon, there would be silence : the peaceful silence of exhaus-tion. Then, already a little recovered, one or two of them would herald conversation with the usual pre-lude, would inhale their cigarette-smoke so loudly, in a manner which was at the same time defiant, it is true, but yet in a way reflective, interesting and friendly, that the sound of it could be heard all over the room, high above the waves, or the comforting, mechanical singing of the electric fan, ever their champion against the lurking, plum-coloured ghost of apoplexy. Finally, though not without effort, and as if at last shaking themselves free of the spray, they would enunciate a few apparently nonchalant words, but ones in reality well-calculated, through long practice, to lead up to their favourite and chosen theme.

Since the liner was India-bound, the greater part of the wayward menagerie upon this voyage was composed of the choleric, military persuasion, very red in face and neck, with antiquated, yellowing white moustaches swaggering like torn regimental banners from their upper lips, and with bald heads, clean and worn smooth by the false, protective egg-shell of their sun-helmets. With them were their well-laundered wives, iron-marked, pressed and flattened, who, in their turn, were usually accompanied by a niece, Doris ; a girl who had suffered that last surviving Victorian emotion, a " disappointment," and was now progressing steadily southward and eastward every year, for having started waltzing in York and Tunbridge, she had since in vain one-stepped at Ostend, fox-trotted at Gibraltar, performed the " blues," all for nothing, at Malta, and was now to " Charleston " despairingly at Simla and black-bottom for nothing in Bombay. Then there were, too, a few self-important officials, who envied, abused in private, yet cringed before the representatives of the army, many rich merchants, who talked endlessly of

rupees and outdid the colonels in their views of the
native question, two or three Hindus, universally
despised and thrust into a corner—although they, on
their side, were very conscious of the loss of caste incurred by travelling across the ocean, especially in such
company, and spent most of their time washing so as to
avoid contamination—while, scattered among all these,
inappropriately enough, were one or two humorous
curates, who despite their jokes and smiles were so
lean and eager that one could only imagine that the
Bishop responsible for their choice had—with the idea
of cannibals always at the back of his mind, and a wish
to disappoint them with a Lenten fare—especially
favoured those with " nothing on them " ; several
silent, bold, esthetic persons of nondescript age and
sex, these latter on the way to Spain or Italy, travelling
in the company of their liquid-eyed counterparts of the
same order, but pretending to timidity, and a good
many nervous and chattering artistic ladies, middle-
aged, dressed in brown camel-like garments that exactly
matched their faces and hair, the latter without doubt
being the actual substance used in camel's-hair paint-
brushes, and who all wore, clasped round their necks,
however ill the calm sea might make them feel, the
identical curved form of the same furry animal. Since
one saw this species nowhere else, it gave them the air
of belonging to a secret society, for the animal was of
curious design and countenance—perhaps, one felt, the
wreck of that rare, egg-laying mammal, the duck-
billed platypus. This camel-corps were determined to

think the best of everybody, and had small cabins entirely filled with neatly-tied-up cardboard boxes, containing sandwiches, paint-brushes, prayer-books, a slab of Rowntree's chocolate "in case of difficulties," a bottle of "eau de Cologne," and a copy of Ruskin's "Stones of Venice"; lastly, but as they would very swiftly intimate in conversation, by no means least, there were two intensely well-informed and much-travelled American women, with their own deck-chairs and names attached—names, one was soon given to understand, that in the other hemisphere conveyed a great deal in the four worlds of birth, art, literature and music. Moreover, it was obvious in the bearing of these two ladies that, setting great store on travel-prestige, they were seldom on dry-land, and spent most of their life nowadays in awarding the prizes for deck-games.

While nearly all the men were resting downstairs, taking in supplies after their labours, these two high-born and cultivated American women would sit placarded in their deck-chairs—which, with the fine eye of practised military leaders, they had placed in just the right strategic position for waylaying the few male survivors from so arduous a morning. Thus labelled, and swathed in furs, rugs, gloves, veils and Asprey-travelling-apparatus, they would entertain a succession of new friends with literary and musical disquisitions, interspersed with fragments of inimitable autobiography.

The smaller of the two ladies, Mrs. O'Looney, combined in her appearance and atmosphere a judicious mixture of skull and fox-terrier. The smile was the sinister, toothy grin of the skull, and in the macabre laugh that attended it the skeleton could be heard jangling its bones : yet the speaking voice, faithful and jolly, the alert eyes and the indeterminate colouring, were clearly canine. Her gnarled, little, tailor-made body, with its abrupt terrier movements, was always, like that of the dog, watchful for unspoken insult against her friend and acknowledged leader. On the other hand, Mrs. Hope-Doodle-Cope, as she elected to be called—the first being her christian name, the second belonging to her dead father, the late Colonel Doodle, the third being that of her husband—was of large, operatic build, rather given, under the outer layers imposed by ocean travel, to pearls, earrings as long as one's finger, Spanish shawls and dramatic velvets. She was for ever softly humming little airs, running over a rather throaty scale or two, or tapping with her fingers on an invisible, as well as fortunately dumb, piano. But the material prolongations of her personality, the rugs, bags and wraps, were not the least interesting part of her, for they represented so many foreign-travel scalps. From having at one time been content to hunt artists and their like, they had become too small game for her, and now whole nations were the object of her chase, whole continents her quarry. And, as though she were a New Guinea head-hunter, she thus wore their scalps dangling from her person, for among her kind they invested her with an immense authority, made it only right that she should be asked to judge of sea-skill and to award the prizes.

Her presence, though, was not without its compensations for me : since one of the few moments of cheerfulness which had visited Tristram since the beginning of his illness was spent in analysing these properties. The piteous silver-fox, he decided, with its dull but flashing bead-eyes, so like those of Mrs. O'Looney, was, as it were, the very pelt of Alaska, the bersaglieri feathers in her hat represented a plucked Italy, the long ruby earrings that jingled over her plate at dinner, exemplified the life-blood of which she had drained Spain, the puma-skin rug was a flayed South American republic, the crocodile-skin cushion a decapitated India, her red hand-bag a still bleeding portion of Morocco, her lacquer cigarette-case, most tragic of all, the entrail of a disembowelled Japan, that, in the confident expectation of the similar reply which good manners must dictate, had perhaps committed *hari-kari*. To mention any foreign country in front of her was an offence : and at the mention of some such word as " Cochin-China," her lips would shoot out with scorn at a curious angle, her eye would assume a bridling but malicious glitter, and she would say, " Well, Mr. Orlander, you must remember that to us Cochin-China is an old story."

But the effect ultimately aimed at in her appearance —and this, again, would constitute in itself a qualifi-

cation for prize-giving at deck-games—was one of
" old-world charm and graciousness." Though still
middle-aged, rather than old, this attempt relied largely
on quite unnecessary quantities of white hair, which, for
ever escaping at unexpected points from under her hat,
by its artificial softness contrived to impart an additional flint-like hardness to the eye, an almost sand-
paper texture to the skin : while, to make doubly sure
that you noticed this " old world quality," she was
always confiding in you stories, pointless, except that
in them people were made to address her in their talk
as " Madame " instead of " Mrs." ; strangers, for example, were made to say, on first meeting her, " This,
Madame Doodle-Cope, is a very unexpected honour."

She had reigned, it appeared, jointly with Mrs.
O'Looney in New York, when there had been such a
think as Breeding, " when there was to be found in
Noo York the noocleus of a cultured but excloosive
society, such as could be found nowhere in Europe."
But alas, the world had begun to alter ! Rich, vulgar
people, of a generation that knew not the name of
Doodle, had started to push their way into this magic
circle, until one day their husbands, Mr. O'Looney and
Judge Cope, had originated a touchingly unselfish idea.
Hand in hand—and, one suspects, without any very
sanguine expectation of success—they had gone to
their wives, and had said, " We have thought things
out together, and a cruel situation faces us. But, Hopie
and Birdie, New York is now no place for two Prin-

cesses. You must travel more. It may be that in Rome or Paris—or even Tokyo or Teheran—you will find the setting that you need : that needs you. Do not let either money or distance deter you. With such an object in view, neither is of any importance. And do you know," Mrs. O'Looney barked energetically at me, " those two darling men don't mind being left alone, they don't mind the cost. Often they write to us, saying, ' Don't trouble to hurry back.' And when, only a few weeks ago, we wrote and asked them, weren't they kind of lonesome, with no one to talk to, they answered —it was in their very last cable, wasn't it, Hopie ?— ' We still have the sound of your voices in our ears.' Now don't you call that just sweet ? . . . And here we are, roaming the world, because our friends are scattered and our little niche is gone. Why, we positively dread going back to Noo York."

Perpetually each of the two ladies would laud the " Social Position " of the other. When not thus engaged, they showed their importance in another way— by remaining in their state-rooms, writing endless little messages to fellow-passengers, demanding, for instance, the immediate loan of the book which they had observed some fellow-traveller was reading at the time. or the return of a volume that they had pressed upon him, however unwilling he had been to accept it. All Mrs. Doodle-Cope's books, incidentally, had branded in her large handwriting on their paper, Tauchnitz covers either the soothing word " good " or the titillating

word " clever." The recommendation never in any
way departed from this formula, for it was to be understood that nothing less than one of these two claims
was to be advanced for any book fortunate enough to
find its way into her hands. The continual notes, concerning such matters, were written on paper emblazoned
by Tiffany with a special monogram—a token of
supreme social consequence—while Mrs. Cope's signature varied from " Cordially, Hope-Doodle-Cope " (a
sound with an agreeable, comfortable, jog-trot-lollop in
it) to (which more suggested, by harmony and association, a bugle-call, a machine-gun opening fire, and a
cheer) " Hastily, Hope-Cope."

Personally, I found this spot on deck a delicious
oasis, but, though at times Tristram derived great enjoyment from it, I feared that on the whole, it served
but to emphasise that tragic background which these
latter months had presented for his mind. Meanwhile,
downstairs in the smoking-room, the heroes of so much
endeavour would be recovering, and thought was now
unfolding its first, tender buds upon the smoky atmosphere. Not to join—unless you were one of the clergymen—in the asthmatic, throaty and spluttering conversation that would follow was to " give oneself airs."
At the same time, the joining-in must be a passive one,
for to say something yourself, except in non-committal
but discreetly rapturous reply, was worse : it was to be
" opinionated."

The tone of the talk differed ; the tendency imparted

by the India-merchants was usually precisely that of small boys at a private-school, boasting after dark in the dormitory of the extent of their fathers' possessions, matching a yacht against an avenue ; while that lent to it by some of the military, was a little more adult, let us say equivalent to that of youths at an army crammer's, burning with the maculate fever of their adolescence and exaggerating to one another their amorous exploits with the wasp-waisted waitresses of the local tea-shop. In fact, happy beings unaware of their own good fortune, unknowing incarnations of Peter Pan, they had never grown up. But the more serious-minded section of the military and the civil-servants discussed politics, much as women do over tea in a ladies' club, though it was to be observed that, as in a Tchekoff play, not one of these more solemn persons ever allowed the direction of his thought or talk to be diverted from the course he had intended it to take by anything another person said : thus it resembled an orchestra in which every instrument maintained its own tune and time against its fellows.

Indian moral deterioration, however, was the chief and favourite theme. There had, for example, recently been an unpleasant incident, in which one of the " brutes " had attempted to hit back ! Unfortunately, when the fiercest of the smoking-room veterans was looking round for someone in whom to confide the details of gallant massacres of old, before the " damned politicians had begun to interfere," it was inevitably, and as though by instinct, to Tristram that he would turn to communicate them. This terrified me, for my friend's mind was indelibly tinged with the poetic, humanitarian sentiment : he was in a very nervous state —worse, it seemed to me, than when we had left London—and I feared an eruption. Forced continually to shadow him, I was several times obliged gently to lead him out : nor did he in the least wish to go. He craved, I suppose, a vent for his emotions. Meanwhile, as somehow or other he was enticed away, I had to make emollient little noises and propitiatory nods and smiles at the flushed, full-blown peony faces round us, angry, one feared, at being cut short in the middle of a tale that had several times ere now interested the cleverest fellow in the " Calcutta Gentlemen's Club." By good fortune, though, they had never heard of Tristram, or trouble would have ensued : for, as a young writer, already famous, and one who was a poet and followed his own bent, he would have ranked almost as an honorary native.

There was, though, a particular incident which might have been deplorable in its effect on him—an episode of a kind that occurs so frequently when there is any opportunity for it, as nearly to persuade me to believe in telepathy or occult revelation. We used rather to frequent the smoking-room, for I thought that watching and listening to the people there would a little distract his mind from his personal affairs. Upon this occasion we were sitting by that table in the centre of the room always occupied by the loud-talking old men, whose wont it was to discuss Indian politics, when one of them unfortunately saw lying by his side a newspaper. By some extraordinary chance, it was the issue, now many weeks old, which contained the announcement of Ursula's engagement : and, as though India no longer existed for them, as if it was the only subject that interested them—though, in reality, not one of them had ever seen the girl—the whole party proceeded to discuss her and the impending marriage, summoning up for their full enjoyment of it every detail of suburban and night-club chatter. There was nothing to be done. I did not attempt in this instance to smuggle Tristram away, for in matters of this kind one could not, I realised, treat him in such a fashion : nor could one sympathise or pretend not to hear. As it was, he did not champion her, did not utter : only the pallor and intenseness of his expression increased. But so relieved was I when the conversation was over, so pleased that it had not been even worse, that it was not until long afterward that my full surprise at his numbness and want of chivalry asserted itself.

Nevertheless, to my mind there is no doubt that this voyage, in spite of its troubles and absurdities, in the end helped his recovery, by providing him with a definite reaction. Until now, for many months it had seemed as though, through long suffering, he had grown incapable of feeling. And then the release from this floating incarceration, when it did come, was all the more wonderful, for on such a ship, even though it is only for a few days, our fate appears inextricably intertwined with that of the other passengers. This is the only world that exists, and all through life their presence, their ideas, their words will hem one in. It will, one feels, be as impossible to escape them in the years to come as it has been in the past to avoid old schoolfellows ; those black-nailed, bullying ghosts. As it was, we arrived sound in limb, and never saw one member of the Indian contingent again.

On the other hand, during our travels, the hard-eyed or liquid-eyed esthetes, the Camel-Corps, and the high-born American ladies were destined, one or other set of them, to haunt us as irresponsibly and inevitably as the chorus from a comic song, emerging suddenly from places the most sacred or profane, coming out of the bathroom in a dressing-gown, or darting out from behind a confessional in some cathedral, but always materialising when least expected and in every setting the most incongruous to them. We need not, there-fore, describe them further for the present, but, what-ever on our journey we are to see, the reader must every now and then introduce this snatch or catch of grotesque melody for himself.

At last, then, we reached Gibraltar. There we found a strong English wind, old ladies staggering under the weight of their enormous ostrich-feather-trimmed hats, English sentries and policemen, Palladian buildings, cactuses, only now growing outside rather than in the cottage-window, prayer-books and parasols, a Government-owned library, into which, by a curious paradox, no one was ever allowed to penetrate, an 1880 Gothic cathedral, and a real English bishop, with a wife and gaiters—in fact, "a corner of a foreign field that is for ever England." We moved on, and almost within a few yards, found ourselves in the Spain of tradition.

That Andalusian spring was an enchanted one, with never a cloud, never a whip of rain. From Algeciras, we made our way slowly to Seville, visiting on our rather roundabout way such places as Ronda and Cordoba and Cadiz, that white city flashing its wings so far out to sea. And, incidentally, it was at the Mesquita, or "Mosquito" as most of them called it, at Cordoba that we re-encountered the Camel-Corps for the first time. On this occasion, however, they were well staged, for the Moorish yellow stone court outside, with its low fountain and flowering orange trees, the pillars of the Mosque itself, springing up like an oasis of palms in the desert, all helped to provide for them an appropriately oriental backcloth.

And then, one day, we saw rising far over a tawny plain, the slender tower of Seville Cathedral, which possesses the same gift of visibility at a distance—a valuable talent in cathedrals—that is the chief attribute of the dome of St. Peter's.

In Seville we made a long stay. I have never been

able to visit it again, but probably it has undergone less change than most towns since those far away days in the 'twenties. Here in any case I can only give a short synthesis of that city as it then was, of its circular bull-rings cut by the sun, just as the sun is sometimes cut by an eclipse, as though by a knife, into halves of intense darkness and light ; its cloistered women sitting round a fountain in a patio, or sometimes issuing forth in their glory of shawls, combs and mantillas ; its serpentine pink, blood-red and lime-green alleys ; its broad, straight terraces, forbidden to traffic, so that Spanish voices can be heard in all their gay hoarseness, and the dark cloaks of the men can flutter round them with a superb precision, born of long and inherited practice ; the narrow streets, full of wine shops that are within like white-washed caves, holding giant tuns from Jerez set up like altars, while out of them sounds a constant drone of music, as though from a church—except here the lively, cast-iron tunes are in the mould of dances ground out ceaselessly with a rolling, jingling and unearthly regularity, by pianolas and penny-organs, to which, as a tin is fastened to a dog's tail, are attached drums and tambourines ; of the occasional whirls and whorls of African dust that rise in the public squares and swell in a moment into twisting, spinning columns and then like ghosts subside into nothingness, of the orchards of orange-trees at this season studded with ivory rosettes and buds as much as with their usual hanging golden lamps, and giving forth a fragrance that, wafted over painted walls into the street, can even combat the pungent oriental smell of Spanish cookery; of its thousand courts and gardens, with their well-watered trenches, full of gigantic violets, growing almost under the swelling hoofs, solid and grey as those of an elephant, of tall, robust and plumy palm trees and of their brilliantly-tiled pavilions; of the height and width of its arched cathedral, in the aspiring but genial gloom of which the people stroll and talk, as well as weep, prostrate themselves, and, during certain days, dance; of the Court of the Oranges outside, with its cloistered passage where still hangs the ancient, scaly lizard;* of the bulls whacked and driven toward the slaughter of an evening, along the dusty roads between the groves of orange-trees, and of the jaunty magnificence of their opponents, when, all decked out and on their way to the ring, they receive the acclamations of a doting crowd; of the miniature chapels painted in dark blue and white, and boasting many a winged pygmy of a saint; of the early mornings, when the rosy rays lie light as feathers along the streets, and when far up, above the harsh cries of the drivers and the vendors, from a thousand contorted belfries of brick, bells without number clatter out their cracked but rhythmic music, thereby startling the placid, white-winged storks nesting beneath, and, finally, of the

---

* The stuffed crocodile which the Sultan of Egypt sent to Alfonso the Learned in 1260 as a formal proposal for the hand of his daughter.

countless Judas-trees, their bloom a vibrant, pink foam, which in these weeks washes the city like a sea, until it draws out of the sky every variation of space and depth, wrings out of it every tone and texture that there is of blue, makes it so distant that it contains within itself all eternity, or so near that it clings, surely, to the feathered branches, and is the very robe and mantle of Seville.

Once immersed in this tide, tingling with the spray of Spanish life, it was as if Tristram had been dipped in the bubbling waters of a healing well. An additional and protective outer skin, as it were, was forming itself, was growing round him. Life was, undoubtedly, renewing the peculiar force that distinguished him from others ; his subtle understanding of people, the fascination which he exerted over everyone with whom he came in contact—so that, for example, and at the lowest level, he was always better looked after than other people in trains and restaurants—his peculiar way of seeing things. And yet, one wondered. . . . If a power that was new had come to him, a resolution which had perhaps been a little wanting, had not, also, something left him ? Had not a quality, delicate and indefinable, evaporated, been dispersed, perhaps for ever ? Surely, far down, a hardening of the fibre, that matched this new protective epidermis, could be detected ? But, one hoped, this new and strange numbness—which, though I may have suspected its existence, had only definitely entered my consciousness when he failed to make any response to the conversation about

Ursula on the ship—would pass away in time. Certainly after so serious a breakdown no man could emerge immediately and unscathed. Moreover, the speed with which he had shaken off this illness, seemed little less than miraculous. Upon the whole, therefore, I was inclined to judge his recovery a true one, a triumphant expression of victory over himself.

At last we tired of Seville—or, rather, understood that if we were ever to leave it, the hour had now struck. Indeed, it was with more than usual disinclination and regret that, mounting the high, dirty steps into the antiquated railway carriage, vast, hot and dusty, we were slowly jolted and trundled through the darkness toward Granada. In Spain a night-journey is always the excuse for a party : crowds came to say good-bye to their friends at each station, and supper and conversation continued until morning came. But for both of us, the journey was slow and sad—for me perhaps sadder than for my friend. Loth to quit this country, and to leave him, in whose return to health I was able to take as much pride as pleasure—just, too, when he was beginning once more to prove himself the most tirelessly delightful of companions—nevertheless, I was forced to think of my return. The actual date of it, it is true, could still be left pleasantly vague : but it was by now the middle of April, my supply of money had nearly run out, and every description of business that could annoy or bother was calling me back to London. Further, Tristram had reached a stage in his bodily and mental recuperation where, not only was he well enough to be without a companion, but soon it might even be of benefit to him. It would probably enable him to sort out his ideas and feelings : while, by renewing his self-confidence, it would recall him to himself, put him again in tune with the world. Actually there was no need for a hurried decision, and I felt that however much better he might be, it would not be right to abandon him before seeing that he was securely and happily settled in Granada ; an austere city, it was said, and one which lacked the shrill life of Seville. Nor did I wish to leave him until Lady Ursula's marriage, and the accounts of it in the English papers—which fortunately we saw practically never—were safely in the past.

The town of Granada lies in a valley, and since the weather was now starting to be hot, we decided to stay up above it, and if possible on the Alhambra hill itself. A small Spanish hotel would please us best, we felt. It would be cheaper. And we wanted to avoid the icy marble walls, tassellated floors, and overheated, glass palm-lounges of the big hotels as much as the stuffy, tasselled sitting-rooms of the pensions, all, no doubt, faintly but for ever sonant with the recurrent chorus of that comic song, which, since leaving Gibraltar, had been perpetually dinned into our ears, and was now beginning to cloy. On arrival, having the whole golden morning in front of us, we determined, therefore, to leave our luggage at the station and walk about until we had found a suitable place in which to stay. The lion-coloured domes and towers sank behind us as we began to climb a steep hill. Indeed, the ascent is quite abrupt, though it lies in a long cleft that runs up to the top between two hills. Now passing under the arch of a robust Moorish tower, we found ourselves on a broad road, leading through a wood. Along by our side a stream ran down, and everywhere in the deep thickets and fastnesses into which led a number of box-edged paths, could be heard the sound of water leaping down the hill.

It is this wood of northern trees—so unexpected a paradise in a hot country devoted to the dry but fleshy riot of cactus, evergreen and aloe—which tinges all about it with an idyllic beauty. Though even its most joyous moments of flowering and birdsong are underlined by a note of faint and pastoral sadness equally unusual in such a climate, yet at the same time it imparts all the genuine life that can be found there to the dead and mouldering plateaus above, where, continual and accusing witnesses to the action and colour that has long left them, the empty courts and flower-clad honeycombs of the palaces rest in their enclosures like so many skeletons lying in their open graves. These straight masts, shattered and torn toward the top as though by battle, wreathed, enwrapped and writhed over by the dark serpents of the ivy, that coiled from one to the other, were yet virginal, and held high above our heads their torches of luminous green, each one so

tender as to retain its own light within the darkness
of the shadowy grove. Rare as the trees themselves are
the copious streams that flow under them. Indeed, the
flash of water, giving life to this stillness, was to be
seen everywhere, at the side of the roads, between the
foliage, and tossed up in silver rings against the sky,
while, cradled in such ideal surroundings, the nightingales, not yet note-perfect, were even now in the full
morning light trying over their exercises, testing their
compass against the roar and horrid mechanic laughter
of the cars, that tempted by so steep a hill to a similar
show of prowess, were racing up and down, making
every species of noise conceivable to the inventive mind
of the young latin male. But when this city-bred
tumult ceased for a moment, it was as though the quiet
of night had come, with no sounds save the varied in-
cantations of the waters, as they raced, whispered and
sang their way down pebble-paved runnels, murmured
and tapped as they dripped their icicles into vast
troughs, or lashed the air with their silver tails till
every glade in this dark wood echoed to a furtive,
loose-lipped babbling, while all the time in that other
dominion, hidden above us, of swaying green pavilions
the nightingales conspired to create a rival singing
world of their own, sending little jets and spurts of
notes to play among the gently moving branches and
causing miniature cascades to tumble through the
fluttering leaves. And these two competing but independent kingdoms of earth-song and air-song meet only

in the open spaces where the fountains, leaping high in the air, unite them.

Apart from the unforgettable beauty of the scene and morning, there was one slight incident—and one often to be repeated—which, owing perhaps to the fatigue of our all-night journey, left upon my mind an ineradicable impression. It was now past eleven o'clock, and the hours of phantasy, which belong to the earliest morning before the sun has donned his steel armour, were over and would not return till he un-buckled it in the evening. The light, then, even when filtered through green leaves, was hard and dry, but, as we ascended one of the broad side paths through the wood, in the very depth of this peaceful place, we met suddenly an apparition, which, though in a sense ordinary enough, indeed material as the light itself, was truly haunting, filled me with a curious shrinking, an inexplicable mingling of alarm and pity. The woman who advanced toward us down the green perspective was middle-aged and very obviously French in her ap-pearance. Dressed neatly, but with extreme poverty, in black clothes, she wore a tattered black mantilla over her head. Everything about her was respectable and proper—with a respectability that held a terrible hint of satire, and with that propriety necessary, let us say, to a murderer—but her face expressed other emotions. Violent fear combined with a thwarted cunning that cannot be too strongly drawn. The whole significance of it was, perhaps, emphasised by her false smile and the dark, piercing squint of her villainous but pitiful eyes. Her countenance, her figure, even the way in which her clothes stylised her body, proclaimed her as born a century too late, for she would have served Goya admirably as a model, not so much for a painting as for one of those etchings of dark, bleak humanity; dank faces, feminine but diabolic. By the hand this figure dragged rather than led an emaciated child : her son, pale, languid and ailing. This small boy of six or seven years of age was neatly dressed in an abbreviated sailor's suit, which set off to perfection his arms and legs, so wasted as to be reminiscent of those magazine advertisements, which represent some infant before he took such and such a patent-food, or of the hideous spectres placarded in an appeal for famine-funds. Merely to look at him, was to suffer. Though his face lacked any inherited villainy, pictured only a dumb despair that was at once weak and ferocious, there was yet about this sad but wolf-like child a horror transcendent—for, just as children can be the most beautiful, so when cruelty or want forces their innocence to yield to craft, to become a commodity on the beggar's market, are they the most tragic and terrifying of all creatures. Already his feeble little voice had assumed the carefully-inculcated whine and drawl of the professionally maltreated—and his questions, his remarks, were infused by this taught and counterfeit innocence.

Directly the mother had seen us, she had stopped glancing from right to left for a possible prey, and, slowing down to her child's pace, had spread a false affability over her other, more natural expression, thereby completing its effect. Now as she neared us, she murmured, as though to herself, in the clear, incisive accents of the French—whose poorest citizens often speak in tones as formal and laid-out as a French garden—" Ah, Messieurs, Messieurs, L'Espagne, c'est un pays dur et brutal. Vous ne pouvez pas croire, M'sieurs, ce qu'il nous a fait. Et Granade, cette vieille ville morte, c'est la ville la plus terrible de toutes les villes d'Espagne. Ah, mais le Bon Dieu ne peut jamais pardonner ni oublier cette manière d'agir." And, as she began this last denunciation, which continued for some moments, she stretched out a greedy, ill-formed hand, appealing to the child as witness for the truth of these vague statements. Her voice, so correct and impersonal, with a tone in it almost religious, spared no mortal within range, but like a sword cleft the air : yet, as one felt awkwardly for coins, it was not the emotion of pity which one experienced, nor of antipathy nor suspicion, but that of horror—for horror is on the grand, inexplicable scale, and there was about her, in spite of the obvious tricks and roguery, a quality that was most impressive. One could not but realise that even though the tones were false, she was telling the truth—part of the truth—and over her hung the cloud of some great, indescribable and antique tragedy, some crime ineffable and beyond belief.

Through the green or golden alleys of the day,

through the sombre blue tunnels of the night, these two figures would furtively make their way along, hand-in-hand. In the next few weeks, sometimes in the hour of sunset, though more frequently of a hot noon, we were often to pass them, were forced to endure this cringing and insinuating lamentation. Yet never once did we inquire of the woman how it was she had come here. Nor were people ever known to ask for her history. An instinct held them back, warned them that were she to comply and speak the truth, she would fill with pity, but at the same time degrade and horrify, the listener. Even the bold gypsies, who frequented the wood selling flowers and " lucky ornaments," and, who, as a rule, brooked no competition, shrank away at her approach, albeit they would occasionally blaspheme loudly from the distance. Her cunning was greater than theirs : further, she was possessed, they were convinced, of the evil-eye. As no one ever enquired, so she never told her story, but was content with her few vague but menacing phrases.

For me the well-enunciated cadences of this strangely sinister yet matter-of-fact refrain seemed to colour faintly the town and all about it, in the same way that a piece of music, once heard, hovers at the back of the mind, sums up and dyes with its notes a person, a city, a garden, or a span of time. Just as the repetitive appearance in unexpected places of the two American ladies, one or two of the esthetes, and members of the Camel-Corps, whom we had first encountered on the boat to Gibraltar, was, because of its lack of purpose combined with inevitability, to imbue all our travels with a certain tone, as though punctuated at intervals by the recurrence of the pointless chorus of a comic song, thus, too, these dragging feet and precise accents, so surprising in such a place and at the same time so appropriate, were to furnish a refrain at once haunting and tragic, full of a significance it was impossible to fathom.

But upon Tristram this apparition produced no effect this first morning. I looked at him : and his face, as he walked, was that of a happy—or at any rate heedless—animal. Perhaps his entire being was taken up with the marvel of recovery, with the unparalleled rush of life back into its empty shell : for if illness and the first tender stages of convalescence refine and render more acute the workings of mind and soul, when full vigour is returning, when the body is renewed, it is the animal who triumphs. And still more is this true when the case is a nervous one, when the mind has assailed the body, made it sick, and when in the end the body has won by healing its enemy.

As we emerged from the wood to find ourselves standing above it on a hill, my mind was still occupied with the strange French couple we had seen. This tableland was a world by itself, entirely surrendered to crumbling Moorish walls, towers, gates, terraces, courts, gardens and palaces : a fabulous kingdom now reigned over by white-moustached officials, peak-capped and garlic-breathing, who doze heavily in the sun. Behind this hill, and almost connected with it at the top—though the ravine up which we had walked divides them further down—is a sister plateau, but this one completely given over to hotels, large and small, and to English and American pensions, their oak-beamed halls magically full, even in this torrid weather, of the drying half-balloons of umbrellas, and set with innumerable goloshes, safe and comforting as the Ark in the Flood. On these twin hills are no banks, shops, or cafés, but by day there flourishes a busy if parasitic activity. All through the hours of light the air is full of the tired, querulous voices of tourists and the insistent, American accents of their cars. But at dusk this life withers in a moment, and the prevailing voices throughout the night are those of the wood, the crystal tongues of water and of nightingale.

Avoiding, then, the hill entirely given over to the riotous purple-faced feasting of the tourists, we were fortunate enough to find, just at the back of the Alhambra itself, exactly the kind of rooms we wanted. The red-painted, small Spanish hotel in which they were placed, stood, moreover, in a most beautiful position. The front of it faced one of the walls of the palace, and the gardens looked toward the flamingo-pink bulk of the PUERTA DE LOS SIETE SUELOS; that sad gate which, after the last Caliph had passed through it, to quit his domain, was at his request sealed up for ever. Above it rose very bare and golden hills, and beyond these, again, the whole range of the Sierra Nevada stood exposed, their planes of snow flashing under the sun like the wings of angry swans. The little garden of the fonda, beneath its shady trees, and with this immense and legendary prospect spread before it, was square and neat, full in this month of white irises that seemed to dissolve as one looked at them from fragile and heraldic flowers into a sheer transparency, so glorious and lucent were they, or into the feathers wafted from those proud and distant swans.

The upper floor, on which our rooms were situated, offered a view even more magnificent. The plain of Granada could be seen washing the ancient walls of the city with a tide of springing, green life, of tendrils, buds and blades all merged into one impression of things flowering in an unparalleled intensity of trembling, living light.

So powerful was this shrill surge of colour and the feeling of growth implicit in it, that though this force could not disguise the melancholy of the Alhambra hill—appeared, indeed, to add to it an especial and subtle quality of poignance—yet it was able, undoubtedly, to smother beneath the vehemence of its assault some other, almost indefinable atmosphere, a deep and hidden sense of foreboding; some elusive emanation that, it seemed to me, could be detected far down under this efflorescence, or hanging over it like a veil through the sombre, invisible mesh of which all objects became darkened. For both of us the beauty we found here far transcended our expectation. But to me, as I regarded the vista of valley, the huddled fragments of the city round the base of the hills, and the snow mountains that lay spread before us, its aspect proclaimed that, in its own right, it belonged more to Africa than to Europe. Was it too extravagant to wonder whether these rubiginous and crumbling walls —on which the cactus's pale jade spikes and angles, the light showing flatly through them, stood set for protection like the equivalent dazzling planes of glass on an English wall—these robust but ancient towers, these turbanned arches, and still more the golden soil itself, the stones, over which the lizards darted like green flames, did not perhaps resent the imposition of a heavy and alien hand ; whether the place was not, even now, African and infidel at heart ; and if an inborn and clandestine hatred did not still run—just as the old religion, it was said, had persisted, hidden away under the new for several centuries—beneath the astonishing beauty of this surface ? But at present none of the uneasiness that beset me so strangely in this lovely world was, I think, communicated to Tristram, and all through my stay I was most circumspect, so that he should not for a moment guess at it. Indeed, I was almost forced to assume that nervous exhaustion was, after all, an infectious illness, which the sufferer could throw off by passing to his companion, so restless and troubled was I, so dark and unusual were now the flights of my imagination. This black under-current—

albeit for hours its existence might be disguised—grew ever stronger during my stay. The nights were feverish and disturbed, either wakeful or tinged with dreams that seemed to hold some gloomy revelation which by daylight could not be recovered. The background of my mind, for some reason not to be fathomed, grew continually more expectant. Yet a month or more was to pass before I could free myself from the enchantment of all the beauty that lay round me.

But just as curious in its way was the effect of this place upon my friend. To say that Tristram Orlander liked Granada would be altogether to under-estimate and misrepresent his feeling for it. From the first moment of his arrival, it made an appeal to him—that same appeal, akin to love, which sometimes one picture out of a whole gallery makes to you, so that for a year or more when entering it, you can see no other. It may be, even, that his impression was a stronger one ; that the place entered into his life with a deep but authentic claim, which he was obliged at once, however dimly, to recognise—in the same manner that some wild phantasy of a dream may yet return to us, as through a mist, days afterward, because of the deposit of essential but hitherto undiscovered truth which we feel to be buried there—or that it struck out of his being an immediate response, just as a casual note of music played in a room immediately calls out of one among a multitude of brittle and transparent objects an answer. It seemed, though, as if to him the silence and emptiness of hill and palace conveyed nothing but the message of their own exquisite loveliness ; for him there were neither shadows nor undercurrents.   Even the spectre of that French-woman in the wood, with her sad, sickly and frightening child, had presented nothing but their material, rather ridiculous shell, nothing but a foil for the beauty of their setting : for though he could still distinguish the grotesque, its grinning and distorted mask now obscured absolutely the face of tragedy.   Formerly, however, it had been in the lifting of this very disguise, in the perception of the infinite number of ties that bind the ludicrous to the tragic, that much of his peculiar merit as a writer had consisted.

But now he found himself living, after all the despair through which he had passed, in an isolated stretch of lambent days that supported no past, presented no future.   It must be remembered that conversation, to one who was so much a master of it, must have been a delight, and that in London, though he was still young, he was a figure, even his entry into a room causing a stir.   Thus I had feared that as he approached his usual vigorous if nervous condition of health, he would like all virtuosos miss the practice of his art, feel the lack of excitement, pine for the atmosphere mingled of fervent applause and execration to which he had become accustomed.   Here, however, he was content and in no way appeared to miss the stimulus either of the admiration of his friends or of the equally vehement dislike of his enemies. Indeed, his advance from sickness to health showed hardly ever a swing-back, swept him on toward bursts of the wildest spirits. No longer did he sit for hours rusty-haired and rusty-eyed, as though the seal of a never-ending winter was upon his soul, but through him, though now apparently only through the outer sheath, ran the radiant flame of life, his new life.

In spite of the glow and exhilaration one noticed in him, there was, too, a change difficult to sum up. The numbness of feeling that I had detected in Seville was, as it were, in a progressive state. Something fragile and delicate had either withdrawn itself or had been coarsened beyond recognition, until even his outlook had become different, grown a little askew. And what most puzzled me was that, when he had left London, though still in a dreadful state of nervousness and fatigue after his long months of sickness, there had been no sign of such a transformation. Surely one would have expected it, were it to occur at all, to have taken place there, and immediately after his illness, rather than now among these towns and landscapes so new to him, and when his recovery seemed otherwise complete ?

Well aware of the torture which for a year or more his state of jealousy had caused him, my mind went back to the terrible, unreasoning—for he held no claim on Ursula except her kindness—scenes that it had been his wont to make. Furthermore, at that time, his knowledge of her love for him had in his sane hours, made him feel foolishly secure ; nor had it, by any means, seemed certain, even to outside eyes, that any rival would triumph.

Knowing his impetuosity, his abrupt alternations of mood, I had, for example, before starting on our voyage, feared that directly he was stronger, a burst of feeling might induce him, at a moment's notice, and without telling me, to charter a car or a special train, if he could obtain the money (or perhaps still more, if he could not), and rush back to England or wherever it was he conceived Ursula to be staying. Once he had discovered her—and how well I could envisage the scene—he would, of course, press her to elope with him, and on her refusal to do so, would create an unpleasant disturbance. Conduct of this sort would have been typical of his behaviour in the past. But no such occasion arose, nor was there any preliminary symptom of it. Indeed now, when he must have known that her wedding was to take place in a day or two, there was no token of jealousy, sorrow, or even of memory. It was not, I was sure, that he was concealing his emotions. No : outwardly there was no trace of her : inwardly there was this new hardness of fibre. Perhaps the explanation was merely that Nature, employing one of her miracles in order to render him insensitive to all regrets, had administered a kind of mental local-anæsthetic, and that this had also influenced his observation of the present. It was no wonder, though, that I had dreaded the possibility of complications : for certainly a prolonged bout of misery had seemed much more likely to be his portion than this curious serenity. And yet serenity was, somehow or other, not the word : perhaps it implies a conquest of suffering. Again, had he vanquished it, or was it really that in his utter defeat, it had been able to impose on him the only terms upon which in future it would be possible for him to live ? But then, one remembered how well he was, how much had come back to him, and was once more confident that this dull, numb scar, too, would pass away with the years.

Such short moods of depression as did descend upon Tristram from time to time were now always due to material causes, and passed almost at once. Extravagant as ever, in the very poorest, cheapest, most wretched hotels, he would usually contrive—one could never quite understand how he did it—to produce a hotel-bill twice as large in amount as my own. As a rule, far from being at all distressed, he would congratulate himself on having been economical. It was invariably less than he expected. But occasionally it would worry him, and he would grow dejected. Then he would swiftly recover ; and would point out, in his defence, that if he had decided to be a stockbroker (though this I took leave to doubt), or if he had only chosen to write badly and vulgarly, he would by now be rich, surrounded by every kind of luxury, universally beloved and respected. His whole life would have been different. An aptitude for money-making, he would say bitterly, only proved that you belonged to a special genus, not necessarily a higher one. You were, in fact, a money-beetle. But whether at such moments of complaint, when he said that his life might have been different, Ursula was in mind, I do not know. Certainly he never mentioned her.

In order to understand or in any measure interpret the thing that eventually befell my friend in Granada, it is necessary for us to explore the scene and its influences, the small happenings that were in themselves so unimportant, with the utmost fullness. But, from this distance of forty odd years, the days that followed merge one into another, and it is often difficult to disentangle them, so apparently alike are they in their peaceful, golden rind. They echoed, fitted into each other, so that in their perfection and interest, as much as in the beauty of rhythm which they built up, my sombre nights, filled often with those struggles for sleep that exhaust one long before it comes, were forgotten.

Often when waking, one would hear what was surely that particular whining at the window which characterises rain in southern climes—a sound quite different from the solid drip and tap of it in northern countries. Well, one could not be surprised. This weather had held for so long. And then, throwing wide the green shutters, one would discover another flawless day, and the sound of water proved to be only the perpetual gurgling and singing of stream and fountain, which rose on all sides from wood and garden. The heat, thus early in the morning and tempered by the fluttering breezes that, gliding down from their soft, white nests in the Sierra Nevada, now hovered above, or beating the air with their cool wings, imparted a gentle shiver and shimmer to every green object, was never too violent, but on the contrary encouraged one to go far afield. It became, therefore, our habit to walk in the morning, before the full droning of the day had reached its climax, or toward evening when all was hushed and silent under the lengthening fingers of the sun. Usually, on our way to the city below, we would pass through the wood, where by a happy paradox, as it grew hotter, the plangent tumbling of the streams would increase in volume, and the leaping of the fountains be lifted ever higher, for in their bounty the Sierras fed every basin and rivulet in every garden. Each day, now, the sun's gaze was melting more of their glittering snow surfaces. From the open, the torrents could be seen wavering down the distant mountain-sides and rocky precipices like the green waving hair of overthrown snow giants, while even to these rippling waters that flung themselves down here and raced under these tall trees, the snow imparted this same tone, which was that of clouded, green jade, for it dulled a little their transparency. Nor was this all that the beneficent snow-god achieved, for brought down on mules by men who made a special profession of it, the snow was converted into dangerous but delectable ices to be consumed by the populace of the city. And, as we walked down the broader, modern streets, we could already see people sitting outside cafés, indulging in this most transient of human delights, while in the little, crooked alleys behind these boulevards, painted hand-barrows were being besieged by shouting, toast-coloured children with the same object in view.

The impression, as you enter Granada, is not so much of the actual city as of the Alhambra hill, which, even when like a shadow it crouches above you looming over the town, continually draws the eye round to itself. The palace that crowns the unimaginably steep tangle of trees, rocks and bushes, rather resembles a more lusty, larger variation of some rose-pink Italian fortress, except that toward the top of one or two of the towers, an arched and pillared window suddenly pierces the blind bulk with an unexpected, jewel-like refinement and hints at the luxurious intricacy that they shelter. No one had prepared us, either for the rough magnificence of the exterior, nor for the exquisite loveliness of its setting, because it was at this time the fashion among persons who loved beautiful things— and no other body of people is so governed and hypnotised by the fetishes itself has set up—to disparage Moorish architecture as fussy and exotic.

As for the first aspect of the city—though, by the character of the people, life there is, and always must have been, infinitely compressed—it was of one much too large for its inhabitants. Before the Spanish conquest, Granada had contained an enormous population, and, though during the nineteenth and early twentieth centuries it had much increased again, even at the time of our visit there was still about it the same grotesque air that a suit several sizes too big for him imparts to the man who wears it. But, notwithstanding that the stage seemed too vast for the action it set, the life, in a sense more severe than at Seville, here had a vivid, bitter quality of its own.

Through the perpetual sunset glow that lingers round the altars in the dark churches, kneeling women can be seen praying in rigid attitudes, their black mantillas streaming back from their foreheads, their arms outstretched in the gesture of crucifixion, while priests, in purple robes, chant and mumble up through the mist of incense. Without, sitting by the huge pillars of the porch, or lying in the cloistered gold of monastic sunshine, a troop of beggars drawls and whimpers vociferously. Only a clumsy, greasy, padded-curtain obstructs the entrance, to divide off the fitful, flickering glory within from the material world beyond. But command is latent in the whining, for until this obstacle to sanctuary is overcome, he who wishes to enter is rightful prey. An innumerable army of the maimed and halt, legless or armless, deaf mutes or men with the thin, blank smile and deep, empty eye-sockets of Breughel's straggling line of blind men—the only ones

in all this host who are pitiful without being repulsive
—worry, fawn on, or jump up like a pack of hounds
at the stranger : and those beggars too deformed even
to crawl up, shout their orders from a distance, or
beckon imperiously with the stump of an arm for
him to come and examine their sores, so certain are
they of their right to a privileged position.   And, indeed, the peace of no church or convent is complete
without the contrast that this contorted and tattered
corps affords.   Outside these querulous courts devoted
to the lazars, the current of life flows strongly.   The
tortuous streets of the old town are full of sound, the
jingle of mules as they strain and stumble over the
cobbles, the hoarse or strident cries of the muleteers,
water-sellers or gypsies, all personal in voice as in
clothing.   Here the town and the life that throbbed
through it, was unchanged : still, in those days, existed
in a past and alien time.

But the wide, modern thoroughfares hemmed in and
pressed back this activity—as policemen clear a way
through a crowd, or stolidly surround an epileptic—
and in them no one except the dustman, busily piling
up and arranging his clouds like an earthly god, seems
at home.

This atmosphere of parody—and one which for me
soon shaded down from the wearying into the unpleasant, and even horrible—it is necessary, but not
easy, to explain.   As we have suggested earlier, the
tendency of life in Europe for a century or more had

been to level, equalise and make uniform. With the ease of modern locomotion, the ideal had been to make the burgess traveller feel equally at home in London, Paris, Nice, Granada, Buda-Pesth, or New York. Spain had never joined with the same enthusiasm as other countries in this denial of soul, but even here the people had to a certain extent torn down their ancient monuments, and erected in their place the nondescript commercial buildings of Cosmopolis.

But, just as this movement was at its height all over the world, it was discovered to the general dismay that it was not a paying proposition. For the locust-like clouds of Americans who now began to arrive in the "backward" countries, though quite as "democratic" as everyone else and justly insistent on American habits of heat, food and sanitation, were absolutely determined to get their money's worth. A rapid review of the sights of Europe constituted then a claim to belong to a kind of *wagon-lit* aristocracy of travel. Each transatlantic visitor had paid down a large sum to a tourist agency in order to become a member of this cultured society, by process of seeing the "Old World," full of picturesque "bits" and "colourful" corners. And here it was, very much like the New, only not so grandiose. Why? Gradually governments and municipalities had been brought round to see the necessity of local colour. The commercial integrity of the travel-bureaux was at stake. It was now up to them to produce the thing for which they had been paid.

Here and now a captive Europe must be forced to alter its tactics. With fantastic speed, the scene was cleared and changed. It had become necessary to resuscitate the corpse. Moreover, in order to placate the great creditor-nation, it was the very oldest, deadest corpse that had to be galvanised : the most ancient buildings which could be found in any town must serve as models for an insensate reproduction. And thus was born the Age of Parody.

Its fruits were manifold and multiform. In Venice pseudo-Gothic palaces sprang up overnight for use as hotels. A big, square barge, surmounted by several plaster Byzantine domes, the highest of which was crowned with one of the peacock's crests of St. Mark's —except that in this case the leaden points had been artfully replaced by little electric globes—was established on the lagoons, so that it could be towed in anywhere, at any moment, to shatter the peace of the canals : for under its canopy blue-lipped, swaying negroes hooted their native American tunes down long golden pipes, while ladies and gentlemen from Chicago, Paris, or London could stagger, and wobble their ill-formed hips, in time to them. In Rome, where space is limited, a beautiful baroque church was pulled down every week to make way for a broken Roman pillar, clamped together by irons and with a rickety, chipped but still over-florid Corinthian capital attached to its top, while the new Government offices were built in a flaccid neo-Roman style, their travertine fronts incised at every point of flat surface with inappropriate classic inscriptions. Thus every city matched against its splendid monuments of the past, similar buildings, but ones which by a butter-fingered exaggeration of their bad qualities, shamed them, or, as it were, made fun of them to their faces, as though one was to see a dwarf or over-fat *crétin* rudely mimicking a great poet or statesman while he was still in the room. Or, again, it recalled the proceedings of " lightning make-up artists " on the old music-hall stage, who with the aid of a cocked-hat and bits of moth-eaten, grey eyebrow, moustache and whisker, gave in rapid succession a series of impersonations of Mozart, Napoleon, Wellington, Gounod, Liszt, Sir Henry Irving and Charles Dickens.

In Granada, where for the last eighty years they had been drowsily pulling down Moorish gates inconvenient to traffic and old towers which were in the way, the authorities were now obliged to run them up again with amazing speed. This process was known as " restoration." Further, any new buildings which had to be erected, of a definite modern purpose—and one quite out of accord with the Moorish temperament and epoch —such as post-offices, stations and gasworks, were designed in a madly misunderstood and distorted semi-Saracenic. The more personal the old buildings had been in their style, the more obvious was the burlesque. And the city was full of it. Every public office, every bank was a-clatter with encaustic tiles of oriental pattern, stalactites dripped from every pillar-box, and even the fire engine bore upon its red body like a rash the caricatured intricacies of Moorish calligraphy. But so dead was that genuine world of spider's-web on its lonely hill, and so far lifted above the town, that few were those, perhaps, who actually noticed the mockery to which this lovely spectre had been subjected, soiled and made into an Aunt-Sally at every street corner.

As you walked up the steep road of shops that leads to the wood, and was the only way for driving to the palaces above, the note of brutal parody was further emphasised. These shops plied two trades. The trap-like door invited the tourist with a quantity of oriental goods, embroidered slippers, brass ornaments, mule-bells, cups, coffee-pots and coloured tassels ; but once enticed within, escape was impossible until the occasion had been, like a fly in amber, enshrined in a semi-permanence, for the window was devoted to photographs of people pitched among those stage properties which they had been so lately, and unwisely, admiring. Fat Spanish ladies, lean American ones, their eyes very shy through pince-nez, English tea-drinking spinsters, with a touch of hockey or the art-school still clinging to them, were here displayed, decked out for ever in the guise of harem-beauties against an appropriately lux-urious background. Usually this consisted of a series of flat screens of honeycomb, stalactite and flowing water, but a few more enterprising tradesmen had even constructed, in a shed built-out at the back, a mimic-miniature of the Alhambra in its full three dimensions,

while to add a further note of cruel and wanton absurdity, the accessories of hookah and coffee-pot were
always ready, standing upon the sham-marble rim of a
sham fountain. A veil, too, hung, like a sheet disguis-
ing some poor corpse, from a nail driven into the wall.
In addition, the necessarily small scale enforced by
the attempt to reproduce a large building within the
space of a tiny shed, was warranted to make anyone but
a pygmy assume the proportions of elephantiasis, swell
out into a cyclopean and apoplectic over life-size. All
these photographs, all these adjuncts, as much as the
lewd and fleering imitations we have described, tend to
bring the originals of so much common fun into dis-
repute, and any time a visitor goes from the town to
the hill, he is bound to pass them. There was something ghastly and ghoulish in this indelicacy, and perhaps it, too, added its own note to the prevalent atmosphere, even for those who did not consciously understand it.

By the time we had walked beyond the shops,
through the gate, into the cool seclusion of the wood,
it was noon. The precise and prophetic tones of the
Frenchwoman which were to become so familiar to
us, could be heard in the distance, accosting strangers.
It was always foreigners she molested. Though the
Spaniards are personally most generous to the poor,
one never heard her approach them for alms. Indeed,
it seemed as if she took a pleasure in the distinctness
of her enunciation for the very reason that her calm

but threatening words must penetrate to any Spanish ears within reach. Often one wondered, whether, if forced by want during the summer months when no tourists came to the city, to beg from the citizens of Granada, she would modify her denunciatory style. I doubted it, because in this sentiment alone was one convinced of her sincerity. Even now I could hear the usual tirade against Spain in progress. Her voice, with its accompaniment of lisping, youthful accents was no doubt succeeding in wringing out of some visitor its pitiful blackmail. The child was appealed to as witness. " Mon enfant, tu es trop jeune pour comprendre des choses pareilles, mais dis à Monsieur, mon pauvre petit, que c'est vrai." Avoiding, if we could, this strange, indeed impressive pair, we would return home to find a meal waiting for us, a meal Spanish in generosity as in odour. But though we had eluded them, yet these two would come back to my mind. As upon the first morning, however, it was only the surface that at all troubled Tristram. He was irritated by the woman begging, but even the recurrence of this apparition seemed to have left no deeper impression upon his mind. But such was the spell that the whole place had cast upon my friend, such the vigour of his newly-established health, that he was at present blind to all except its beauty.

After luncheon, we would go out again. Fortunately the hill on which the Alhambra stood was almost free from the mocking parodies we had seen below, though on the twin hill opposite rose a Moorish *Caravanserai* : the Hotel Boabdil, which insolently mimicked the old palaces, inside and outside and all the time. But every sitting-room in every ordinary-looking hotel boasted some similar blasphemy. Once on the Alhambra hill, however, this other genuine world was the only one which existed. All the long, golden-skinned after-noon we would, perhaps, explore this plateau, a place enchanted even in the most material of hours, and un-der the hardest of lights. Its magic seemed able to defy the laws of time, and even of weather, just as the loveliness of its palaces had set at nought the laws of architecture. By this not only do I intend to signify the survival of these buildings, so delicate as in itself to constitute a miracle, but that up here time moved differently, even when compared with the city below. One hour became five, five hours passed as one. It had its own pulse of time, lazy but majestic.

During the hour of siesta, when the hill slept, when even its guardians, the peaks of their caps pulled down over their eyes, dreamt on their rush chairs, when the gypsies were silent, wrapped, no doubt, in swarthy slumber, and, what was more, there were no children playing and shouting under the gold-disked trees in the Plaza de los Aljibes, we would walk there or rest in a corner of one of the palaces. This plaza, rec-tangular in shape, lies between the palace built by Charles V—but never finished—and the high old walls of the Moorish cistern. The other two, narrow sides are usually bounded only by the cries that float up from the city beneath. But at this hour all was silent : leaning on the broad stone shelf, we could watch the now empty city below, its streets appearing to tremble under the heat. From here there was no sign of parody, and all the ancient streets that climb and circle round the cathedral were revealed. Under, just under us, flashed the river Darro, singing almost lustily at this season of melting snow, and across it, on the slightly lower hill opposite, was the Albaicin. There, half-smothered by a gesticulating riot of prickly-pears and cactuses, a horde of gypsies lived in electrically-lit caves, that gleamed with coffee-pots and copper pans, heirlooms and only relics of a formerly vagrant existence. The whole of the Albaicin hill had been surrendered to them. When the siesta was finished, one would see them flaunting out of their burrows, like some mysterious creation of gaudy tropical insect, half-ant, half-parrot. They would strut along the paths through the huge plants, taller than themselves, by which they were surrounded, just as insects move and creep along little tracks in their miniature jungle of grass. Hence issuing, in their dignified but audacious clothes, crinolines and flaming shawls, further enhanced by all the tourism-encouraging apparatus of high combs, barbaric bracelets and a flower tucked away above the ear, now they would once more scatter over Granada and its environs to importune and worry the visitors.

For centuries driven off from every respectable door,

hounded out of every town, and even from the desolate
heath, with special and ferocious laws enacted against
them in every country, and, moreover, in this particular one, the appointed prey of black-hooded inquisitors
and continually given over to torture, suddenly these
gitanos had been encouraged, almost forced to stay,
had found themselves converted into an industry, into
the very essence of local colour—though never really
had they belonged to any locality. It was a prodigy,
scarcely less surprising than if we were to-day to find
a dragon, tethered and tame in a cave, thoroughly
domesticated, the flame of its breathing harnessed, used
for the lighting, heating and cooking-ranges of the city
below. By a curious perversion, these gypsies, originally impelled by their poverty to wander, were now
implored, and even paid, to roam no more ; were here
kept, an entire people, to amuse a new race of moneyed
nomads : the bird of prey had suffered its pinions to
be clipped, while to the lamb had been given wings.
Yet there was a difference : for not only had the gypsies
to amuse, they must also frighten the loads of steel-
accented or curatical tourists rolling up the hills in their
iron ships. The visitors expected to obtain a grand-
guignol, as well as the purely romantic, thrill. It was
not enough for them to admire the clothes and dances
of the *gitanos*, it had also to be possible for the green-
faced guide of that period, with his huge tortoiseshell-
rimmed spectacles and Berlitz-American accent, to point
out one or two of them as the heroes of crime no less

than of passion. The dagger and poison-cup had always to be ready in the cause—could be used with knowledge of a sure impunity, should the feuds in which they had been employed prove sufficiently melodramatic and " colourful."

And yet the *gitanos'* ornamental profession of wheedling and violence was not a pretence. So native was the villainy of these nomads, bound to their caves by golden chains, that the fact that they were now officially encouraged to wear particular clothes, learn various dances, and to exhibit an occasional violence in order to extract money from the " gorgios," the very roguery of this whole proceeding lent to it a certain reality, gave them a genuine zest for it : while no amount of municipal, or even governmental, employ could ever subdue their proclivities to dance, thieve, or knife. Thus the only change, from their point of view, that modern life had forced on them was that they were being paid for doing something, which, though forbidden, they had formerly done for nothing, and were more or less guaranteed in their profession —or rather their want of one.

And most beautiful they were, these people who haunted the woods and alleys of Granada, ogling and whining, and who grew in every shade and colour from lemon-yellow through green and mauve to black. Their arms, unsheathed out of the flower-like brightness of their sleeves, were as brown as coffee-berries, their hands dark and scaly as an eagle's claw. But they, too, imparting a tone of cunning and dissemblance, added their note to the entire district.

Even as we watched, fragments of snarling song, hoarse above the singing of the river, would be wafted to us from the hill opposite, and we could see half-naked, burnt-black children dancing among the aloes and southern plants. But, interesting as was that hill to watch, we had to turn away, for soon the siesta would be over : and at this hour, when all men still rested, when pavilion, court, and alley were enshrined in a radiance so intense that it seemed almost as tangible as the long-fingered gold-lacquer rays on a Chinese screen ; when, outside, the marble paving glittered and shone, and myrtle and box exhaled their warm, comforting scents more pungently than at any other moment of the day, loaded with who knows what memories of other gardens and other times, while, within, the sun played his beams down through the upper windows, upon every pattern and design of wall and marble-floor, and these in their turn reflected a watery glory upon the golden honeycombs of dome and ceiling, and through all, and above every chirrup and clamour of bird and insect, could be heard the wayward voice of the water, that never absent chain of life and movement, which with its silver links binds the whole world together, room to garden, palace to palace, and remote past to present and future, then was it still better to linger among the courts and chambers of the Alhambra. For these halls seemed woven by the faultless instinct and fabulous industry of a myriad silk-worms and transcendent spiders, in conjunction with a race of giant, gold-liveried bees who, having abandoned for architecture their honeyed economics and proclaimed Beauty as their god, had lavished upon this palace every hoard of flavour, scent and sun-colour : and how else, at any other and more magic hour, was one to imagine that these walls, these gardens, were anything but a dream, just touched by nightmare ?

And now, while the dragon guardians yet slept, their breath droning resonantly under the domes, until it became allied with the warm song of the drowsy courts, it was possible to walk through the palace unmolested, to lie undisturbed and talk in a cool corner. As we rested there, our backs against the tiled dados, the uneuropean conception of the place was accentuated. Not only were these buildings apparently mutable as the velvet and silk tents of the African conquerors, out of which they had been evoked—so fragile a creation that only by thus spinning and weaving them within a fortress could they have survived—but, as Tristram was the first to point out to me, every arched window, divided by its slender column, of itself bore witness to how evidently it had been created for a race whose habit it was to sit cross-legged upon the ground. Because, if one sat down on a chair, like a Christian, the two pointed vistas it enclosed were meaningless and muddled, but, from the level of the floor, there was suddenly revealed a new and artfully entwined perspective of tiled walls, balconies, arches, with, as its focus, an ever changing and dissolving composition of water and light, which together played a thousand vibrant variations on the fronded tracery of ferns, the open, translucent shields of lilies, and the silver-backed glossy leaves of the ilex.

As the water-cooled air fluttered in at the window during this calm hour when the sun was at its height, all traces of uneasiness in the atmosphere were momentarily banished. Now in their beauty these pavilions could defy the aping world of caricature and burlesque by which they were encircled, and sunk in a peace that both cleared and lulled the mind, removed that utter fatigue which was settling on me in consequence of so many restless nights—for as sleep was coming back to Tristram, it appeared to be fleeing from me in my turn. Indeed, my misery was aggravated by the fact that I dared not complain, dared not reveal the obscure state of inquietude in which I now existed, to one who was himself only just convalescent. There was no other person in whom I could confide, and, if there had been, who but Tristram would have understood? But as we sat there, in that strange and complete kingdom which enclosed us, I was quickly able to forget the hours of darkness. We talked of the many things that interested us, for we were then not old enough to have forfeited the seriousness of the young, nor to have acquired the flippancy, under a serious manner, of the middle-aged. We discussed the current movements in art and literature, their probable development in the future, and applauded the revolt against the ennui of academic vision that was so evident and widespread, as much as we deplored the intolerant counter-movements, so powerful in politics and social life, which threatened at the time to overwhelm that little vitality still left to an exhausted and impoverished Europe.

Yet some, I thought, of his seriousness and some of his wit, seemed to have deserted my friend : or would it, perhaps, be more accurate to say that his point of view had fallen nearer the level, that his mind no longer illumined the subjects it played upon with the same steady radiance, a radiance all his own, in which consisted both his wit and wisdom ? In this decline, I began to think it possible after all to detect traces of Ursula—not of herself, it is true, but of his love for her—even if this passion had died. For though still extravagant as he had ever been, he now talked continually of money : to hear him it would never have been suspected that this was the rock upon which he had let his happiness be broken, or that he had played, in connection with it, the part of the artist-ascetic. There were other parallel and more superficial changes in him, but these were quite as odd and surprising. His personal style was, as I have said, of a careless, untidy elegance—though this was, of course, dependent on a certain quality of good-looks. After the sorrow and misery that had overwhelmed him, one would have expected, were any alteration to manifest itself, an increased emphasis upon the note of negligence. But, on the contrary, it was plain that he had become increasingly concerned with all the exterior details of his appearance, as though, just as much as in his opinions, thus too was he now anxious for an outward conformity. He was, however, so individual, so essentially different from other men, that these symptoms might have gone unnoticed, except that to anybody who had known him well for many years they were unmistakable. Of what they were indicatory, was not so clear. Yet in talking with him, it was impossible even now not to be carried away by his flow of ideas, and by the vitality transmitted into those wild fantasies that his mind improvised so easily and lightly.

Another thing I had noticed. He had begun to rely very much on wine and brandy : not that he was a drunkard, but he craved the feeling of excitement which they undoubtedly bestow on some people. To him it restored life. Nor was I at all worried at this or inclined to interfere. His recovery was in many ways miraculous, and in spite of any medical opinion to the contrary, I have always found that alcohol is to an extent a cure for the nervous exhaustion that follows on misery. And certainly it seemed to suit him, for he looked wonderfully well, I thought.

No sound penetrated to us from the courts beyond, save the droning of sun-heavy insects and the song of the birds as they bumped up toward the golden

fretwork through the open arches or shrilled in unison
from their thickets on the hill. Then, all at once the
siesta-hour would end, and the silence, so doubly silent
for the little sounds of sun and garden that broke it,
would be destroyed completely by a sudden explosion
of steel-clad clamour. A thousand machine-made
voices, rising up and down with the smooth but grinding clatter of their native elevators, or with the raucous
infallibility of electric-drills, would shatter and splinter
these plaster palaces to pieces, sterilise them, deprive
them of every scrap of life and colour, make them as
tawdry as a Christmas-window-decoration in a New
York store. A thousand tourists had arrived by chara-
banc from Gibraltar. Each male would be armed with
his own film-machine, then as indispensable a part of
the " hundred-per-cent-American-he-man " apparatus as
the " plus-fours " which now, in old fashion-plates,
look to the younger generation so effeminate and funny.
Picking out of this choice gathering a female as unsuited
for the process as possible, he would prepare to hand
her, hair-net and all, and looking self-consciously romantic out of compliment to the setting, down to an
interested posterity. There she would stand—while
her admirer peered into the little black box, and busily
turned a handle—move, smile, in the Myrtle Court or
by the Lion Fountain, until a guide would run up,
barking like a sheep dog, and worry them back into the
flock. It was time to dash down the white roads to
Seville and Cordoba. Soon they would be herded on

the return journey to Gibraltar, propelled from there to Naples, Rome, Venice—films, this time, of doves fluttering round coarse, ringed hands against a skyful of domes—Athens and Constantinople, there to desecrate with their false pleasure and profane with standardised praise these sacred and ancient places. Meanwhile, the instant they were gone, the Alhambra would recover ; and with much more speed than many of its more substantial peers of wonder in those other cities. Within a moment, a wailing voice, a guitar or two, and the sound of water had placed beauty back securely in her home. But hardly had this rescue been effected, before there could be heard a hissing splutter and deep guttural booming, and in place of those just gone, would be deposited as many German tourists, still wearing their yachting-caps, in addition to having donned for the occasion their most impressive pairs of spectacles. Sometimes, again, it would be a party of our sibilant fellow-countrymen, more awed and aloof than the continental or transatlantic travellers, tapping and scratching the walls, and always breaking up into units of ones or whispering twos.

As we grew to understand the life of the hill—or, rather, the embalming rites decreed to this lovely corpse —we would wait until the first invasion, and then claim sanctuary in the empty, roofless palace of the Emperor Charles V. There we were safe, for tourists were at that time forbidden by their guides to admire any building on these heights erected after the expulsion of the

Moors, and its logical and geometric beauty, like that
of a passion-flower, is sternly opposed to the coloured
intricacies of its wily oriental neighbour.

Here, in fact, is to be found the hymn to freedom of
the Spanish soul, at last rid of an alien nightmare and
about to install its own. No palace was ever so cool
and dark and yet so full of sunshine, so silent yet full
of birdsong, as this unfinished one. Moreover, though
such pipings and flutings were the only strains to which
it echoed, it seemed essentially created, deserted as it
stood, for the appreciation of music.

And one day, suddenly, we were able to provide
that which had been lacking. On this afternoon as
we approached our refuge, we noticed a little crowd
and heard a sound of singing. Greatly daring, and
in rebellion against their shepherd, a few isolated
American tourists, laughing and shouting, were standing round a blind man, and throwing heavy Spanish
copper coins into his hat. This beggar, about whom
was nothing repulsive, but, instead, a stern, almost
biblical beauty, at their command was playing very
badly on his guitar the most blatant American tunes.
As he sang a few jumbled words, the deep sockets of
his eyes, with their blank and awful gaze as of a stone
head, stared resolutely toward some inexpressibly far
horizon : indeed his body, and the whole tilt of it,
had acquired the balance, the sightless immobility, of
stone : and his long thin hands, too, even though they
moved to touch the strings of the instrument, were those

of a carven saint. After his clients had shuffled and bellowed themselves into the distance, we inquired whether he could not give us any Spanish songs? At this, his manner altered, and immediately he began thrumming deeply on the guitar, drawing out of it the menacing insect-like dronings that herald Flamenco music. We helped him to stand up, and carrying the wooden box which had served as pedestal for this singing effigy, led him into the palace, seating him in the centre of the court, circular like the arena for a bull-fight.

As he wailed these old songs, of such vigorous but mournful beauty, the stare thawed, expression flickered for a moment over his sallow and lined face, the body rocked and listed till his voice rang out, startled the nesting birds by drawing echoes out of this resonant emptiness. While he sang, we could stand in one of the lofty windows, the ledges of which were brushed by the rustling tree-tops or climb noiselessly up the moss-grown, broken steps to the gallery that girdles the court, and has only a circle of blue sky for roof. Against this radiant ceiling, the various flowering weeds, which imparted to grey-green stone and marble, dank and bleached as though they stood in the depths of ocean, their sole touch of colour, showed very definitely, and could be seen to stir as they were ruffled by a gentle wind. Never had a palace been created that was so consciously European, so much the child of Greece and Rome, as this one that had blossomed at the expense of the conquered Africans—paid for, even, out of the fines levied upon them : while in the same way that the Spaniard stood over the Moor, or that the jolting and American-made tunes were displacing the native and haunted music to which we were listening, so this palace rested heavily upon the ruins of Moorish pleasure-houses. The sun coming through the windows would touch first one bas-relief and then another, call out of the inlay of serpentine that framed them, a tone of rusty green, or would for a moment sculpture with its percipient fingers the upturned face of the blind man, as he sang this melancholy and cruel music that was not, it seemed to us, either western or eastern, but of a beauty that produced an homeric impression of illimitable age and distance. Though songs about the Riff War were still, at that day, being composed—songs that differed not a jot from those handed on for centuries—this music, alas, was dying, its idiom and flavour too acrid for modern ears. Visitors accustomed to the fussy, buzzing trombones and lank, jiggy clarionet sounds of northern street-music, disliked it, though they would pityingly bestow upon the singers a coin, under the impression that the timbre of voice and manner of singing were unintentional : then they would ask them if they could not play, instead, one of the popular American tunes of the time. And only at night, lying on their tattered cloaks under a grape-blue sky, gypsies, tinkers and beggars would sing it still for their own pleasure.

Luckily for us, the blind man had so seldom been asked by foreigners for Flamenco songs, that he was flattered at our demanding them : and since we formed a great liking for this strange music, he would often return here to sing to us, until about four o'clock he was fetched by a child, with huge sombre eyes, to be led down to who knows what hidden den in the city.

Sometimes, again, if his music failed us, we would walk above the Alhambra, between the two long white hotels that mirrored each other in a comfortable French way at each side of the road, past the Generalife, huddled among its cypresses, and at this season nearly obscured by the very temporary pink sails of almond and peach-trees. Above its pavilions, pools and orchards stand, grey and faintly golden, mountains that are like downs, save that these are more dead than any hills that we have seen. On them and in the valleys that divide them, grows no plant, no blade of grass. They are wrinkled, round and grey as an elephant's back, intimidating and silent as those mountains to be distinguished in the golden Hunter's Moon, significant as the livid, bone-bare hills, riven by a sunburst, that compose the background of so many of El Greco's pictures. As we passed them, and could see them rolling away higher and higher to become entangled in the more ordinary cliffs, glaciers and crags of the Sierra Nevada, I thought of the old Spanish legend that quite near, but deeply hidden in these forked, icy and inaccessible mountains, cut off from interference by precipice and deep ravine, and thus invisible to the Christians, there yet lingered some thousands of dark-skinned infidels.   Certainly hiding and secrecy were to be felt in the atmosphere.   These grey-golden downs above us, majestic as they were, we avoided : for, oddly enough, out of all the mocking and incomprehensible things in Granada, however much they attracted, they yet at the same time sounded for Tristram the only note that repelled him.   To wander there alone, he said, would fill him with an illogical alarm, while it would be impossible to take anything but a solitary walk, since no one would wish to break that unearthly silence with the very human sound of speech.

Soon it would be time to walk in the wood, again—in this hour, more full than ever of the song of birds and water.   Each warm day, as one looked back on it, had passed very swiftly and ever so slowly, had held within itself a world of long and indolent experience that made it appear pleasantly endless : but at this moment, when it was nearly over and was joining itself on, one more day added to the golden avenue of days spent in Granada, the perspective was so foreshortened that one could almost touch and feel even those furthest away.   The last rays of the sun were now piercing the undergrowth.   There the purple flags, of which it was chiefly composed, were beginning to flower very subtly, so that at first the recurrent but casual repetition of mauve, rather more intense in tone than the shadows, seemed merely some more vehement blossoming of shade among this mass of green daggers. The gypsy women, always in wait for foreigners, would stalk in and out across our path. Whichever path through the trees we chose, one of them would be there, waiting to pounce out from the shadows and decked out in her full parrot's plumage. Whining, wheedling, but very certain of herself, she would never cease her importunings until she had sold us a small bunch of violets or a rose, which she would insist on pinning into our button-holes with her thin, ferocious claw, meantime unctuously assuring us of the Spanish equivalent of the fact that we were " pretty gentlemen." But no sooner had we by this surrender bought back our peace, than would be raised from one of the thickets that voice which to me had become the very rhythm of this hill. The flat French cadences, more terrible in their truth even than in their insincerity, enunciated with such deliberation and practised elocution, could be heard at an altogether unexpected distance. Now we would turn up toward the Plaza, and still, from there, the oracle could be heard : each word of it, dropped into the wood, broke, as it were, the silence in enlarging circles, just as a stone dropped into a pool will ruffle its surface long after it has sunk.

The light was dying. Every city has its own beauties of light and darkness, but when the sun has set and its last dragon's breath of fire has been extinguished, there comes to Granada a moment that no other city knows. From the further parapet, upon which we leant, it was possible to see almost the entire town, swinging and curving over its rounded hills. For about seven or eight minutes a deep blueness, a blueness the transparency of which is scarcely believable, lingers over and encloses the world. All else, hills, houses and town, irradiate a light golden or primrose tone, that is yet flat, but is heightened by the lights that, in mimicry of the stars above them, are fluttering out in all directions below. The very ground itself appears to share in the illumination, for each gypsy-cave opposite winks an electric eye. And on such breathless evenings, and during these few minutes, the whole town is borne up to the watcher on the hill. Dominating this tapestry of sound is the deep voice of the Darro, rolling its snow-fed waters below, and with it is woven in harmony every note that can come from an ancient city : singing mingles with traffic, the bells ring out their silver or tinny music in clattering patterns, there are the deep, throaty cries of the muleteers, sometimes rising for an instant to a high falsetto scream, the formalised recommendations of pedlars selling their wares, and even the echo of conversation by the water's edge. All these different sounds take to themselves wings at this hour, fly up, soar and dip under the weedy cornices of the ruined palace like so many birds giving out their notes. It was only, perhaps, when hill and city found this magic union that I hated to leave Granada so soon.

Suddenly the primrose glow dwindled out, the singing of the city died, and it was time for us to return to our *fonda*. Though there were only two or three people besides ourselves staying in it, already in preparation for dinner amazing sounds of seething and frying, as though an army were to be fed, issued from the kitchen, while through the open door, the large proprietress could be seen majestically moving, like the deity, through a column of fire and smoke. In the little garden outside, the cups of the irises were now pale and stationary moths that floated a little above the darkness ever grew paler and more opaque, until with its first rays the moon renewed their translucence; the air entered in warm gusts through the wide open windows, and brought with it, in the intervals between the rattle of plates, the trilling of the nightingales still employed in the never-ending exercise of their music.

After dinner, from time to time, we would visit the other hotels in order to drink coffee and remark our fellow-tourists : this last purpose being nearly allied in origin to the fakir-like prompting inherent in man, which led saints and anchorites to practise self-torture. But Tristram often felt the need to be in—though not of—a crowd, and was never really so happy, though probably he would have denied it, as when able to examine one. Indeed it gave him even more pleasure, I think, to be surrounded by people whom he did not know than to be among his numerous dear friends. Out of each group, each inhabitant of a strange hotel, he could weave himself a story, grotesque or tragic.

But the settings offered us for our modern martyr-

dom were limited in number, and not always satis-
factory. That cluster of English pensions near the
Generalife was too far off to make us wish to walk
there at the end of the day, and we knew, without
seeing them, their plain, white-distempered walls, their
" artistic " unstained chairs, and their tables laden with
pale-lipped crocks, out of which drooped the rusty,
wire-like stalks of a few faded wild-flowers. Moreover, such rooms were too austere for smoking or
drinking : and assuredly the comic song, first heard at
Gibraltar, would echo and re-echo for us under every
sham rafter and over every chill tile. On the other
hand, the nice, clumsy white hotel that mirrored itself
rather inanely, a road edged with streams dividing it
from its reflection across the way, was too full of stuffy,
little Saracenic sitting-rooms—padded sitting-rooms as
though for the reception of maniac Moors—on the
walls of which, doubtless to calm them and make them
feel at home, were hung yellowing, time-stained photographs in coloured oriental frames of veiled beauties,
camels and palm-trees. There was no space here for a
wide range of observation.

The only one which offered a real field for discovery,
then, was the Boabdil Palace Hotel, a new affair of the
grandiose and expensive kind, its intercoiling knots of
dumpling-like domes and dumpy minarets visible for
many a mile. Like Don Quixote and Sancho Panza,
here we were forced to charge the windmill of a
swing-door, installed there to separate the true, golden

grain of the tourist from the chaff that consisted of touts, guides and beggars : or, again, the swing-door, outward and visible sign of hotel luxury, might be said to have confronted one much as a trap confronts for its enticement an animal. Once in its grip, escape was impossible : while to guard against the contingency of such a rash attempt, placed at its side in the little lobby was a large box-like booth, with an opening toward the top—as it might be the window of a booking-office, or the stage of a street puppet-show when the curtain rings up. To aid this last simile, the being who inhabited it was continually ringing bells, as though this were a trick he had recently been taught, and of which he was so proud as to be completely unconcerned as to both the cause and result of his action. The booth was unlike the usual concierge's desk. The management prided itself on the way in which the decorative themes had been carried out even to the smallest detail, so a few stalactites and honeycombs had been thrown in to stylise it, and it was portentously painted in red and blue that suggested more than ever the frame for some antique miming by minute figures. Alas, all the drama that this stage sheltered was the modern, expensive tragedy of missed trains, telegrams unsent or dispatched and delivered to the wrong person, motor-cars that broke down in the mountains, and an occasional faulty airplane. Sometimes on entering the hotel nothing was visible at first save an artful vacancy, for the porter would be stealthily crouching under it, pretending to examine the numerous shelves for the many things lost or mislaid, and then all of a sudden the head and shoulders would pop up into their square frame, and the face of the very God of Muddle himself would be revealed, surrounded by all the properties necessary for his symbolism, telephones upon which to cut off the speakers, telegrams to mis-send, letters to be unposted, time-tables to be misread, bells to be struck, pulled and pressed in order to conjure up the correct atmosphere of pandemonium, and, which was evidently to him a new and pleasing adjunct to the possibilities he had already established, a pencil that swung stiffly on a chain, like the miniature corpse of a malefactor suspended from the gibbet.

The head and shoulders of the being thus caged, meagre as they were from the point of view of a lover of proportion, were too large for their framing, yet, as we watched him indulging his antics with a fine dexterity, considering how limited was the space allowed him, we wondered how it was that the proprietors had not selected a more magnificent figurehead. The features were mean and indeterminate, and though by the energy of his abrupt and jerky movements, he was no doubt still young, his face was curiously ageless, might have been taken at alternate moments for that of quite an old man or that of a boy. He had no hump to his back, only a slight stoop, yet it is but fair to add that as he leapt up into his booth there was something of the grotesque air of Punch about him :

and when wishing to attract attention, he had formed the habit of rapping the ledge under him with a pencil, much as his prototype uses the baton. The head, moreover, for ever turning woodenly from side to side, as though in search of something it had just lost, was that of a controlled automaton ; it was held a little down, while its eyes, unable to look straight at others, disclosed a perpetual, idiotic but malicious flicker. A wooden lid appeared to move over them from side to side, their rolling regulated by some invisible showman. Every moment one expected the act to end, and the head and shoulders, with that last, derisive shriek of the Roman clown, to declare themselves sawdust, and flop forward, loosely swinging over the shelf.

It was, in truth, almost impossible not to dislike this poor comedian, his qualities emphasised as they were, by an unctuous, ingratiating manner that yet harboured an obvious, if subdued spite : while Tristram, from the very first moment of entering the hotel, had conceived for him a rare and deep aversion, but one of which he was rather ashamed—an aversion such as one might entertain for some species, repulsive because akin to one's own, the same that many a human being feels for a monkey, and every monkey, it is said, for a seal. Yet both of us appeared to exercise over this puppet a genuine fascination—perhaps the reverse side, the response, to our own emotion. Directly we entered the hotel, he would pop up into his window, run out of his booth and fuss round us, hindering us as we took off our coats by the futility of his help, so that the extrication of even an arm was an impossibility, talking pointlessly and with too much affability about the weather or the guests, and ringing countless bells to have us led to the sitting-rooms. Indeed, the statement that he imbued the whole hotel with an air that transcended inefficiency and became sinister, would be no exaggeration.

Out of the lobby, the lounge-rooms opened, one leading into another, and all, one knew, just caught in the gilded but guttersnipe act of imitating the Alhambra directly its back was turned. The hotel had, of course, been conjured up because the American tourist insisted on having his pound of flesh richly sauced with local colour. Every ceiling was hung with meat-red and vein-blue stalactites, that, even when aided by the most glaring illumination, looked darkly gross and corrupt ; every wall was crowded with blinding incised patterns, or with slabs of larder-like marble and tiles, upon which were displayed pictures of veiled, though scantily draped, females, with lustrous but lustful eyes, ogling one against a background of poached-egg and date-palm sunset, so that often this combination of ceiling, marble, tiles and white limbs with muslin over them, must suggest the premises of a hygiene-loving millionaire-butcher. Against the acceptance of such a conclusion, however, were the vases of tall, preserved palm-trees, very dusty and septic, and the number of cushions and divans, and mascots, so half-witted in conception as to make the sensitive visitor blush, which to the directorate spelt luxury. For the rest, every table was oriental as an elephant, every chair poked a sly, Moorish finger into your back, and was so made that when you got up, it overturned with a resounding crash. At first the manufacture of such a chair for a hotel may seem to have been an extravagance, for doubtless many were broken in the process. But, in reality, it was a business proposition, for the shame and noise of such a somersault stunned the visitor, rendered him quite incapable of those methods of calm addition and subtraction for which the management harboured justifiably so profound a distrust and resentment. For the further bewilderment of their guests, over this surfeit of decoration and upholstery which we have described, there darted in the daytime little patches of red, blue and orange, for stained glass is linked fast to the orient in the hotel-management mind. All round the walls, in Moorish open-work wooden cases, was a great show of silvered radiators, which in the winter must have frozen the visitor with their likeness to some organisation of frost on a stone, but which by now were sweating profusely, imparting to the room a musty and mildewed odour. Throughout the years these pipes remained resolutely tepid, for just as that degree of temperature in winter is the most cooling, so in summer is it, conversely, the most heating. Nor was this all the benefit the guest would reap from them. There was a radiator in each bedroom, and all night long it would sing, gurgle and croak like a mechanical nightingale.

One evening we were spying, after the fashion

described, on the assembled tourists in the lounge of the Boabdil. As we sat there, drinking Turkish coffee out of a pseudo-Arab egg-shell cup resting in a mount wrought of Algerian brass, we discovered three friends sitting immediately behind us. All of them were writers of a certain distinction, and great friends of Tristram, for whose work, besides, they cherished an immense admiration. We stayed there talking with them, as much as the hotel orchestra—that, frantically lurching, was engaged in serving out an individual species of semi-jazz, coated richly with Spanish idiom— would permit : but the sounds were so thick and close together that to convey your voice over them resembled an attempt to cross a tropic jungle, and, again, one would suddenly, after being completely hidden by these noises, find oneself without warning perilously conspicuous in a clearing, the voice uplifted, nude and distinct, into the open golden space of silence. Eventually, however, our three friends managed to communicate the fact that they were leaving Granada very soon, and to suggest that we should dine with them the following night.

This invitation was most welcome to me, because it was for the very evening before my return to England. I had feared that were we two to have dinner alone at our hotel, in an atmosphere mingled of packing and farewells, Tristram might all at once be overwhelmed with anticipation of his loneliness. It was true that there was now no reason to defer my departure. Ursula's marriage had taken place the previous fortnight. He had seemed unaware of it, and was in any case, I felt sure, quite unscathed and happy. Himself was resolved to stay on in Granada for another five or six weeks, since he held that one should see countries and towns at their most typical : Sweden under snow, or by the light of the midnight sun, London in a fog, and the English countryside exposing its fresh verdure, like St. Theresa her flesh, to the arrows of the rain. He wished to see this lovely place in the full spangled tide of the heat. But, setting aside his own inclinations, it was absolutely necessary, so the London doctors had told me, for him to be alone a little, when well enough, before returning home ; imperative that he should grow used to looking after himself once more and develop again that confidence and self-reliance, the failure of which had been largely responsible for his long illness. He loved Granada, so it must be a good place in which for him to stay : and one really could not let one's own obscure and morbid fancies become entangled in a matter so vital for him—yet I could not be altogether satisfied at leaving him ; would not have done so, indeed, unless lack of money and pressure of work had compelled it. For, in spite of his apparent health and happiness, in spite of every favourable, almost too favourable, circumstance, I could not feel entirely at peace.

Our last day together in Granada stands out very

clearly in my memory. The morning and early afternoon we spent much as usual, lingering among the palaces and gardens of the plateau. Before tea, however, we started to walk down to the city by a road that was new to us. It coiled round the back of the lower hill behind us, beneath the grey and golden downs which roused in Tristram such a feeling of repulsion. But we were anxious to examine this shallow, mound-like tableland, because it presented a peculiar phenomenon, framed in to perfection its own peculiar life ; one quite as legendary as that of the hypothetical Moors in the Sierras. This flat hill-top, then, was smooth and polite, while looking out of clumps and tangles of tropical plants, rose the surprised and spectacled faces of several English pensions : buildings of lath and plaster, reminiscent of " Shakespeare's England," but so flimsy and temporary as to be obviously no more than the transient tents pitched by a conquering race. Alas ! this ruling caste was already riven and split, and from such impermanent shelter waged a dignified, but none the less deadly, internecine warfare, which, like the Crusades was one inspired less by mundane motives than for the sake of spiritual prestige. These hostilities, further, had recently grown more acute—so we had been told—and had taken on a thousand new guerilla manifestations. The reason for this intensification of the campaign was that the newest pension had set up in its grounds an English chapel of its own, a very exotic affair of red-brick and white cut-stone. This daring move had been received with consternation, and was felt to be a violating of every unwritten law, a flouting of every code that had hitherto prevailed. People who acted thus, it was felt, would stoop to anything and stop at nothing. In fact it ranked as an atrocity. Yet, undoubtedly, it constituted a tactical advantage, for the denizens of the other shelters were obliged to seem pleased at it, and unless willing for the moment to pretend to an artistic and care-free atheism, excusable since it was adopted for the purpose of a more relentless prosecution of the war, must even attend service there.

The extraordinary loyalty of the English, their team-spirit, now proved itself, for each visitor would at once willingly range herself under the banner of her pension, determined to fight to a finish, though only a few days before she had not even been aware of its existence. It should not, though, from this statement be assumed that such gallantry debarred a combatant from entering on any personal feud in her own pension, or from any denunciation of its management for exorbitant over-charging. But in face of the enemy the ranks were solid.

As we approached these hives of unrewarded industry, these battle-grounds unsung, many old dragons, some armed with canvases and brandishing paint-brushes in a manner suspiciously expert, others a little bedraggled, carrying embroidered tambourines from

which fluttered tags of coloured silk, as though returning tired after some dionysian frenzy in the hills, were
marching back in search of fresh adventure to their
inconceivably artistic lairs, there to gorge themselves
on tea and toast. We entered in turn all the rival
establishments, and found them practically interchange-
able. Each one was as half-timbered as anything could
be, each one had the same few wild flowers in a pottery
jar that we had so surely foretold—poor, wilting wild
flowers, still hot and parched from a gloved grasp—
while, where the rooms were not " simple," they were
a-clatter with majolica plates, a film of blue-bottle
lustre across their surface. Many bowls of rusty, dusty
pot-pourri filled each sitting-room, whatever the time
of year, with the wintry if English music of a sneeze,
and there were placed in all the corners tall jars of
dried flowers, thistles and the like, to give a " home-
touch." Then, of course, there were pots of musty,
mildewed " home-made " marmalade, and " American
Fudge," oozing with the heat, for sale on a little table.
Competition had further established in each rival
pension, the protoplasm of a lending library, every
page in every book of which had been tea-stained and
tear-stained beyond legibility, challenge to, or cause of
homeric contest. Voices even now could be heard
raised in protest against alleged favouritism, or in
denunciation of a torn page.

Finally we selected that pension which seemed to
us the most fully-armed, formidable and aggressive,

and there drank tea, strong, black, Indian tea. Conversation was irate and artistic. For Tristram's identity had been discovered—revealed by a member of the Camel-Corps who had taken up her abode here, and sat surrounded by a litter of paint-brushes, prayer-books and torn leaves from library books. But angry glances flashed across the clinking cups, for the industrious amateur is even sworn foe to genius.

But now comes the surprise—leaving the pension, and turning the corner of the downward road to Granada, a few feet, a few inches almost, under these English ladies, the whole hillside, we found, had been burrowed by gypsies, and this time by authentic, unsalaried *gitanos*, living in a primitive whirl of dust, dirt, knives, tambourines—though ones very different from those in the rooms just overhead—vermin and bright colours. The whole place was a hive of cigar-coloured children. By the side of the road, at the cave's mouth, a brown mother would be nursing a cocoanut-coloured baby at her breast, and men would be fighting and singing.

When above, and perhaps a little tranquillised by a glass of Malaga, the English dragons were from custom warming their toes at a non-existent fire, regarding the orchidaceous blossoms, which, in the manner of Indian magicians, they were now with arthritic fingers conjuring up out of the blank, moon face of the tambourine, indulging in one of that infinite number of card-games and pastimes which our race has invented to strangle the infant hours at birth, grumbling, very rightly, about the food provided for them, or discussing the loss, possible theft, even, of a prayer-book with a watered-blue-silk marker, what impetuous scenes, what turbulent orgies, what dramas of love, robbery, rapine and murder, were not in progress a few inches under those wistfully tapping toes ? Or, again, of an afternoon, when the gypsies were dreaming away their siestas, out of the sun in the cool dimness of their earthy caverns, what to them unimaginable feats of ice-blooded rancour and rain-bred religious fanaticism were not being enacted, what subtle threats and cunning insinuations were not being made, a few inches over their dusky heads in " lounge " and lending-library. Each world was incomprehensible to the other, invisible, withal, as though only frequented by a race of spirits. Of these two systems of alien conquest and romantic valour, one stood imposed above the other, and in this exemplified Granada. Thus, too, had the infidel squatted for centuries over the Christian, until the balance swung the other way, and the Spaniard had dominated the Moor : while even now the Palace of the Emperor Charles leant heavily across its Saracen foundations.

From an inspection of these two symbolic and fasci-nating worlds, so flaunting yet self-concealing, we walked on to the town below, more than ever golden in these last hours of sunlight. The trees which lined these broader streets and plazas were in the first fresh-

ness of their green, and at this hour a coolness crept
through them, and made their young leaves sparkle in
a waver of silver. But from the bull-ring, as we
passed it, a hot and suffocating din tore the air, and,
as if in sympathy, the frayed edges of the sky, where
they touched the earth, began to assume a tone of
dusty red, until an effluvium of blood seemed to over-
cast this exquisite place, and in imagination one could
see the sand being used, just as with men is religion,
to obliterate the tell-tale stains of animal blood, blot
out the facts of death. In the magnificent ritual of the
Corrida, with all its sound and colour, as much as in
that of the Church, even the novice onlooker soon for-
gets his horror. Who can think of those tense moments
when, for instance, the matador first enters the arena,
or when before the new bull inherits his domain of
death, the animal last killed is drawn out at a gallop
by three mules, without a memory of something wonderful ? But, thus passing by, with only this brutal
clamour of shouting in its defence, the situation showed
itself more clearly, disentangled from the arts of outward show. Tristram said, rather in jest, though there
was some significance in his words, that his sympathy
lay with the bull rather than with the mutilated horses :
for the bull could not delay, could not be late. There
was only one way out of its dark shelter—into the
arena : only one way out of the arena—as a stiffening
corpse. The frenzied noise sank down suddenly to a
dead silence and was then renewed. But soon we could

hear it only faintly, as we walked along the shud-deringly-white roads, between the grotesque ranks of gesticulating prickly pears, toward the plain.

Now we turned our steps toward the Cartuga, a con-vent deserted save for beggars and a sacristan, that lies about a mile outside the town. That the throng of deformities, which huddled itself in the lingering sun-shine of these courts, shall still haunt this place, was perhaps a sign of the conservatism innate in beggars : for no doubt it was merely because in former times they had been fed there at a grating. Both parties of Spanish sightseers came here, too, from time to time, and like the people of all southern countries, they are generous to the poor, never ignore the claims of the crippled. Yet they never give as much as the foreigner, and owing to the prejudiced preciosity of English and American travellers, there was no plenty of alien pence for this grotesque company. The building, alas, shel-tered an Ishmael architecture, outcast and unlike any other.

The passages of the Monastery, incidentally, were decorated with a series of pictures that portray with true Spanish realism, with that same not so much cruel love as impersonal observation of blood which has also inspired the bull-fight, the various details of ingenious torture inflicted upon Spanish saints by members of the Church of England and other kindred and equally implacable organisations. It was obvious that the mind of the Spanish painter had been very much impressed by the great part played in these torments of the holy men by female heretics, for each panel demonstrated at least one member of the frail sex experimenting with some novel ingenuity of Methodist or Episcopal torture. After being brought up on English history books, these revelations might at first have surprised one, had it not been that the ferocity of the dragons at the pensions had just prepared us for almost anything of the sort. Spain, perhaps, imparts to the English visitor something of her own fanaticism, but translated into more dour channels. Certainly, we decided, between dragon and torturer, always making allowance for the difference in dress, there was to be detected a distinct outward resemblance, and we wished that we could have invented some plan to lure them down to survey the work of their ancestors. Tristram held that an inspection of these paintings might even help them to a few fresh ideas in the prosecution of their war over the new chapel. Alas, they were not to be inveigled hither. The ghost of Ruskin barred the path.

One thing in the convent I remember particularly. There was leading out of the church, a little side-chapel in which stood a great collection of saints' relics. Gilded glass cases, full of bones decorated with coral-pink ribbons, and of skulls with false wreaths of orange-blossom clasping their bone-brows, stood endlessly, one above the other, round its walls. This last gruesome and cynical conception was horribly effective, and, as will be seen later, must have burnt itself into Tristram's consciousness.

We walked out into the courtyard where the grey

branches of an old wistaria coiled like serpents about the ledges and balconies, and its soft, rain-coloured flowers distilled their mysterious sweetness for the beggars who were bawling, each attempting to out-shout another in the effort to advertise that particular sore or deformity which he justly considered his chief claim to interest.

Soon I was climbing for the last time the steep road, lined for the tourist with shops, even their doors covered with cheap oriental trumpery that rattled and banged in the evening breeze, their windows displaying egregiously coy old American or English ladies, per-petuated by the camera in that wanton moment when, intoxicated by local colour, they had allowed them-selves to be posed as *houris*.

We passed through the wood, its leaves faintly stirring, and through the hot, fluttered silence again rose the voice of the Frenchwoman. And, as I hurried on to the Plaza de los Aljibes, for once my resolution dwindled, and in a moment of weakness I turned to Tristram, and owned how much this sombre figure, always trailing through the wood with her wretched child, affected my nerves. Directly the words were spoken, I bitterly regretted them. But Tristram was quite unaffected by them, laughed, and may have felt, perhaps, that my confession was the measure of his own recovery. One thing alone in town and landscape caused in him any other kind of feeling—the austerity of the forgotten hills above, grey, bare and rugose as the hide of an elephant : these, indeed, woke in him a faint, indefinable apprehension, which must, he thought, be the last vestige of nervous disorder. But the tide of new health was washing over his body and mind ever more strongly, and with it had been heightened his love of the place where this good had befallen him. Though he was to stay on here after my departure, he hated the idea of returning to England.

After changing for dinner, we made our way toward the Boabdil Hotel. It was about a quarter to nine, rather early for this meal in Spain, but we were to have cocktails with our friends first. The wood was now very dark, and as we emerged from it, the lighted-up swing-door glittered for us like a cubist orange divided into four quarters. It sounded for us its revolving, caoutchouc music ; soft prelude to the modern hotel's full symphony, of which the chief components then were the tattooings of constant hot and cold water against the inverted, white porcelain kettledrums of three hundred basins, frenetic hammering and loud coaxing of boilers, the metallic tongues of three hundred or more radiators dripping their aluminium music, the buzzing—half dragon-fly, half airplane—of electric fans, incessant tintinnabulation of telephones, despairing ringing of bells by visitors, clattering, banging and finally breaking of china dishes and plates and rattling jangle of metal ones, the mingled xylophones and castanets of glasses and spoons being knocked together, the muffled, hurried yet systematic percussion of ice in cocktail-shakers, and, finally, dominating ever so quietly all other themes, running under and over every orchestration, the relentless, synchronised ticking of three hundred implacable electric clocks, mowing away the minutes as though with the twin-bladed scythe of Time and Death working in unison.

Once the difficulties of the door had been negotiated, we were greeted by a fatuous ringing of bells all round us, and, as we passed his brilliantly-illumined Moorish booth, there sprang up—for as usual he had been grovelling inanely under the shelves—the head and shoulders of the puppet-like concierge, directing at us the malign, if silly, flicker of his eyes. The look which Tristram directed at him in answer most plainly expressed the rekindling of that antagonism which had been aroused in him at the first sight of this liveried manikin—an inexplicable hostility, for pity rather than hatred ought, surely, to have been the emotion to which this acting should have appealed. This, however, was but the first note struck in an evening that, beginning in the grotesque key, to the end maintained it, though within itself it allowed of an enormous range.

We entered the lounge safely and found our hosts, without too much interference from the officious mammet. But no sooner were we seated in front of some orange-coloured cocktails than there was wafted toward us one part of that preposterous refrain from the comic song that had at intervals rung in our ears ever since we had left the ship at Gibraltar : for there, materialised for the occasion on cushioned divans in an Arabic recess, who should recline except Mrs. O'Looney and Mrs. Hope-Doodle-Cope ? Alas, their presence served at once to banish the fevered oriental imagery of the hotel directorate, and, in its stead, to induce in the lounge—despite all Mrs. Cope's velvets, pearls, shawls, and the various highly-coloured ribbons that girdled, or perhaps secured, her hair—a salty breeze, redolent of deck-chairs and deck-games.

It must be admitted that, though we had met frequently since our first encounter on the boat, we had spoken but little. Alas, on this occasion we deceived them. Seeing us in an expensive hotel, they concluded we were staying there, and their hearts warmed to us. Moreover, they felt, *we* at least must realise their importance, for they had personally informed us of it : while, up till now, there had only been time for them to impress it on the hotel-management, and not as yet on their fellow-guests. They beckoned to us, therefore, alluringly from their couch, then shouted, and finally roared at us to come up and introduce our friends. The presentation, apart from the subsequent inspection and the numerous, very searching queries that ensued, occupied some little time. Eventually, however, we were passed safely through this moral and mental *douane*, and found ourselves, as it were, on the right side of the barrier. And because our friends were also writers, and one of them—it was Otho Fitz-Maurice—was already very well known, we had the good fortune to be treated to a discourse on art and literature that was particularly full of a personal flavour. Turning to Mrs. Cope, Mrs. O'Looney first coughed, the little, dry, hacking, workmanlike cough of the practised orator, and then, coming straight down to business, said, "I think, Hopie, that it would interest Mr. Orlander and his friends—for, after all, they are literary men, and here we are, together, in Granada—to hear about your Mother, Madame Doodle, and Washington Irving. What a power that man had, Mr. FitzMaurice, for expressing the sublime in terms of Spiritual Magnitōōde, without ever losing sight of the Locality, or of the Oriental Vōōpoint on Fate—or, as they say, Kismet—which such a Vōōpoint entails. I often think that in this particular respect, he compares favourably, even with such a literary giant as Russell Jenkin Jones, with whose work you are undoubtedly *ac*quainted." After this little preliminary announcement, Mrs. O'Looney stopped, and cleared her throat three times, moistened her lips with her tongue, after the manner of a professional party orator, handing out a well-known but precious exordium, standby in many precarious situations, and formally opened the proceedings.

"Mrs. Hope-Doodle-Cope's Mother, as you are doubtless aware, held a Commanding Position in Nōō York Society, when that little band of friends signified Something that could be found Nowhere else in the Wide-World—(though, since those days, Mr. Orlan-

der, it has become *very, very* little). By birth a Boston
Boosum, as a young girl she became known, throughout
America, and even Eurōpe, as the Wild Rose of
Massachusetts. Her husband, Mrs. Hope-Doodle-
Cope's father, of whom you will also have been told
much, was—whether owing to his Social Position, or
to the Interest that attached to him as one of the
Victors of our Civil War, it would require somebody
cleverer," and with a little laugh, " oh, yes, cleverer,
Mr. FitzMaurice, than *Me* to decide—naturally extremely intimate with all literary men and musicians.
Madame Doodle's house soon offered the setting for a
group that, though composed of people of very retir-
ing disposition, soon became famous all over the
Civilised Globe. It was there that Lincoln met Eliot
Poole Fiske, on that very celebrated occasion : and
there, too, I was privileged to hear Hopie, while still
quite a young girl, sing a duet with Patti. And my !
but Hopie's top-notes beat hers. She as much as
acknowledged it. (Don't frown at me like that, Hopie,
you know it's the truth.) Why, I heard her say with
my own ears, ' *Sangue di Diavolo*, I won't go on singing with that girl. I can't keep pace with her.' Why,
it's my belief that they weren't even in the same key !
Ah ! when Hopie married, the world lost a Very Rare
Artist. Often, Mr. FitzMaurice, Matrimōny Spells Loss
to Mankind, don't you think so ? And do you know
what I put her genius down to, Mr. Orlander ?—Why,
it's her French Blood, of course it is ! You see Hopie

was born a Doodle, and the first Doodle, who settled
in Nōō England in 1582, was the rightful Duc de
Doudeauville—only he didn't know it, and the other
pioneers never found it out! Isn't that queeeer?
But Hopie's father, though French, you would have
said, to the very backbone, never let you forget for a
minute that he was a Citizen of our Republic—and we,
as you are aware, do not hold with handles to our
names. Why! a thousand times, I've heard him sit up,
as an old man, with several other Veteran Victors
round him, and say, 'I'd rather be plain Colonel
Doodle than any Dook de Doodoveal in the Worrld.'
—But I was telling you about Hopie's mother.—Well,
as I have attempted to convey, her drawing-room was
like a Beacon to many lonely souls, artist, author and
musician. On his return from Granada, Washington
Irving was, of course, taken to see her.—And do you
know, that though she came of a *very*, *very* ancient
Massachusetts line, he mistook her for a Spaniard?
Why, yes! Now that was queēr, very queēr. I wish
you boys could have seen her. I loved her, just as if
she were my own Mother! But, oh Mr. Orlander, her
end was a terrible one. For three years that beautiful
woman lay paralysed and on her back. But Hopie and
I knōō our dōōty; we never left her for a moment.
Day and night, we stayed by her bedside—talking, talking, talking—while she lay there, unable to move,
unable to answer back."

At this point, the duke-descended Doodle could keep

silence no longer, and burst out with, " Oh, but you'd all have just worshipped Oliver Wendell Holmes. So simple and impressive : never seeking to be original : no pose, only poise, and saying the beautiful things that lay uppermost in his mind. But aren't you English funny ? Only to-day, Mrs. Popham (is that her name, dear ?) mentioned Lewis Carroll to *Me !* But in Birdie's father's house, we met all the most celebrated writers of children's stories of the epoch. Many of them were actually written for Birdie. You remember that lovely little tale of Wilfred Arbuckle Johnson's— ' The Chestnut Girl '—well that was written to Birdie : and in America We look upon it as the chief contribution to child-literature. But, you see, we no longer read ' Alice in Wonderland,' for we consider that Mr. Lewis Carroll was not sinceēre."

Knowing by experience that it was hopeless to attempt flight from the two ladies before each of them had been given time to broadcast a testimonial to the other, we had made no effort. But now, thankful that at present we were not compelled to share the fate of Mrs. Hope-Doodle-Cope's mother, we rose with determination, said good-bye, gulped our cocktails, and entrenched ourselves at a table in the dining-room.

I can still summon up the scene to my memory, as though it were a matter of a few days ago rather than of nearly half a century. Our table was in a corner, under a portentous dome, from which dripped every possible species of stalactite, nor had any shade, tone or colour been allowed to go unrepresented. Opposite me sat Tristram with his finely-drawn face and witty eyes. I noticed that he was altering a little, the small lines round the eyes, and running from nostril to mouth were now a little incised and accentuated. Next him was Otho FitzMaurice, almost as definite in character as Tristram, but encased in a very different shell. Swarthy, large and placid, with broad hands and clumsy gestures, he would have resembled a farmer more than a literary man, had not his eyes broken up the whole façade of his appearance by betraying the presence of the person within, an acute and observant prisoner. Then there were the two younger men, Robert Mainworth and Lionel Foley, rather silent, attentive and eager. Much of what was said on that evening has escaped during the years, much of what was then new, controversial and prophetic, has, since its fulfilment, become obvious and indisputable, but from my journal I can reproduce a little of it.

To be at his best, Tristram must either be faced with a slightly hostile gathering, which called up in him every reserve of strength, gaiety and sagacity, or with such an audience of a few people in sympathy with himself as upon this occasion he obtained. Because of it, or perhaps in consequence of his long rest, his power of vitalising others, of making them as communicative and revealing as himself, together with his gift for directing the conversation without ever appearing to monopolise it, were manifested in the highest degree.

Further, the literary *causerie* to which we had just been treated, and with no certainty of ultimate escape, proved, even from this distance, a gay and fantastic prelude. Tristram maintained, I remember, that it was a complete justification of his outlook.

T. O.—Since the war,* he said, modern life has grown so essentially grotesque that the writer of this time is continually obliged to soften rather than exaggerate, as hitherto, the outlines. Dickens, whom, by the way, I admire enormously, used during his life to be accused of caricature, yet his methods, if applied to-day, would seem lamentably tame as compared with that which he was drawing. And this change, I think, is a new one.

O. F.—I'm not so sure, Tristram. The tendency was always there, waiting to be developed. Dickens, the first novelist in England to deal with modern life, may have detected its existence beneath the surface, and though he has minimised it, no doubt this was actually responsible for the cry of " exaggeration." You know I started life as a doctor ; and one of the few things that interested me in that career was the study, then a new one, of the germs that lie dormant in the body. For many years, for example, the microbe of pneumonia may lurk in the nose or mouth. Then one day its chance comes. The bodily resistance is weakened in some way, or an anæsthetic, perhaps, frees its passage into the lungs, and it starts on a career of

* First World War, 1914-1918.

conquest. So it was with the war, which gave every microbe of folly and meanness the opportunity for which it had been so long on the look-out. To take one instance only : toward the end of the war everyone not entirely demented must have been aware that the news in the daily papers was controlled news ; in other words, lies—but for the sake of excitement and for the fun of believing the same thing as everyone else, most people deliberately *chose* to believe it. It amounted to mass-drugging.

T. O.—All the same, what delightful stories they were ! German spies putting down concrete beds for guns in every seaside town, the Crown Prince seen in London, in disguise, the theft of a grand piano from a French village by the Kaiser in person (imagine any German wanting to steal a *French* piano !), babies crucified head downwards in every direction, German corpses made into margarine for the workers, and all the rest of it.

Self.—And yet are not such atrocities possible ? The mildest people became demoniac in wartime. Towards the end of the war, a friend of mine wrote a letter under an assumed name to a newspaper. In it he stated that he was a country clergyman, and would like to do his bit toward winning the war by making a sugges-tion. Would it not be possible and helpful at this juncture to put out the eyes of all interned Germans ? Contrary to his expectation, the letter was published and very well received. Many persons wrote saying that it was the suggestion they had long been waiting for, and, thank God, there was one Englishman man enough to put it forward !

T. O.—It is certainly curious to compare the attitude of our countrymen during the last war with that adopted by the aristocratic English Government in the seventeenth century. During the Dutch wars, several of our fellow-subjects turned up from the Dutch colonies with magnificent tales of the atrocities committed by the enemy upon the defenceless bodies of English women and children in those distant outposts. The persons who carried these stories were immediately arrested, tried and condemned, on the ground that it was obvious to anyone who knew the Dutch that they were incapable of such brutal behaviour. The stories were, therefore, lies : and lies of a political order endangered the State. And even now I believe that unless the Government, when at war, almost forced its subjects to believe lies, the English would be found to be the most sane and least credulous of peoples. It is hardly fair to accuse them of *wanting* to believe. After all, any man who announced publicly that he considered war wrong was thrown into gaol.

O. F.—Yes, but it's odd that while the public grew enraged about such minor and imaginary atrocities as we have been talking about, it regarded the actual and gross atrocity of the war itself—which made such things as these credible to millions of sane people—without turning a hair. " The war was inevitable." Apparently any atrocity that is inevitable is right.

T. O.—But the harm done by such widespread

mania, and its accompaniment of lies, goes for little by the side of the more intense evil that befell the country through the desertion of its intellectual leaders. Men of the most remarkable gifts and of the utmost integrity were corrupted, began to believe and publish their belief in the very thing they had been denouncing all their lives. Even Anatole France was driven by the emotional rush of the war into upholding it for a month or so : though after that time had elapsed his intelligence and his principles again asserted themselves. In England Shaw and Bertrand Russell were almost the only two well-known and respected writers of the elder generation who kept their heads. No wonder that with no one but Bishops and Generals to guide it, the British Public stampeded. On the younger, self-thinking minority the result was disastrous. It was discouraged, made irritable or apathetic : and where it was not destroyed, was thrown into so vehement a reaction that it, also, became a little demented ; defiantly bizarre and removed from reality in a different direction. Exaggeration, on one side or another, has become the normal thing and goes unrecognised.

R. M.—But is it correct, Tristram, to lay the blame of the whole thing upon the war ? Surely the changing of wealth from one set of hands to another is the real cause of this caricaturing ?

T. O.—Well, anyhow, the war speeded it up. Besides, before the war the sceptre was passing from the British to the German middle-class. The war presented it, instead, to America, which was not ready to receive it. When wealth was in the hands of the English, education for the rich was optional. Only games were compulsory. But the new rich in America have become rich so quickly, that speed is to them a god, and every miracle a possibility. They believe in education for themselves as much as for the poor, but they expect to finish the process in a fortnight—like children in their quickness, their memories have the same unusual tenacity. Names, though maltreated, are seldom forgotten. On the material plane, the results of this "quick change" wealth are very queer, too. One moment a family lives in the slums : the next it feasts continually on terrapin in huge Gothic halls, lined with dummies in suits of armour, that look like stuffed bears holding trays, and lit by artificial sunshine falling through rich and ancient stained-glass windows. The whole setting is placed, probably, on the top five-storeys of some cliff-like skyscraper. Thus equipped, the owner becomes an authority on art, and of course on literature.

O. F.—Only the other day I sat next at dinner to a woman, who opened the conversation by turning to me and saying, "Now tell me all about English Poetry." To my shame, she forced me to say something about it, and when Swinburne's name occurred, she suddenly assumed a new, authoritative manner, and declared : "Oh, Mr. FitzMaurice, I prefer to regard Swinburne as a prose-writer." She had, of course, never read a line of his in either prose or poetry : but she was a person widely known for her cultivation, and her sincerity was almost a career.

T. O.—In any case, a leisured society, on which the things we care for have always been said to depend, is now to be found even less among the rich than the poor. It is an age in which hostesses, and those who aim at salons, spend all their time having nervous breakdowns from overwork. The intense energy required of them becomes a habit, a kind of St. Vitus's dance. And such a life is as bad for the temper and manners as for the health and appearance. Gone are the Lilies of the Field : and in their place are the organised armies of the bee, ant, and money-beetle, with an occasional wasp like you and me, Otho! And so we have the fatiguing spectacle of " Hopie " and " Birdie " travelling madly round the world together in order to keep up with others of their sept. It reminds one of that story by Kipling of the man who tried by continuous travelling to add an extra day to his lifetime. As I looked at them to-night, decked out in their spoils under a Moorish alcove, I realised that no such spectacle had been possible since the passing of Imperial Rome. But, once written down, it transcends belief. And this is why the word " satire " is so seldom off the critical nib. Petronius Arbiter was, I am sure, faced with the same problem. Very likely it was responsible for his mysterious suicide.

O. F.—But of course the word " satirical " has really

reversed its meaning. It is now only applied to an accurate presentation of modern life. The ancient school of fiction, puny and degenerate, still goes on, though it is as unreal and conventional as one of Leighton's old " Flaming Junes," and is praised as being " a straight picture of the age " or " true and realistic." Hardly ever does anyone denounce it and tell the truth ; which is that it has no basis in life at all, is utterly unlike anything.

T. O.—And as a matter of fact the new life has its qualities : majestic absurdity, idiot-strength, speed, unfathomable sadness, inimitable silliness. These demand their own treatment. One method would be to apply to the age a prose, a machinery of thought and description, as fast-moving as itself—for even if the brain's no better, at least it acts with more speed ; another would be to apply to life the scientific method of the microscope, which lets us see a universe within a drop of water. Under such an instrument, hero and villian can no longer exist in their fullness of other days, since each of their actions and thoughts is seen to be built up of a thousand subsidiary ones, varying in motive. After Dostoiefsky and Proust, Prospero and Caliban must always be played by the same actor. Just as in actual engineering, so in the understanding of thoughts and actions, our generation can throw bridges over chasms, which were formerly impossible to span, and connect them together. With our perceptions, our knowledge, we can, like detectives, see the meaning of associations that have hitherto appeared casual. We can burrow under, build over and round thought.

O. F.—Such statements are fun, I know. But what do they amount to ? How are you to overcome the chief obstacle to the writing of the modern novel, an obstacle rooted in the nature of democracy ? During the last fifty years or so, it was realised that a peasant could be of as much, or more, interest than Sir Willoughby Patterne or Richard Feverel. It has now come to be assumed that, *ex officio*, he must be so. A snobbery of a perverted kind has arisen, which does not comprehend that ignorant millionaire, ignorant peasant is each as boring as the other. And Balzac's titled ladies, Proust's Dukes and Duchesses and dethroned princes, D'Annunzio's Roman nobles and exotic poets are often more human, and certainly more interesting, than English, Scandinavian and, above all, Russian peasants, in spite of our modern prejudices.

T. O.—That's scarcely fair, Otho. Titled heroes and heroines are still as popular as ever, both in Mayfair and with the masses. Only the intelligent minority despises or distrusts them, because they have been so long associated with trash in the way of books. But I *must* say that it does seem as if the novelist is determined to write of types that are dying, peasants, top-hatted, gold-watch-chained merchants and the whole horde of their insufferable descendants, or the captains of sailing ships. And, after all, it is difficult for a grown-up person to take much interest in the psychological reactions of a sea-captain in the South Seas : both individual and background have long been more notorious for action than words or thought. For Heaven's sake, if you're going to write a story about the sea, do it on the level—let it be a sea-story. The nearing taps of Long John Silver's wooden leg on the frosty, moonlit road, the grotesque fragments of rum-stained song in " Treasure Island," are worth all the headaches that later salts in fiction have brought down on themselves by sustained, unnecessary and unbecoming hard-thinking.

L. F.—Still, if the peasant is unfortunately, as you say, Tristram, becoming extinct, if the lamentable day is approaching, when, as I know you think, all agricultural work will be controlled and muddled from the cities, under the guidance of chemists and their like, carried out by machines, surely you will admit that a fully authenticated description of one will always be of interest ?

O. F.—Only to the antiquarian, Lionel. Hardly more exciting than some prehistoric novel in which the hero, instead of a man, is a diplodicus or ichthyosaurus. Supposing that Greek and Roman authors, instead of men, had taken the Dodo as their constant theme, we should not read them much now.

T. O.—Well, for one thing, we don't : and for another, Dido is not much less stuffed and inanimate than the Dodo. The ancients were for ever writing of gods : and religious literature is difficult to read. Unless Man makes God entirely in his own image, he is apt in a book to be a bore. And why should a novel or long rhymed poem about a Dodo be sillier than a poem about any other kind of bird ?

Self.—You're quite right, both of you. While the novel belongs to the peasant (it would be so much better if he'd got the land instead), poetry has become a bird's nest. A decadent rusticity is responsible for this condition. In each instance, Marie Antoinette can be seen at her dismal and silly pretence of dairymaid.

T. O.—Yes, it's true that a process of petrifaction has set in, and has to be broken up. Poetry in England has come to be regarded as a kindly method of fossilising birds, or rather of setting them, like a fly, for ever in the transparent and gluey substance of routined rhythm and rhyming words.

O. F.—But poetry is outworn as an instrument. That's the trouble. After all, the best modern prose has taken all that was good from it, leaving poetry to become an old-fashioned medium.

T. O.—That's absurd, Otho ! How can you think that poetry will ever take a lower place than prose ? It is true that it's in transition, and that few poets attempt to give voice to their own age and aspirations, that few use their own personal accents—for the rhythm of the voice in poetry, as much as in prose, is all important. But that has always been so. There are still poets writing. T. S. Eliot, for example.—

How many great poets do you expect in an age? The only interest that ever attaches to prose as prose is when it is written by a poet *manqué*, like yourself.

Self.—To revert for an instant to peasants—who are growing rarer even than poets—the worst of it is that now not only are they becoming extinct, they are also becoming self-conscious, apt to stand about a little awkwardly before the Angelus gives them the cue, apt, in England, to be too merry or too grim. The revival of smocks and morris-dancing has nearly finished its deadly work. By writing of them, novelists have falsified the virtues of that very type they so much admire.

O. F.—It's exactly the same with the negro in America. The perverted snobbery I was talking about has, as you all must have noticed for yourselves, found its most typical expression in the cult of the Negro, now made the hero of so many fashionable novels, operas and plays. But the only virtue that separated his race from others, was a child-like simplicity of character. Through a long course of mingled abuse and over-praise, this has been crushed and flattered out of him.

T. O.—Yes, first he was made colour-conscious, and then class-conscious : the only kinds of consciousness that destroy. When I was in New York a year or two ago, I was invited to attend a coming-out ball given by a rich negress for her two nieces. We were conducted into a room furnished in the style of the Second Empire, the ceiling being made of pleated rose silk, drawn up to a gold rosette, like the roof of a tent. On the tables lay all the latest French and German books on Negro Art, but bound very evidently for the negro market, for their covers were a-flutter with gaudy ribbons. Our hostess, large and black as life, stood in the centre, a majestic figure in elephant-grey silk, with a Grecian fillet round her shiny hair. One dusky *débutante*, dressed in the latest Paris fashion, clung each side of her. The guests stood round in a circle. The proceedings were of a grace and formality that recalled Versailles in its most august days. The introductions were particularly complete. " Mrs. Jenkins, the wife of Dr. Jenkins of Ohio : may I present Mr. Orlander of London, Eng. ; " but no lady would shake hands until she had first fully mastered both my name and place of origin. Until her information was perfect on these points, the dark hand would be kept, in an attitude or readiness, but rigid at her side. If necessary she would ask several searching questions. Afterwards, when I was sitting out with one of the nieces after a dance, she turned to me suddenly and said in her rich, dramatic voice, " Excuse my asking, Mr. Orlander, but are you High-Class ? " I was rather nonplussed as to what answer I ought to make, but decided it was best to lay claim to this distinction. Reassured, she replied, " Well, I'm glad of that. You see, all of us here are ' tip-top ' : and though I have no colour prejudice, I *do* think the classes ought not to mingle."

O. F.—It's dreadfully sad that they should have had

attention drawn to them. After all, in spite of his physical perfection, which city life will soon destroy, the negro is of far less importance than any spectacled clerk. It's quite time that a run-down and sick Europe —sick only because of lack of confidence—asserted herself. After all, in spite of the arts of China, Egypt and Mexico, the classic line of Europe has been responsible for more beauty, outward and inward, in the world, than any other principle evoked out of human consciousness. We must return to a classic line, but one again enriched by experience, and drawing its life-blood from the age.

T. O.—But we must remember that diversity is the essence and tradition of Europe. And at the same time we must make in life a determined onslaught on the standardising dollar-system, demand our own customs and habits of thought. It is important to keep the life itself untainted and on lines natural to itself. That this can be done without the paraphernalia of imperialism is very plainly to be seen in Holland, or in Sweden, the only other country besides the United States that has a superb modern architecture to express its national life. At the same time, an English writer must never be self-consciously national. He must draw his inspiration from every quarter, need never bother to be English since what he borrows from alien sources is converted by his very blood. Look at Shakespeare, influenced as he was by every idea that came within his reach. You cannot, even if you want to, deny your

inheritance.   The birth-mark will show itself.   But
it is necessary to turn once again to the Continent, and
as usual it is to France, rather than Russia, however
many geniuses she has produced and will produce, that
we must turn.

O. F.—Perhaps it's too late.   The novelists, of the
end of the nineteenth century and of the last two decades, have rolled the heavy and ungraceful bodies of
their children in such a mire of misapplied psychology
that the old lines have been obliterated.   A new form
must arise for the novel.

T. O.—Yes, but in a sense it will design its own
form.   One can no longer wipe out of existence every
character on the stage, as it was possible and right
for the Elizabethans and Greeks to do.   In the same
way that I was suggesting just now that in future
there can be no heroes or villains, so it would seem that
no novel, unless it is a fantastic one, can have a definite
beginning or end.   Each omega to us contains in itself
a thousand alphas.   But the average reader has not yet
accustomed himself to throw away these props and read
without them.   And no doubt this partly accounts for
the new popularity of biography—so often quoted as a
sign of grace—with its inevitable alpha of birth and
omega of death.

O. F.—I think that phenomenon is due to a much
sadder and more serious cause.   Seventy years ago, fifty
years ago, the supply of those who read books was
limited, but its quality was good.   Excellently educated,

if after a peculiar pattern. Now it's larger, more heterogeneous, but without education. The rage for biography is rooted in the universal ignorance. The fact of there having existed—and so near our own time —such a fabulous genius as Napoleon, comes to the reader with all the shock of an agreeable surprise. It is to him like visiting the Natural History Museum, and finding there an enormous extinct animal that is only just dead : safe, but so exciting. " Good gracious," he exclaims aloud as he reads, " and ending like that at St. Helena ! Why has no one ever told me about it before ? " Puffed up with his new knowledge, he rushes round to boast to a friend. The friend buys the book too. Its popularity is like a snowball.

T. O.—Yes, and conversely, if the reader is already aware of the identity of the character about whom the biography is woven, he is all the more pleased. Queen Victoria is, for instance, a buoy to whom all can cling, on the sea of ignorance on which they are being tossed. They know who she was, and hated letting go of her. Hurriedly they buy the book, are again lulled into security. Yet democracy does not like its leaders to have been unblemished. Only the average man is now, by his own consent, perfect.

I have often pondered on how much of what was said that night, especially as to literary tendencies of the day, has since proved prophetic : even as I write this book, I see how right it is that only in a biography, or a true story such as this one, can the form still be dictated by a definite beginning or end.

The talk went on for some time in this strain. Tristram had now obtained the full self-release that wine offered him. Indeed, in their anxiety to do him honour, our hosts had provided a veritable fountain of liquor : and if we were all forced, or forced ourselves, to drink more than was good for us, it certainly aided the buoyancy of our spirits—up to a point.—But the truth is that when Englishmen are alone after dinner, be the company the most intelligent, or the most lewd and imbecile—and always supposing there is enough to drink—there comes a moment of gravity. Women often believe that when they leave the men, the conversation takes a ribald turn. But much more often it is devoted to such matters as, at the lowest level, dreams, coincidences and ghosts : at the highest, the possibility of the survival of the individual after death, the question of free-will versus predetermination, relativity, and the composition of the atom. Only when thus keyed up does the Englishman dare approach such subjects, though it is evident that they make a deep appeal to him. And when dinner was over and we had begun to smoke, I noticed the familiar symptoms that preceded such a conversation. A silence, and then all at once the talk had taken on this darker hue.

We discussed at first the distorted mirroring of the future that sometimes occurs—or perhaps only seems to us in days after to have occurred—in a dream ; a distortion similar to that evinced in one that follows certain events upon which obviously it is based, except that in these cases the order is reversed, and the dream precedes the happenings upon which it is founded. FitzMaurice held that if this predictive distortion could be proved and studied, much was to be deduced from it as to the nature of Time. Time, it might be, was like a great river, of which the main stream rushes down, past our landmarks, with ever-increasing speed, but which has, if you can reach them, its quiet backwaters in which many things are reflected, though very seldom in their exact likeness, as much as its eddies and falls where the turbulence of the waters forbids mirroring of any kind. A period of quiet, uneventful life was absolutely necessary in order to obtain this gift, however muddled and fragmentary, of prophecy. Again, the witches, sorcerers, warlocks, saints and diviners were probably half-wits (myself had seen a half-wit Moorish prophet, who had foretold the arrival of the French in his country; a special pavilion had been erected for him by admirers, though when possible he escapes, remains naked in the cold and refuses to eat), but if this was proved against one of them it was regarded by most Europeans as a complete refutation of any claim to such a power. But might not the exact opposite be the case? Might it not be precisely the fact of their weakness that aids them? Is it not possible that an intelligence, however low, a soul, however debased, that swings loose and unguided, is more likely to pick up fragmentary impressions of the future than one that is carefully trained and skilfully directed toward certain points of interest in the present ? Owing to the faulty powers of expression, the feeble mind may have that difficulty in accurately transmitting which so often appears to obscure prophecy : but then it may be that the ability to concentrate, which would enable these things to be correctly expressed, might keep them out altogether. In sleep, this power of concentration, so carefully cherished and developed, leaves us, and we are in those deep, idiot caves where prophecy may enter. When awake again, the active intelligence may, perhaps, want to banish such an intruder, one who is so dangerous, so much older and more subtle.

Tristram, at this point, reminded me of his childish gift, to which we have alluded, of being able to foretell minor events : and one of us suggested in explanation of it, that if you either wanted or dreaded something sufficiently, you exercised on it, through the concentration that took place, an unconscious influence, equivalent to that of a magnet upon a nail, which would surely, though without your knowledge, draw it toward you out of the future. If you wanted it strongly and with insistence, and were innocent and whole enough (that is to say of one piece, without distractions) to concentrate upon it in this unknowing fashion, then when this thing or event came to you, the nature of the power you possessed would elude you, and would appear in the guise of divination of the future. Similarly when you had, in the same manner attracted to yourself some calamity through your attempts to stave it off, this process would seem to have been a foreboding of it.

To this, Tristram replied with a theory of his own : " It is my conviction," he said, " that circumstances conspire, will, indeed, go to almost any lengths, to take advantage of us. Combine the two popular sayings : that misfortunes never come singly and that money goes to the rich. I mean, if already poor, we are certain to lose what money we have with greater ease and rapidity. Something will occur to justify the emotions which for the moment we entertain, for circumstances ' play up ' in the most lamentably hypocritical manner. Let us consider a slight but nauseating example. You remember, Osbert, our first day in Cadiz, and what happened to me there. I was still nervous and ill, and felt particularly unwell that morning. Long before I went out, a sense of southern squalor had overwhelmed me. It was as though one was being suffocated by the heat, dirt and poverty : though, thinking over it, it is plain to me now, that apart from the incidents I am going to relate there was ever so little justification in fact for this feeling, since Cadiz, so open to sea and air, is not a sordid town. However—as we walked away from our hotel, by the side of a church I noticed a man, sitting down, with a wooden bucket in front of him. It contained a mass of bright green worms, wriggling about in a little

sea-water.   At that moment, a Spanish sailor came
up, gave the man a coin, and taking up a handful of
them, very much alive as they were, swallowed them
down at one gulp, and said to me at the same time
in broken English, ' Very goote.'   He may have been
right.   Really, I suppose, there was nothing disgusting
about it : probably it was no worse than eating oysters
or winkles or the things that people eat everywhere
abroad by the seaside.   But in the state I was in that
morning, it made me feel ill, and I decided to rest for
a little in the cool church by my side.   Hurrying toward the steps that led to it, though, I nearly fell, and
looking down, found I had tripped up over a dead
piebald rat (the only black and white one—I'm thankful to say—that it has ever been my lot to meet, alive
or dead).   This was really too much for me : and once
in the church, I realised that nothing except a bath,
a book, and my hotel bedroom could comfort me.   It
was extremely dark, impossible to see anything, but I
plunged for where I could just distinguish the opposite
door, seized the handle—and to my utter horror found
that instead I clasped in my hand the outstretched
stump of a beggar's arm.   These three minor, but re-
volting and cumulative, adventures had occurred with
the most amazing swiftness, as though timed for the
signals ' One-Two-Three.'   And for a time I was completely bowled over.

Then again, one Sunday morning, a year or two
ago, I was walking in the Tuileries Gardens.   Armistice

Day was being celebrated, and the noise and sound of firing was intense, and for my part, I felt nervous, full of premonitions, though these sensations I attributed to the general noise. However, I remarked to my companion, ' I feel very uneasy this morning, and can't stand it any longer,' and started back to my hotel. Suddenly there was a smaller sound, a crackling fire, within a few yards of me. I had witnessed, almost before I knew it, a murder and suicide. Now I hold that it was not a premonition which I had experienced, but that because I was in the state I have described, I happened to see something to justify it. Those who feel nothing, see nothing.

But that is only one side to it. What befell me in Cadiz, the crime I saw in Paris, was genuine. On the other hand, things will take an immense amount of trouble to appear to be something which they are not, something that you are expecting. Think of the Corean Bear. In that obsolescent land was found a small animal, ursine in habits and appearance. It was, in consequence, very naturally supposed to be a bear by the naturalists, who having heard of it, were first fortunate enough to capture one. And it was only after many, many years had passed that it transpired that the little creature was not of this genus at all, but belonged to some extinct tribe parallel to it, the sole survival in that part of the world of a much more ancient creation. The story of Dr. Bode's Leonardo wax-bust contains a similar warning. He was the only great connoisseur to expect to find a work of this category, and one immediately sprang up to fulfil his expectations : exactly the kind of bust he had expected, but of another epoch and by a later hand. For, perhaps, if you ask a question of destiny, you will receive an answer in keeping with it ; but the answer is in reality only the echo which the question calls forth. If you are inclined to be frightened at night in an old house, it will reply to you in that strain. There will be a sudden, an inexplicable commotion and turbulence in the blank darkness, or you will be roused from your first timid sleep by a startlingly distinct footfall, or by a door slowly creaking open at the instigation of an unseen hand. Thus that which actually appears to happen, and the previous fear of what might happen, are made for a moment to coincide. It is as though the hallucination of a madman were, for an instant, and because he suffers from it, to be translated into the semblance of reality, to be verified by an actual, indisputable occurrence, so that the last poor gleams of truth which filter every now and then into his mind must assure him, not of his deranged condition, but, instead, of the essential truth and rightness of his particular delusion.

Finally, let me try to explain what I want to suggest by giving you, in illustration of it, a sad experience of my own. There was living in London, a year or two ago, a Scandinavian friend of mine. I'm not sure if any of you knew him, but he was a poet, rather a good one. While still a boy, unable to bear the bookless

and suburban atmosphere of one of the smaller northern cities, he had run away from home—but, alas ! not
before his native climate had made its first and final gift
to him, a passion and craving for the strongest drink
he could find. At last he drifted to London under the
antiquated impression that its streets were paved with
gold. There he starved in various professions, for he
had no money of his own, and was incapable of prolonged effort at anything but his own work : and, since
he preferred drink even to that, he was an undoubted,
but always talented, failure. The regime in which he
persevered, of continual drunkenness combined with
starvation—for he could never afford to indulge in food
and drink at the same time—eventually succeeded in
upsetting the balance of a brain always more rich in
imagery than reason. His lunacy began with that favourite malady of artists—and one for which, incidentally, there is, in England, often only too much
excuse in fact—the delusion of being persecuted.
Henceforth Nielsen existed in a tortured world of melo-
drama, on the ill-proportioned, haunted quality of
which no shade of reason could impinge. His mind
became incarcerated in this nightmare-universe it had
created, a spider fast caught in its own web. He told
me of people climbing up the outer wall of his Bloomsbury lodging-house, in the black but early hours, so that
they might look in at the window of his fourth-storey
bedroom, of implacable enemies who from their lairs
were able to switch electric-currents through the wire

springs of the mattress upon which he was lying; of dire threats from cocaine-loving curates, and of a thousand such unexpected occurrences. But, above all, he was for ever telling of anonymous persecutors, always armed with black umbrellas, who would surreptitiously approach him in the street—no matter what part of London he might be in at the moment—tap him on the shoulder, murmur an unintelligible message and then vanish, soon swallowed up by crowds or darkness.

His was a most difficult case, for he was a determined man and would not do anything that was suggested to him. Obviously he had eaten nothing for days. I tried to quieten him, and arranged with a small non-licensed restaurant near where I lived, so that he could have a series of meals without drink. It was hoped that with regular food prepared for him, here in a peaceful neighbourhood far from the centre of his hallucinations, he would be able to eat, and that with the renewed physical strength that should follow, his dormant reason would once more assert its sway. In addition, I decided to take him one afternoon to be examined by a doctor, to whom the case had been explained beforehand. For a long time Nielsen was closeted with him. Eventually the doctor called me in, and said, " I want you to hear what I am telling your friend. He has now confessed to me that the occurrences which he has been talking about are not real, but invented ones. He admits and knows it : and I have warned him of the appalling danger he runs by indulging in such fancies. You tell me he is a poet : well, let him utilise his imagination in another way. Trees, flowers, nymphs, by all means—but don't let him pretend that people with black umbrellas come up in the street, tap him on the shoulder and speak to him. They don't do anything of the sort. And he has given me his word to drink no more alcohol for a year. Isn't that so, Mr. Nielsen ? Now you'll remember and make a fight for it ? You've given me your word, mind. You'll be all right, quite all right.' And the doctor, patting him on the back in a way that was no less professional than friendly, propelled us into the passage, where a damp parlourmaid juggled perpetually with hats and gloves, there being always more of them than she could ever keep in the air at the same moment.

Even as we left the house, I could see how different Nielsen was, cheerful and sensible. His eyes, too, had lost their expression of vacant but cunning fear. We walked slowly down the whitened steps—steps that are in the morning the bane of so many lumbaginous charwomen—that led from the house into the street, at this instant of twilight lying beneath like a dark, foggy, lamp-lit canal which we were forced to enter. But, directly the door had been shut behind us, I recalled that, confused by the hat-and-glove-act on the part of the parlourmaid, I had left my walking-stick in the hall. I had, therefore, to run up the steps again, ring the bell, and seize my cane : all this business, however, in reality only occupied a second or so. I came running down the steps again and saw Nielsen, waiting for me safely under the nearest lamp-post. He was looking in my direction. Then, all at once, I saw him turn round swiftly. As he did so, a nondescript figure, carrying a black umbrella, sidled up behind him, paused, tapped him on the shoulder, mumbled a few indistinct words, and rapidly shuffled away into the darkness. The man was perhaps himself mad or drunk —I do not know—but the fight for Nielsen's reason was from that moment lost : for this incident, which had so often befallen him in his own mind, with every illusion of reality, had now been enacted in front of a witness. I could not deny what I had seen, for to have done so would have been to sap still further his belief in me and in the world of common sense. One shadow behind his sick brain had taken to itself substance, and had thereby supported, and guaranteed the existence of, all the other spectres stalking in the background. He was able, also, to assume the triumphant ' I told you so ' air of one, hitherto unbelieved, whose tales have now been proved the truth before all men. Things, not persons, had plotted : circumstances had conspired to clamp the fool to his folly. Yet he became more secretive as to his hallucinations, deeming those who would not place credence in them unworthy of his trust. And this casual verification of fiction by fact was in the end responsible for Nielsen's death, for before a month was past he had killed himself."

I have always remembered this story, told us, when a young man, by a most remarkable writer and my most intimate friend : and in years long after, when events brought it back to my mind, I have often wondered whether thus, too, circumstances may not have conspired to frighten, and finally to crush, my acquaintance, that famous, elderly writer and man-of-the-world, the late Tristram Orlander—for, in accordance with his theory, the mere holding of it would tend to make it appear as though substantiated by facts.

But in those distant, golden days of which I am talking, there was no herald of any calamity. Tristram's spirits soon veered, and the conversation followed them. The curious, after-dinner interval of gravity was over. If it were possible to plan out the future, he had decided on his, he said, and proceeded to give us an inimitable forecast of it. He intended to be rich, honoured, and a great figure in the land. No thread of beauty, no adventure of thought should mar his work, which would sell in thousands. A nabob of literature, he would reap a fortune from the tropic jungle of sex through which he would drag his readers, though never would he put forth a new idea on it, or allow a beam of intelligence to play upon its density and reveal the nature of its growth. He would buy a flotilla of islands upon which to live, and was already deep sunk in the cushioned cars and airplanes of the future. With a vast variety of walking-sticks, guns, fishing-rods and gulf clubs at his disposal, he would at last make peace with his relatives, cultivate all his own special bores, and in the end lead the life of a gentleman. In this sketch of his career, that he developed with so much elaboration, there was a satiric note, which, one felt, must, like an antiseptic, always preserve him from any such decay as he was describing.

At last we got up from the table, and walked out into the warm air of the moonlit wood. Many people were walking there on this hot night, but the nightingales, high up in their dark, swaying towers ignored the hoarse splutter of talk beneath them, and calmly continued their practising, weaving their own elaborate but pure variations on the themes enunciated by stream and fountain. Far away, too, one could detect the tragic, sordid refrain which haunted this paradise of trees and water. Raised up in denunciation, the neat French voice, all the more menacing for its outer-coating of politeness, and in its level tones quite impossible to escape, seemed convincing and convinced as must have been the lonely voices of Isaiah or Jeremiah, and equally conscious of the doom of mankind. Under it, too, could be distinguished its dreadful, lisping accompaniment : and now anger was added to my other emotions, for though not always in agreement with English doctrine, I adhere most strongly to the national faith that small children should be in bed by six o'clock.

The rest of the party, I think, did not disentangle these two particular contributions from the complex of sounds that arose, and the accurate little rings of speech settled into the night, overwhelmed by the nightingales, bubbling waters and the near-by clatter of thumping and jumping gypsies, with the insect-like droning that inspired it : these last frantic rhythms issuing from the white hotel, where these strange people were no doubt bounding about in as savage a fashion as possible—though never without grace—for the edification of mild and timid visitors.

We sauntered past the long, trough-like fountain of the Marqués de Mandegar, its fruit-crowned masks now sprouting silver beards in the light of a half-moon, and turning up a turbaned archway, found ourselves in the Plaza. Unlike the wood, it was quite deserted. We walked on toward the far end, past the unfinished grey palace, past the forum-like field of ruins, tangled and meaningless foundations, behind which rose the robust walls of the Alhambra. Under the green illumination it was quieter than ever—for at such hours it was always closed, except that for the few days of the full moon susurrant droves of tourists were allowed there after payment of an extravagant sum, but never in parties of less than a hundred persons—and now we could regard in ideal silence the never-failing wonder of the town sprawling over its slopes. But as we gazed down below, suddenly, in a rush of stupid spirits, Tristram declared that he must visit the Alhambra by moonlight, and before anyone could stop him had vaulted the palings and was racing across the enclosure. The only chance for his safety was to pursue him.

Even as we ran across the confusing black and white bars formed by the fence and the moonlight, we could hear watchful barking, occasionally degenerating into mournful howls, from the hill opposite, and the Spanish dogs of the South are as vicious as those of Greece or Sicily.   If we shouted, we should wake the night-watchmen, ferocious and fully armed.   They would imagine us to be robbers come to steal the famous vase, and if we were sufficiently lucky to escape being shot in any affray, yet a single night in a Spanish prison would be enough.   However, it ought to be no easy matter to enter the precincts.   But good fortune— from the point of view of the escapader—generally attends such escapades.   No great monument is ever allowed to be entirely free of scaffolding, and work-men had been, as usual, repairing the walls.   We had almost caught him up, when Tristram discovered a long ladder, and climbing rapidly up it into a cradle of planks, hurdles and matting, discovered in the wall an aperture just large enough to admit of his getting through it.   We could not abandon him, and were forced again to follow.   It was easy enough to climb through : and there he was, waiting for us in the little entrance court, where in the daytime visitors obtain their tickets.   There was a lamp in the upper storey —the lyke-wake, evidently, over this lovely corpse— and we could hear the guardians talking, their voices raised, no doubt, over wine and cheese, and discussing, perhaps, various questions of Spanish punctilio.   If our situation was somewhat precarious, there was yet about this oasis of pleasant, lamp-lit conversation above the wilderness of black corridors and of chambers, now as silent as the deserts out of which they had blossomed, a quality that was at once comforting and olympian, making us loth to leave it. Our intrusion, however, compelled us to be lucifugous as bats, and we crept onward. The light was blacked out, and we were in the Court of the Myrtles, a world native to these sequences of milky whiteness and grape-bloom shadow.

The palace is so complete in itself, so independent, even in its daylight vistas, of the outer world, that notwithstanding its deadness, it is as though one were put in a bottle whence the wine had been long poured, but in which at certain hours the fumes still linger. Further, our houses are made to live in, and for the daytime : but these pavilions were different. Never had a palace been created so purposely for night, and as a frame : and at this moment, the moon had torn reality from us, and placed us in a scene, set it may be, for soft action, but certainly for a drama of life, of which there was none now, until it seemed as though this ever-empty, waiting theatre welcomed even our burlesque entry. The stillness round us was made all the more taut by the countless little sounds and crepitations of a southern night, which were, in themselves, admirably organised as an accompaniment for the miming action which the place and hour demanded. In the very low back-ground of this silence could be distinguished far away the notes, immeasurably old, of frogs croaking out their Aristophanic laughter, while the cicada and their allied tribes were supplying a more strictly local touch by a continuous clacking of casta-nets : bats pricked the general effect with their needle-sharp cries, and, ever so softly, over all hung that song which can never have left this hill since its creation, the song of water murmuring in a thousand different tongues, dripping, singing, rushing, rippling.   But all these sounds only served to set off this nearer silence that was no negative thing, it seemed, but positive. Round us, their intricacies made softer, their golden honey-combs now gleaming with points of silver light, against the vitriolic green-white of the white walls, stood loggias and pavilions, domes, turrets and arcades. The dark, herb-scented air in front of us trembled, all flecked with golden specks where the fire-flies darted and hovered.   And under it, down the middle of the court, stretched a length of transparent, marble-paved water, on the surface of which floated little jugglers' rings of silver, where any moonbeam touched a ripple. If we had not by force stopped him, Tristram would have bathed here.   It was as if some demon of per-versity and stubbornness had taken temporary posses-sion of him, making him wish to do everything that was most infantile.

We wandered quietly through into the Court of the Lions.   In the middle of it, the little marble bunch of lions that support the water-basin had grown silver hides and manes, and roof-deep the silence rose all round us, except that now and then, ever so far outside this enclosed and distant world, a dog could be heard, grating its voice against every brick and stone. In the darkness of the four lofty pavilions, and in the endless, labyrinthine corridors that led off and under them, a thousand swarthy and stealthy ghosts were surely mustered, sighing, rustling and shuffling softly in their palace-slippers. So strong was the emanation here, that even the author of this foolish joke was now anxious, I think, to return to the comparative life and more easy silences of the open air. We stole back, through the Ambassadors' Hall. One of us gently pulled back a shutter—and instantly there rushed in, to shatter this sly silence, an indescribably welcome gust of life from the Albaicin opposite. Lights flashed out of dark caves, and there was the inevitable uproar of dancing and quarrelling, and voices wailing out their music. So keen in its edge was the moonlight that the prickly pears could be seen guarding the caves with their frozen, cautioning hands.

On our bare feet, we now ran swiftly through the little court, down the passage, up through the place of repairing, across the meadow : once more we were safely beneath the trees in the empty Plaza. The lights of Granada were sprinkled across the hills, and a tide of vibrant life washed the base of the dead hill and splashed up to us. The shrilling and chattering that was wafted from the city seemed a portion of the night, exactly matched the orchestration of the cicadas, frogs and of the countless little insects that make their innumerable minute sounds by the regular folding and unfolding of their wings, except that in the human counterpart we found, as we stood there silent and listening, a warmth and comfort that transcended experience : for it was as though we had travelled an incalculable distance.

And this was the last time I saw Granada at night. The next morning I left it in the company of our three hosts of the previous evening. Before going into Tristram's room to say good-bye, I had wondered whether our adventure—if that description can be applied to a matter of atmosphere rather than of happening—had in any way tinged his mind with that same dark shade which it had imparted to mine. I found him, however, lying on the outside of his bed, drowsily stretching himself in the hot sunshine that fell upon it, with all the unthinking serenity of the animal world. His slow smile crept over his face : yet as I looked at his head, so beautiful and distinguished in its own manner, I asked myself whether some alteration was not to be noticed in it, whether the flame had not been a little dulled down.

From the low window, so that he could see it from where he was lying, the whole wide view was visible. The lion-coloured plain was now a shade more tawny than when I had first beheld it, the green patches now fuller and deeper in their tone, the light, sunrise wisps of almond and peach had been superseded by cumulus clouds of apple and pear sailing heavily toward the horizon, while here and there, where the light air already danced and trembled with the heat, there was all the appearance of water, so that the blossoming trees over these stretches of African mirage actually seemed so many full-rigged ships. And out of this plain grew the clusters of gold towers, the turrets, the courts of monasteries, the outlines of street and square, fitting the lovely lines of the hills, and filled with an exuberant sense of growth, yet for me all, all darkened, caught in the black mesh of a veil of foreboding. Could it be, I wondered again, that some illness was about to attack me, that Tristram had really contrived to shake off on to me the burden of his nerves : for here was he, happy and content, while I was filled with an unparalleled restlessness till my mind harboured many idle portents of disaster ?

But once the train had started, once comfortably settled in the roomy carriage—a carriage, indeed, so roomy that it made me feel like Jonah, so much did it resemble the red-plush stomach of a whale—the perspective of my stay in Granada, never clear when one is in a place, began to arrange itself. Having left Tristram in the best of health, happily installed in the place which he owned to liking best in the world —I discovered that it was yet about him rather than myself that I felt anxious. As new country, rocky chasms and old, tall trees sped by the window, the scent and flavour of the place we had just left grew more distinct. It was then that I was certain that it was no place in which for him to be alone—and here was the discovery, for *him :* who loved it. Yet what could I do, what could have been done, to dissuade him from staying on ? No reasons could have been urged, except such ones as would probably, in his present mood, have made him laugh : if not laugh, then have disturbed him and so have injured his health.

Still he was well now : and the delight and surprise of his friends to a certain extent soothed me. They had, they now told me, thought that any revival that might set in would be an affair of years rather than of months, and never, in any case, had they expected to see him again so entirely spirited and happy. Yet having been near him continually through the long months of illness and convalescence, only myself could estimate justly the extent of the collapse that had occurred, and though quietened by this confirmation from outside of the extraordinary improvement that was manifest in him, nevertheless I could not be extricated from the current of uneasiness that ran under my other feelings.—Far away, there still sounded for me through the grinding and jolting of the train, until it seemed to take the actual rhythm of her voice and accents, that clear, incisive oracle, and the words : " Ah, Messieurs, Messieurs, l'Espagne, c'est un pays dur et brutal. Vous ne pouvez pas croire, m'ssieurs, ce qu'il nous a fait. Et Granade, cette vieille ville morte, c'est

la ville la plus terrible de toutes les villes de l'Espagne.
Ah ! mais le bon Dieu ne peut jamais oublier ni pardonner cette manière d'agir."

*　　*　　*　　*　　*　　*

Tristram had no such misgivings. To him it seemed
that his old craving for crowds, friends and excitement
had passed away for ever. He had, in fact, never
owned to its existence or for an instant admitted it to
himself as a feature of his temperament, but had chosen
to regard it as the result of circumstances, of an urban
life. It was impossible, he would maintain, to be lonely
except in a great city, or during a long period of bad
weather. The restful nights to which he had been so
long unaccustomed, had filled him with renewed vigour
and self-reliance. That event which he had known
would ruin his life—Ursula's refusal to marry him—
now proved to have counted for nothing : nor was
it at all as though his sensibilities had been paralysed
by shock. On the contrary, he felt that the strength
which had accrued to him was a new strength, and
thus could not, would not, feed the old emotions. The
dead wood had been cut out of the tree and it was
healthy.

And here we reach one of the inner qualities of
selfishness that brand the sensualist. He was relieved
to find that he no longer regretted her or her marriage :
that which had in reality wounded him much more
than the loss of the woman he loved was the fact that
he was wounded. Just as, at the time, his sorrow had

doubled itself, so now it had been halved.   The astonishing speed of his recovery could thus be accounted
for : he had felt himself whole again, and had become
so.

Then, too, Granada struck out of him that strange
response.   But had a note in common in their being.
The alliance of desert and tropic growth, of real and
artificial, the combination of luxuriant plain and snow
mountain, of absolute death and negation with an
acrid and strident life, made an acute appeal to his
senses, drugged him, as it were, with a quality of beauty
that was new to him in this particular materialisation
of it, made him blind to the corruption that lay concealed within.   Hence he felt no need for a friend to
be with him, and found that here he could wander for
hours by himself, though he had always ridiculed the
solitary walker " communing with Nature," and had
hitherto regarded walking as necessary exercise and the
medium for one of the pleasantest forms of companionship and conversation.

No longer, even, did the down-like mountains that
swelled above the Alhambra—and which had once,
alone of all things about this place, communicated a
vague feeling of disturbance—repel him.   Now he
would climb for hours among these hills, that with their
grey furrows, were rough-skinned as an elephant.
Round the lower slopes there would be a few clans-
women from the pensions, standing looking at the
view, with camp-stools beside them, on which lay a

posy of withered wild flowers. Long veils hung down
behind them to protect them from the sun's hot pursuit,
and their hats were spattered with the naïve blossoms
of English millinery, till their gaunt but gallant figures seemed to offer some degree of blasphemous likeness to the flower-sprinkled and light-footed goddesses
in Botticelli's " Spring." Or again, as he passed them,
they would be wistfully sucking the point of a paint-
brush, looking at him out of the bloodshot corner of a
timid, very human eye, while at the same time appearing to fix on the distance a calculating parrot's eye of
cold hostility and contempt : a ruse born of long torture
at the hands of the cruel but ingenious children of
the Latin races (for, alas, "picturesque old bits"
always abounded in such diminutive demons, who, with
so much sport ready to their hand, soon brought to it
all the technique and gay assurance of the practised
bull-fighter : and, while it was absolutely necessary for
you to watch what they were doing, if for a moment
you permitted them to realise that they had succeeded
in their efforts to fret and distract, all further hope
of peace was over). Then there was also the male
equivalent to this type, jolly, sabre-toothed men under
panamas, anxious to discuss the weather and deplore
their difficulties. Yet strewn over the broad flanks of
the gold-grey hills, these artistic parasites were from
above scarcely visible. Only a faint disturbance of
colourless movement showed itself.

As he climbed higher, never a living creature would

he meet, except once and again a goatherd, sitting on a stone, shaping a stick for himself, while his dark flock cropped the thyme and other herbs, with their trembling blue lips of old men. And he would rest, and let the silence and isolation wash over him and enter his soul.

One day, however, he reached a hill-top which looked down on the Generalife and the courts of the Alhambra—from here minute as those of a doll's-house —when he noticed in the ground by him a large cavity. It was in no way fenced off, and peering into it, he was amazed to discover that in reality this hill was as hollow as it looked, was full of broken masonry, ruined chambers and staircases enough for an entire hidden population. And all round on the flattened tops of the hills there lay, bleached and dry as skeletons, the pleas-ure-tanks and paved-pools of the Moors. Here, cen-turies before the Alhambra had crystallised into its innumerable cubes and pentagons, had risen a vast palace of boundless fame and beauty, the almost leg-endary Daralharosa. Once this hill, too, had been fertile, given over to flowers and waters set in the odorous shade of cypress alleys, myrtle bosks and orange groves. Indeed, across the water in Africa, those bearded, white-turbaned figures who declaim poetry to the sound of drums and vellum-covered gourds, still tell of this palace, of its silks, velvets and precious stones, its gilded hanging lamps and perfumes, and of the quicksilver sea upon which floated the

Caliph's couch, so that he might sleep the more softly ; though now there was only an impression of seared earth, as if it had been sown with salt.

At first Tristram enjoyed wandering among these mysterious survivals, the bones of a dead world of pleasure. Yet, as he grew to know them, their tragic aridity began to penetrate his mind, to revive in him again that curious instinct of repulsion. However, no sooner had this sense of unease reasserted itself, than he was spared further trouble from it. Summer flew down suddenly with an indescribable flashing of its hot and sequined wings. In a day all had been changed. It became too warm for a walk of any description. Most of the ferocious but artistic tribes-women from the pensions ceased painting, and went home, laden with peasant pottery, so that when, with a great bumping of heads against rafters in the Cots-wolds—a constant, dull music that it seemed must be the accompaniment for some weird savage rite—each trunk was opened, it was found to resemble a Neolithic tomb more than an ordinary portmanteau. The library books were dusted and put away : the " home-made fudge " melted in its glass jars. Outside the white hotel the elderly American judges started to drink spirits at nine instead of ten, and several old English colonels, never before evident, appeared in sun-helmets, as though the heat had all at once caused the long-forgotten dragon's teeth to bear fruit. In every field and on every hill the spring flowers were dried to black sticks, while in compensation each day round the river beds more oleanders kindled their gentle pink and white flames. The gypsies, their arms now resembling charcoal, deserted all their posts save those in the wood. Down in the city even the beggars lay under the porches of the churches rather than advertise their distinguishing deformity on the burning steps that led up to them ; refrained, moreover, from the exercise of their ritual whining until the panting, green wind of dusk came to release them from the necessity of such self-restraint. And all those citizens who united strength with leisure (the possession of this last blessing appeared to be general) would now walk up the steep hill through the woods, and linger all day here or in the tree-sheltered plaza, thereby making these places crowded and noisy.

Under these new conditions Tristram used to carry a book into the cool seclusion of the Emperor's palace, the weedy galleries of which seemed to have been created solely for the trapping of any breeze that might flutter by. Even here, though, he found it difficult in this torrid weather to fix his attention. There was to be felt in the air an unusual blending of drowsiness with excitement. Into his sanctuary would penetrate the splutter of Spanish laughter, or there would be a silence in which a voice could be heard wailing the lost glories of Granada and the valour of the Christians, and in that sound the warring plumes of the paladins triumphed anew. Then, again, the cars would hoot up and down the hill with that increased pleasure in speed and uproar which is born of heat.

But if, during the daytime, the whole town was on holiday, picnicking in the hills, at sunset all was transformed. Then down in the city, voices and guitars sounded without lull, and the breathless hill was deserted save for its own music of nightingales, waters, and the orchestral background of the insects drumming and beating their wings. And during the nights, so calm and beautiful, Tristram began to find that sleep was once more becoming as difficult for him to achieve as it had ever been ; that when for an hour it might settle down on him, yet it brought with it no rest. Further, his dreams swept him off to a monstrous and distorted world, the very thought of which in the daytime appalled him. Against this sleeplessness that was creeping back on him so remorselessly, against this sleep which filled him with terror, he battled equally and with all his might : but in vain. For the means with which these two enemies sought to defeat him were most subtle ones. Even though he dreaded sleep, he longed to lose reality in it for a little : even when asleep, however far dragged down beneath the level of consciousness, he was aware that he but dreamt— (though this knowledge never in any way softened the horror of the dream)—and longed to escape back into a world secure and sane.

The succession of restful nights which he had enjoyed recently had been so long a one, that it had become his habit, for the first time in his life, to go to bed early. Now, though, he was forced to reverse all this, and endeavoured to evade the demons that beset him by staying up till two or three o'clock in the morning. Many times by so doing he avoided sleeplessness at this stage, and would fall at once into a heavy slumber—but the dreams that visited him would be as menacing as ever in their warped reality, and after, as it would seem, a whole lifetime of agony, he would wake to discover that he had only endured it for an hour. And this would end his sleep for the night.

The scene and atmosphere of his dreams would, in whatever key they had begun—for often one of them opened very delightfully so as to entice him on, down to the lower dungeons of the subconscious from which it was more difficult to fight his way out—swiftly assume their familiar and sinister aspect. Though in no sense sequent, they all most plainly belonged to the same creation, proved that many things of which he had at the time appeared to miss the significance had most surely reached him.

Nevertheless, the days spent in Granada were still pleasant—often pleasant enough to induce temporary forgetfulness of the nights. Sometimes, after daybreak, he would obtain a second spell of sleep, peaceful if short, from which he would wake up to the comforting drone of voices in the heat-spangled wood. Furthermore, his health had so far recovered that a certain buoyancy was soon able to extricate him from the depths into which he now fell at night. From time to time, too, his frayed nerves would offer him a single long night of the undisturbed slumber of exhaustion, or he would fall asleep as he lay safely enfolded by the full light of afternoon, in the cool, grey galleries of the unfinished palace. These exceptions, though they might render the disappointment and torture of the ensuing nights more unendurable, yet made the process through which he was passing one that was ever so gradual. In the air, too, was a new stir and gaiety that helped to support him : for spring, most melancholy-beautiful of the seasons, had yielded to summer. The city and its hills remained disconcertingly lovely, even if there pertained to them less magic and more common sense.

It was, though, in this very season of common sense, that Tristram for the first time began to understand that there were other facets to this beauty which had called out in him such an immediate response. Many things which had been elusive, defined themselves. He noticed himself regarding with a growing distaste the public buildings of the city below, and the furnishing of the hotels, with their constant repetition, their blatant and inane hammering-in of Moorish themes. It seemed to him now that, just as a waxwork of a great man has about it a quality horrible as well as insulting—one that consists in an approach that is so near to life, and yet lacks the movement and breathing that should animate it—something, it may be, almost of black magic, so had these hard, inanimate and fly-blown imitation palaces. There were sides, too, to the older life for which he felt a deep antipathy. He thought of the deformed and crippled beggars lying outside their churches under the pall of white dust that ever and again a wind lifted and flung round them, and of the blood so rapidly blotted out by sand in the arena. But not only did such genuine and inherent attributes of the place repel him, the temporary ones of the tourist season, the few old women from the pensions who still remained here steadfast to their dutiful routine of Sunday church and weekday water-colour, the last, belated charabancs of square-jawed, ox-eyed tourists, inspired in him an equal hatred. He loathed the swindling, wheedling gypsies, and, as for the voice in the wood, he, who had never heeded it hitherto, now grew to entertain for it a dread that transcended my own. It held for him the hollow warning of something he could not escape. So painful was its effect upon him that he sought to analyse it. Now he remembered how, on my last day in Granada, I had confessed to a repugnance for this respectable, black-clad figure, with her expression of mingled fear and cunning. Yet as he considered the picture of the two figures, moving through the dark-green tunnels of the wood, which he summoned up in his mind, he perceived, too, that his impression differed from mine. So inseparably associated in any memory of them were mother and child that at first one regarded them as an entity. But, when he had a little succeeded in disentangling his image of them, he was astonished to discover that, though her voice served as oracular utterance for both, it was toward the languid and ailing child, piteous for all its craftiness, rather than toward the villainous mother, that his instinct of abhorrence directed itself. And though this appeared silly, illogical and unkind, he could not conquer it.

It was curious, moreover, that the sense of uneasiness, of something being wrong, that seized on him at this period, had come to him, not through his direct observation of the persons or things themselves, but from their materialisation in his dreams ; strange erratic ideas, never entirely brought out into the full light of memory, but wafted up without reason from below his mind. Little by little the queer, other-world accuracy of his subconscious interpretations had begun to tinge his thoughts in the daytime too. The Frenchwoman and her child, the silly little Jack-in-the-box hall-porter from the Boabdil, were so much nearer to truth in that world, it seemed, than in the waking one. Each figure was possessed of an intense reality of exaggeration, was so much more true than truth, so much more like than a mere likeness could make it.

There had always, of course, been, in opposition to the general trend of his character, a superstitious, even a mystical side to his nature. It was, in fact, sufficiently developed to have made him afraid of it, so that he had rather deliberately closed his mind to any aspect of life with which it might be related. He could not, it must be admitted, banish his superstitions : though many of his friends thought them a pose, for he purposely ridiculed them to himself and to others, treating them as a laughable manifestation of weakness. Cut off, after this manner, from their roots in the deeper region out of which they had flowered, they became worthless as he made them appear. Thus now, when his perceptions warned him that some strange and hitherto strangled sense was encroaching on its fellows, it was with an accentuated enjoyment and of intention that he turned toward the substantial comforts of the five legitimate senses, which were in him so acute. Alas, these tried and valued friends betrayed him. Even if the days were still agreeable, with sights and sounds, with rest and books to read, yet in this more material mood, he grew to be disgusted with the dirt, breeding and swarming in this heat, with the sadness, squalor and emptiness. In the burning, everlasting afternoons there came moments of unbearable longing for a well-arranged, comfortable life, and of yearning for home and friends. He thought of the people he loved, and it seemed to him he was dead to them, dead and alone, imprisoned within the trivial barriers he had set up for his own safety—such things as food, drink and smoking. Yet though the place and the thoughts it bred began to oppress him, he could not make up his mind to leave it. With every reason to go and none to stay, he must remain. Something remorseless and inevitable held him here. For him to say, " Now I am going," was as difficult as it would be for an iron nail to leave the magnet to which it it attached. And, indeed, himself discerned this curious attraction at work.

At other times, it is true, he acknowledged that these were merely the morbid fancies born of insomnia and an enforced idleness. If only the doctors had allowed him to work, his condition, he believed would have been different. The nervous superfluity of the artist would have been unloosed into its proper channel, his overfine perceptions would have aided, not injured. But he had been forbidden to write for many months : and now that he was unwell again, still less did he dare to disobey.

Soon a change came over the land. The weather, which for weeks past had offered an endless chain of flawless days alternating with transparent, grape-blue nights, broke its habit. The heat, still increasing, became insupportable, but a peculiar black fog* brooded over this beautiful world. Out of it, the Alhambra hill could only a little lift its head. Gone was the flashing of the Sierra's swan-like wings : the skull-coloured hills above the town had become black shadows in their bareness, and from the terraces only the towers of the town, rising out of this murky sea, were visible. Within the hot and breathless wood,

* A phenomenon that is occasionally to be met with in this part of Spain during the summer.

the singing of birds, the running gurgle of water, the sound of any voice, charged the air with a new and ominous intensity. For several days this curious blight persisted. It seemed to owe allegiance to no season, and, since it also obscured the world, removed men to a time and place of its own. Moreover, it exercised an undoubted influence upon the mind—more especially, we imagine, upon one as susceptible as Tristram's —fortifying in it all that was in tone with such darkness. The physical discomfort, even, was considerable. It was rather as though he had been carried off suddenly to another planet, and was forced to breathe in an atmosphere that was differently composed from that to which he was accustomed.

Every day that it continued, this blackness drove more visitors out of Granada : and as Tristram saw them go, his loneliness was thrown into relief. Yet he did not move. Every day his longing, if not for love, at least for companionship grew more ardent. At first this was vague in its direction. But then it grew more definite. For just as his new distrust of the place had originally floated up to his consciousness through the warning symbolism of his dreams, so now it was through them that his old love for Ursula, which he had been convinced was dead, again asserted itself. This passion permeated the fevered and fantastic world to which, for however brief a time, each night transported him ; and he knew that there was a wound in him which could never be healed. And during these black, suffocating nights, when every star was muffled in a heavy veil, the other, distorted world became yet more real and vivid.

One night, after walking in the wood to try and find some hidden breeze, he went to bed. It was about two o'clock, and instantly he fell asleep. He dreamt that he was walking in a valley among the grey, down-like hills above the Alhambra. He experienced a sense of hope and secret elation, as he went, rather fast, up the narrowing defile. At one side of the little track was a hut, with a sham-Moorish window, wide open. As he neared it, the head and shoulders of the puppet-like concierge from the Boabdil Hotel leapt up into the space. As the meagre, minute creature executed his trick, he turned on Tristram the shifting glitter of his eyes, across which the lids seemed to fold from side to side like those of a reptile, and emitted a harsh triumphant cry, similar to that with which Punch swings up into his miniature proscenium : that cry which is so ancient and malign in its apparent folly. Now he had projected himself up and out of the window, and was running along in front, with the bounding, stiff-jointed action of an automaton, looking furtively round from time to time and beckoning. Even in his dream, it seemed to Tristram rather strange that in spite of this hurrying, whooping, preposterous figure, which continued to beckon him on to the unknown, and at intervals to utter its acrid shrieks, yet within himself he should still have this inner glow of contentment and happiness.   He pretended to ignore this officious little comedian : but, not in the least disconcerted, the porter ran on, still acting his part.   Tristram now noticed, for the first time, that round the base of each hill there were scattered several swathed figures, sketching—some of them with the folds of their veils and the trimmings of their hats arranged in Saracenic patterns, stalactites and honeycombs.   At this point the concierge became very excited, stood still and gesticulated violently, try-ing, obviously, to indicate one particular figure.   He even ran back to lead him up to her.   Tristram at first refused to look in this direction at all, but when at last he did so, to his joy he recognised that this heavily-veiled form was Ursula's.   As he approached, she rose and walked away, in front of him, with that light step that was so characteristic of her—indeed, in the dream, he recognised the sound of her footsteps—but, however much he implored her, she would not speak a word, or turn round so that he could see her face.   Mean-while, the concierge was running on ahead again, with his odd, wooden rhythm.   As Tristram passed the other veiled figures, looking so determinedly into the distance and sucking the ends of their paint-brushes, he saw that they were holding them with the slender but thick-knuckled fingers of a skeleton.   Their resolute gaze was the unseeing stare of empty sockets ; their mouths had the cruel, straight smile of the skull.   Now the defile grew narrower and the hills towered above him : but when he looked up at these heights, it was only to find that these gaunt artists had somehow or other stolen up there without his perceiving it. Swollen to enormous dimensions, they seemed to be standing on guard against the skyline. Still the concierge led on. Tristram, however, realised that his feeling of elation had dwindled away; so greatly was he distressed at being unable to attract Ursula's notice. Suddenly, rounding a corner in the ravine, they met the French-woman with her son. "Messieurs, Messieurs," she started—and as she began to declaim her lines, the porter, his eyes sparkling with spite, danced up to Tristram, and, pointing at the child, said with mock courtesy in broken English (Tristram had not heard him speak before): "It is the child, sir, to whom I want to call your attention. Mark him very carefully. You need not mind the mother, but be careful never to forget the child." These words he spoke, as if they would convey some secret but expected meaning. Then he muttered a sentence or two to the undersized and lisping boy, who, at this, looked up at Tristram very deliberately and intently. Tristram, for his part, felt that some power was compelling him to study the child's face, as though he ought to memorise it, and gazed back at the pale little countenance, which was unpleasant in its pitifulness. As the mother reached the end of her denunciation, Ursula slowly turned her head toward him (and it was only now that he saw she was wearing, not a hat and veil, as he had thought, but was dressed as a bride, with a wreath of orange-

blossom, and, falling from it, a long veil of white lace).
Slowly she turned her head toward him, parting the
veil as she did so. She was going to kiss him—but it
seemed as though the lovely face was coming to him
from a great, an immeasurable distance. And as he
watched, as it approached, it, too, developed the lipless,
snarling grin of the skull. Slowly, slowly, nearer
and nearer, larger and yet larger it came (and, though
it was now a skull, how clearly that skull belonged to
Ursula), nearer and nearer, until it reminded him,
though he dreamt, of a close-up at a cinema. How was
he to get away? He turned round, swerved, and saw
the Frenchwoman and her child blocking the path
behind him (and, while he looked, the child all at once
grew up, and became the concierge, dressed in his
uniform). Above him the dreadful Death's Head
Corps was still on duty. In his sleep he groaned aloud
and battled, for he was aware that he had only just
time enough, only just will enough, to escape before it
caught him, to run back down that endless alley between the ogre-guarded mountains to the light at the
end. He made a rush for it—but here, suddenly, a
dark and turgid stream obstructed him. An old boat
swayed on these waters menacingly, and rocked in his
direction, but he would not get into it, for he saw a
huge three-headed dog, with fiery, bloodshot eyes,
watching him from a cave opposite. With an enormous effort, a vast exertion of will, he leapt over these
haunted waves toward the light, and even as he landed,

he could hear the terrible, frantic baying of the monster. He had woken, his feet kicking convulsively against the bottom of the bed, as if, in all reality, he had jumped from one world to another. Outside somewhere, a dog was barking : a comforting sound, it seemed now. Yet for several minutes that were hours he was utterly unable to stir, so much alive and genuine to him still were the incidents of the dream, could not even move his hand to switch on the light. When at last he had gathered up sufficient strength, he looked at his watch. It registered three o'clock. The entire excursion had taken up less than an hour of our time.

He put out the light again, and lay sleepless and hopeless in the black silence. The dog had stopped barking ; but presently the first cock began to crow out a sly, counterfeit greeting to dawn. And to Tristram, as he listened to the air being drawn taut by this sound, that always must suggest the mocking, challenging witness to a great treachery, it seemed as though he had **indeed betrayed himself**, giving up his life to the things which no one valued, and which were, after all, of no use. If he had worked for money, rather than for the sake of beauty, was it not certain that he would now be happy, successful, respected, rich, with never a moment spared him out of the general chatter of the parrot-house for loneliness ? But in his bitterness, there fell upon him the old longing and aching for the people that he loved, and the places that he knew. How distinctly he saw his friends, what each one was doing, what each one was saying—and even this was alluring in the mood which had seized him.— Here he lay, poor and alone. A stupid cloud of self-pity descended on him. And then, as it dissolved, London, London at the end of May, swept down on him with all the haunting, languorous but triumphant nostalgia of a Tchaikovsky waltz.

The whole city was in flower. The first impression was one of blossoming. And over all and above all sounded the magnificent, lion-mouthed roar of the traffic. The grey, busy streets and circuses, ablaze with the swift, raucous yellow and red flames of the omni-buses, were further sprinkled with the gigantic, Vic-torian bouquets of the flower-women. Through the elegant screen at Hyde Park Corner, through the graceful arches between the pearly, stone-pillars, the old trees could be seen once more waving their green fingers on the spring breeze, that struggled under them like a bird. Beneath this quivering shade, the first warm sun of the year had caused to flutter out from their cells and hives every kind of brilliantly-coloured insect. The drone of talk lingered on the warm, cigarette-scented air, while not far away there sounded a continuous accompaniment in the muffled thudding of cantering hooves. Almost extinct specimens, boast-ing every kind of check, gaiter and whisker, were trot-ting sternly up and down, as though this action of

theirs must convey a vast amount to a great many
people, as though, for example, they were carrying an
all-important despatch to the Commander-in-Chief,
while every now and then a riding-master would go
past, instructing the cluster of children round him just
as a duck teaches her young to swim.   In the great
yellow squares, the crooks and dry sticks of the
shrubberies were breaking into little rosettes of shrill
green or posies of pink-and-white that spread their
ephemeral wings on the mild spring air, while the innumerable soot-stained iron-railings that guarded the
faint, Persian torches of the lilac, already a little burning down, for once clearly showed themselves too solid
for their delicate work.   The statue in the centre of
each garden had assumed a new and wistful coyness, as
it struck its heavy, oratorical pose in the midst of so
much lightness of leaf and petal.   Even the houses
round seemed to be blossoming—a great smell of paint
being the scent that these ponderous flowers exhaled—
for the residences of the rich had just been dizened for
them, while in some cases the process had not yet been
finished, and up ladders, on planks and round the tops
of the houses, the white-coated workmen were still
forming their own ever shifting but hieratic friezes.
This smell of paint fought against the country scents
gently breathed out by every young leaf and crinkled
blossom, and mingled with that of tar and petrol, for
cars and taxicabs were purring swiftly over the watery
black surface of the roads, shining and smooth as

canals, through the amber and clouded heat of a hot London morning. Outside one square block of a house, a red and white awning was already being erected ; large, rectangular vans drove up on their tiny wheels, and men hurried in and out. And Tristram thought of how, in the evening, the gondola-like cars would glide up to the house with a lacquered inevitability, and cascades and showers of golden light would splash and shiver down from the wide-open windows into the darkness. From them, too, would float the over-sympathetic hooting and sobbing of saxophones, as they gurgled and throbbed out those tunes which, in spite of their self-satisfied brazen rhythms and savage gorilla-like drummings that pretend to constitute an incitement to worship before Venus, have yet under them a good solid bottom of hell-fire ! For beneath every jazz rhythm was hidden the mournful whining of the Wesleyan Chapel, the austere howlings of the Pilgrim Fathers, as much as the comfortable self-righteousness of " Hymns Ancient and Modern " : as dance-music, it was, in fact, comparable to the daughter of a clergyman who earns renown by playing an unexpectedly daring part on the music-hall stage. Still, the traffic, even at this hour, would roar loud above such melodious thumpings and moanings. At night its waves would arrange themselves into their wonted tiers, each one serving a different need or pleasure of the town : there would be the after-theatre wave, the later one of the pleasure-seekers returning home, both westward : and then the lorries, piled up with vegetables and provisions, would pound and lumber eastward.

All these sounds, from which he had so often suffered, Tristram dwelt on lovingly in his imagination. As his passionate materialisation of the things he loved faded away, and the five senses returned from their temporary delirium to imprison him again within the narrow walls of his bedroom in Granada, each moment made him more wretched. Outside, notwithstanding the renewed promises of dawn which the cock crowed out every moment, black night maintained its domination. And his restless imaginings again wandered to other scenes, his brain racing without control.

It is said, as some may think too often, that to a drowning man comes a sudden, ultimate flare-up of the memory, and of that mysterious power which interprets it ; that his whole career, with its trend, passes before him for final judgment. So now it was for Tristram as though a life were ending. The golden procession of the years once more filed past him, its phantasy realised with a cruel preciseness. Yet, despite the accuracy of focus which these rapidly merging scenes assumed, despite their apparent verisimilitude, there was in the selection of them, as much as in the way they were presented, if only he could have detected it, an unfair stress and emphasis. The inner and invisible censor, now turned torturer, displayed a certain bias, continually minimised or exaggerated in accordance with his prejudice. Thus the death of Tristram's parents, which had overwhelmed him as a child, was glossed over, smoothed out. He was allowed to rejoice in the love they had given him when young without being permitted to grieve at their loss. The sale of his family home, too, was practically erased : while the lesser miseries, the appalling ennui and littleness of school-life, the melancholy, vague yearnings, and even little distresses, of adolescence were romanticised or altogether omitted. On the other hand, the beauty and hopefulness of the past were continually magnified, so as to intensify the unhappiness of the present.

How calmly it had begun for him, how friendly it seemed now. He saw himself, a small child playing, drenched in that glow of summer-evening sunlight which illumines all childhood. Perhaps this particular evening had constituted his first esthetic impression, just as it had marked his first revolt against authority. So beautiful had the late afternoon seemed to him, so fragrant the air and the flowers that powdered all the ground, so immense the green, tall trees, so enticing the faint breezes that trailed through them, and above all, so manifest was the sense of vital mystery, though he could not guess the nature of it, with which the whole earth was imbued, that he had run away out of the schoolroom where he had been learning to read. The dismal " CAT—RAT " of it still tapped woodenly in his ears. But here he was, securely hidden in the green, rich grass, tumbling among the familiar meadow-flowers ; flowers that were then so familiar and large, because so near him. They were always the small, yellow ones of the sun, ragged deep-yellow-maned dandelions, hard, glazed yellow buttercups, cowslips with all the taste of summer on their gold tongues, and daisies with their clear yellow eyes wide-open. He knew, as he rolled there like a young animal, that he could not be seen and that it was well ; since his father was looking for him angrily. The fact that he would no doubt be found in the end was too much buried in the future to allow him to think about it. Moreover, he felt a sense of security, because, though he knew he could not explain in words the quality of the almost religious impulse that had conquered him—for words had not so very long been within his reach—grown-up people were so clever that they would of their own accord understand. Then, besides, there was his Mother to help and support him. Round him revolved the wheel of a machine that, though ancient, was still in working order. From where he lay in the grass, could just be seen the classical pediment of the stables, that temple of Irish life, and he could even hear the stamping and snorting of the impatient iron-shod gods to whom it was dedicated. He could see, also, the thatched roof of the dairy, round like that of a beehive, but stored and scented with other riches than honey, cool as ice within, and smelling suavely of rich cream and butter. Near-by were the neglected gardens, great hedges growing awry, and sundials and fountains broken and crumbling. In the house, too, was to be felt the faint pulsing of a life that was continuous, even if the fullest beat of it was in the past. Portraits of wigged gentlemen, pompous and stately in their gilded or silvered frames, stags' heads, rows and rows of musty calf-bound books, fossils, bits of armour, and the cruel angular faces of legendary fish from the lake below, all made their own contribution, yet were part of the same thing : a thing rather frightening because so ancient and sure of itself. How many memories asserted themselves !—There was the morning when his nurse had locked herself and him in the nursery, because the new cook, who had only arrived the previous evening, had been found drunk : and drunken people were dangerous. From his high, barred window he saw this almost mythical villainess leave, stumping down the drive, a fat figure in a black dress and bonnet, holding a bent umbrella in one hand and a prayer-book in the other, as though going to church, and singing loudly on her wild way beneath the green waving trees. Behind her was borne her bright-yellow tin trunk on a hand-barrow : which imparted a processional and symbolic touch to the dreary but strange departure of this bacchante.

Then, once more, he looked out on the park in the autumn mornings, when through the trembling golden mists he would be taken to search for mushrooms. And they would examine the tall tufts of dew-spangled grass until they found in some of them, hidden as though in a primeval forest, these miniature stone-henges, covered, it seemed, in white kid, and smelling, too, of that leather. Or, perhaps, there was fruit to be picked in the walled garden. Now, again, he was a year or two older, learning to ride on a fat-bellied, rough-maned pony that flew over the ground, so that, as he galloped, his knees clutching the centre of the circular belly beneath him, it was as though he were trying to maintain his balance seated on one spinning globe, while that, in its turn, and perhaps in obedience to some stern but incomprehensible law of nature, was lightly skimming the surface of another. The groom cantered a little ahead, and as he strove to catch him up, he could feel, once more, the sweet, young air beating its wings against his face.—But, all of a sudden, this background was snatched from him, just as it had been in real life (except that now the process appeared to have been a painless one), and he jumped over the years to find himself a small boy, strolling and slouching round the grey walls, neat or prickly, of Windsor Castle. From the Long Terrace he looked down. Just under him the birds skimmed and darted, leaping out from their copper-blue-green citadels; then, a long way below, came the streets, neat and demure, the serpentine river dotted with boats, that from here looked like water-beetles paddling their way on the surface of a pool, the school-buildings headed by their monumental white sheep, and, beyond again, the Thames Valley, studded with little golden villages, under tall trees, rolling away into a haze of heat. He remembered how one day for an instant his eye had rested on the central red court of the school, with its tiny green-stained and theatrically-posed statue, holding an unwieldy sceptre, of the monarch who had built it—that long-dead king whom, for all his weakness, Shakespeare has endeared to England for ever. At the thought of this, a flame of enthusiasm that no school, for all its cold water, could quench, had swept through his body : already he had decided on his own path of life. A poet was to him as Nelson and Wellington combined, with a dozen or so cricketers and racing-motorists thrown in for full weight, would be to most boys. His head sang with the music of words, the words of Marlowe, Marvell and Shelley, and the long, swinging rhythms of Swinburne, that in their outward glory and inner first must now ever be the first poems to capture the ear and imagination of an English child with an undeveloped instinct for beauty : poems that will lead him on to love the work of other poets, and so induct him into a whole new world for which he has been waiting. Already his pockets were full of what he considered his own verse, though actually at this stage they exactly and immaturely echoed the thought and music of the last poet he had read. As he gazed upon the landscape now darkling under the weight of mountainous thunder-clouds—which endowed this homely plain with just the necessary touch of inspiration—while yet objects suddenly blazed out of the gloom below with a sullen green flame, as though for a second illumined by the enormous, irresistible headlights attached to the chariot of an approaching god, first one huge old tree and then another being singled out, or a patch of river taking on abruptly a livid and menacing sheen ; as, then, the nearer leaves under him fluttered and shivered in their own rhythm upon the faunal air, the passionate germ of all poetry had stirred to life in his heart. And in that moment of revelation, he had known that he, too, was indeed a poet. One day he would be able to trap the strange, un-netable lines of poetry, that even now flashed like bright birds through the warm darkness of his dreams. And this darkness, too, the strength of the emotions which were now waking in him, these bewildering passions which had rushed down on him without warning and had shaken him to the foundations of his being, he recognised as being part of the same power : for poetry only blossoms in warm blood. Golden and sempiternal, the future stretched before him. And though, even then, he had realised that poets, in this like soldiers, never grow rich, the torch of his ambition burnt steadily. What did he care for the anger of guardians or for poverty ?—But now childhood and adolescence were past. War spread the evil shadow of its bat-like wings over the country, and he returned to Ireland. The scenes flashed out quickly. He was writing already and it was London. His first success had been so pleasant, because such a short time before he had been a nervous, uncertain child, while now he was conscious of possessing an influence over people. He could lead, and they must follow. Yet this success had, as well, been disappointing (and, at this juncture, as though in ridicule, every sombre bell in the city beneath began to gabble out its clattering metallic music, with that syncopated fervour peculiar to southern peals, which have always in them a suggestion of crockery being broken). Now ensued the period when he had first begun to live too much on his nerves. But his early love affairs of these years, presented to him thus and for his own purposes by the inner censor and producer, came back to him shown in the most favourable light that was possible. He preserved enough of his own judgment, however, to conclude that in reality some of them had been sordid, as nearly all had been silly. Yet, he comforted himself, all the time he had as an artist remained scrupulous and ascetic. Even while he congratulated himself, though, his satisfaction was shattered, for of what use was this incessant labour, from which, it was true, he had achieved a certain distinction, to what purpose this wearing thin of the nerves, when it had ended, not only in constant worry over money-matters, but in this utter loneliness, this lying alone unable to reason or sleep? But if he had sold his talents, would he have been happier, would she have married him? He understood that the warm blood of the animal which had, alas, in the end snared him into this love, had also made it impossible for him to interpret life save in his own special manner. The habitual cheapness and ease of his amatory successes— he saw it now—had led him to this fatal love affair, not foreseeing the possibility of defeat, or that such a result must end love in his life, since it was a failure from which it was obviously destined that he should never recover. He had sprung from a long line of unbridled and sensually-victorious men—which origin indeed was responsible for his abilities as much as defects—and, because he could not have his way, had lost her soul, which had always belonged to him, and had gained nothing. Why was it, he wondered, that his senses had always sold him in this fashion, making him believe that the body was the gate of conquest to the spirit that animated it, so that he could not have one without the other? For, however sensual, he had never regarded physical love as an end in itself. His imagination had given him a great power of self-deception, and like a god, he had in his career bestowed souls upon many who, finally, he had discovered to have none. But his defeat appeared, moreover, to have been possessed of magical qualities, for it had been able to extract the virtue out of everything for which he cared. Nothing that he valued was now left to him in life, nor were there any material compensations. But all this went for little (and this he fully realised) as compared to the crushing tragedy that had in the end come to pass, when he had succeeded in forcing her to love him, and when, frightened at the strength of her own passion, terrified that it might break up the design of her life, to her more important than anything else, she had married another man. Again jealousy aimed at him its poisoned arrows till every wound burnt and stabbed him.

Now the scenes which he had so dreaded being shown were re-enacted in his mind. He saw Ursula as he had first seen her, reviewed the years of their friendship, comprehended how suddenly it had turned to love : a transmutation, he perceived, which ought surely from the beginning to have been expected, and, furthermore, to have been expected at the very time it occurred. Those skilled in such matters can predict that at a particular season a butterfly will emerge from a chrysalis : and in the same way this metamorphosis was in reality only following out some natural law ordained for it.

And soon he was provided with a wonderful series of physical materialisations. It was scarcely credible that things remembered could be so actual. He could almost touch her. All the attributes of her personality came back to him, the turn of her small head on its long neck as she fixed on him the blank, blue gaze of her lovely, far-seeing eyes, the fluttering hands with their long thin fingers, the cold but ever so moving music of her voice, the swiftness of speech which translated that of her eye, and the deep, almost harsh laughter. He recalled with utmost truth the expression of her face at any given moment, as she looked at

him when he first tried to make love to her, as he
watched her listening to music, much moved by it, or
as, the peacock element for the time predominant,
she prepared to enter the ballroom, rejoicing so plainly
in her own power, every expression that flickered in
her eyes or across her face seeming to light up the
room, such the radiant force of life behind it. He lay
there on the bed, watching and racked. The mingled
ice and fire of their love scorched him anew. His
whole body ached and throbbed and burnt for her.
Gusts of passion attacked him, so that, in spite of the
fever-heat of the night, he was left with chattering
teeth, and it felt as though his heart were being held
by invisible steel fingers, as though a very real, acute
pain was there. But the emotions, through which he
was whirled so rapidly, now again altered. His longing for Ursula became a morbid longing for companionship, any companionship at however low a level,
physical companionship that with its feeling of warmth
against his body would at any rate deceive him in the
long, lonely nights, communicate a false glow to ease
his heart.—Outside the first light had slowly changed
from grey into a watery green, as though the earth
were once more rising from an evil flood : but not until
the sun had firmly grasped the hill opposite with its
red-hot claws did sleep and a little peace come to him.

When he awoke, it was to a day of great brilliance.
No breath of the blackness that had engulfed this

lovely region during the last few days lingered about it. On the contrary the sun shook his golden mane in every open space with an evident pleasure : and a new elasticity and vigour was to be felt in the crystal air. Yet all day he walked the wood and terraces, still with this pain, this aching at his heart. As he paced backwards and forwards under a burden of loneliness unimaginable in its weight, he vowed that henceforth the riches and comfort which might mitigate it should be his object. In his bitterness, he reflected that he, who had given so much of himself to others, would have been grateful for any word thrown to him, even a fatuous and anonymous " Good day." Even one of the spectres that in London so insistently aired their claims to his affection—based on the fact that not only had they bored him for a lifetime, but his parents before him—would have been welcome. But the foreigners on the hill were few, and none spoke to him. And as the evening approached, he dreaded the darkness that was sweeping up toward him from the valleys. He was as conscious as ever, though, that he could not leave here, could not escape. The unknown power of attraction still held him fast.

Dusk came, and he walked up and down along the terrace that led to the Hotel Boabdil, above the gypsies' hive. Indeed, from below were wafted at intervals great, warm gusts of shouting and laughter, the sounds of a dense mass of life huddled together. At last Tristram could bear his isolation no longer. He must go into the Hotel Boabdil, and find out if, by chance, anyone he knew was staying there. He wondered why he had not done this before. He might easily, he thought, in so large a hotel discover, if not a friend, at least someone he had met, for all that the place was emptying of visitors. If only there was someone to whom he could talk for a little, no doubt this stupid sense of loneliness would leave him. After all, it was childish to behave like this, when he was so much better, and so many of his troubles were in the past. He would go in and look. He felt too nervous, though, to sit in the lounge by himself, watching the people. The best thing, then, would be to walk into the hall and ask to see the list of guests.

As he decided to do this, the thought of the concierge, the image of him that rose up, tinctured as it was by the dream of the previous night, almost persuaded Tristram to desist. Further, he was shy by nature and would have to think of some name for which to inquire, in explanation of why he wished to look at the register. Still, he must not turn back now : it was too important for him. Perhaps the best method, and one that might at the same time intimidate the horrible little porter, should he still be on duty, would be to ask for some high-sounding name that did not exist. He must be inventive. It made it so much easier if he could ask the porter for some name improvised by himself : for, then, when told that no such person was staying in the hotel, he could reply that this must be a mistake, and demand to see the register. Thus he could find out exactly who was staying in the hotel. The idea amused him, too, and for several seconds he forgot his loneliness in the childish game of making up names and titles. Finally, after selecting the best of these creations, he turned firmly toward the hotel. He was no longer nervous, for he was armed with this weapon of his own invention which could not, he knew, be used against him.

A curious deep hush and silence prevailed. The birds had stopped their full-throated chants, and even the singing of the waters was low and weary. Not a leaf stirred in the woods behind him, and the sound of each football crackling there acquired a new value, an almost augural significance. As he approached the hotel, surely he heard, far away, those tones which he had grown to hate, and which, though they denounced the place, seemed the very voice of it ? So far away were the words, that he could not be certain of their reality—yet he was tired, and in this state the sense of hearing becomes infinitely acute. Surely the voice reached him : " Monsieur, Monsieur," it said, issuing from some distant thicket of the wood, " prenez garde, prenez garde, parce que Granade est une ville terrible, où l'on se trouve parmi des choses macabres."

He fought his way through the maelstrom of the swing-door and entered the hall. It seemed empty. Not a servant was to be seen. This he had not expected and it rather disconcerted him. But even as

he looked round for someone, the all too familiar head
and puny, uniformed shoulders of the porter bobbed
up to the surface and flopped over the edge of the
miniature proscenium. Tristram was again reminded
of Punch by the action of it. The eyes flickered sideways, as was their wont, and then gazed at him in-
quiringly. Tristram was once more the prey of the
vague nausea that this little creature never failed to
arouse in him. He wished heartily that he had never
come. It seemed to him, also, that in the quivering
eyes he could trace a new expression, a look, as it
were, of malice gratified. Now the concierge spoke :
and as he did so, Tristram was astonished at how
accurately he had anticipated in his dream the oleagi-
nous texture of this voice, at once impertinent and
servile. Never to his knowledge had he heard it before. But the man was asking him something, and he
must answer. He was asking him, of course, what he
wanted. But one of those abrupt alterations of feeling
to which my friend was liable had overtaken him. He
had lost all confidence : and the result of this was that
now he could not even remember the name and title
of the fictitious nobleman, whom only a moment or
two ago it had given him such pleasure to create. He
stuttered, heart and memory failing him. Moreover, in
these few seconds he suffered a curious sense of double
reality, as if these trivial things he was experiencing
had happened to him before. He tried to recall the
occasion, but it eluded him. Defeated as he must

appear, though, he ought, he realised, to make an effort. He understood that he must say something, could not allow the moral victory to go to this hostile and detestable puppet. In a flash, as he thought of inspiration, he decided what to do. He would ask for himself! He grasped at once the security which such a question bestowed on him, in that he was certain of the answer, and thus held the last trick in his own hand. Pulling himself together, therefore, he said resolutely, " I've come to see Mr. Tristram Orlander. Is he in? " The name, hanging suspended in the echoing air, seemed both strange and familiar. It was as though this question of his, too, was but a repetition. If he had asked for himself before, though, somewhere or other, surely he would have remembered it! And he laughed, for he was suddenly recovered, and it was hardly probable—absurd, in fact. It came, no doubt, this sense, from being overtired. Many people have experienced it at one time or another. He had heard doctors say that it was because the two lobes of the brain were not acting together properly; a symptom of fatigue. After all, he must not forget that he had spent a dreadful night . . . He was thinking in this fashion, not attending to the concierge or to what he was saying, since he need not wait, except in appearance, for the answer. Yes, a dreadful night—but suddenly something penetrated his consciousness, something odd and unforeseen. The porter, though he had blinked and allowed the pupils of his eyes to oscillate feebly, but yet violently, from side to side, had smiled at his question, had almost given the impression of being ready for it—Tristram had noticed that. But now the puppet had answered, had said, "Yes, sir, I believe he's waiting for you," and darting out from the side of his booth, was leading the way down a passage. The only thing was to follow—there was no time in which to think, and the shock was so great that Tristram was ushered out of the lift and down another corridor into the lobby of a private suite, almost before he was aware of what he was doing. He was in a stunned condition from surprise. But even if he had in this moment possessed the courage, the mere initiative, to refuse to enter, he would yet have been forced to go on. Of that, far down under his mind, he was fully cognisant. As though this were death, there was no retreat from it.

After knocking at the inner door and throwing it wide open, the porter had left him. From the doorway, he could see a rich, ridiculous apartment, red and blue honeycombs and gilded stalactites glowing warmly under the shaded oriental lamps. A voice said loudly, "Come in." Sitting at a low table, a book in front of him, which he must just have put down, was an elderly, bearded stranger. At first Tristram could not see him well, because though the room itself was softly lighted, there was a concentration of light upon his own face as he entered, for one of the shades was tilted up at an angle. For the instant he felt as though a spot-light had been cast upon him, and he was entering a stage, before which stretched a large, invisible audience. But as he advanced into the room, and passed beyond this brightly illumined circle, he could see well enough. His first impression was one of expense. This dignified, elderly man, was so beautifully trimmed, groomed, and dressed. The beard acted a little as mask, but the eyes had in them, surely, a tired, strained look, as though the owner of them had been waiting a long time. The immaculate figure, against this luxurious yet ludicrous background, exhaled an elegance peculiar to itself, but which yet reminded him of someone . . . While he was mechanically observing these details, the tall stranger rose, and in a voice which it seemed to Tristram he had most certainly heard, not only before, but constantly, every day—(or was he merely experiencing again, he wondered, that repetitive sensation which induces you to believe that this same thing has occurred, this same person been encountered, at some previous time which you cannot recall ?)—he said, speaking with a curious, but unpleasantly conscious charm, " I was expecting you, but not yet : you, who always ruin yourself through being too late, are for once too early."—Tristram did not pay much heed to the words, for as he enunciated them, the stranger, raising the angle of his head so that the light gilded its outline, turned his eyes full upon those of the younger man. During the brief time that this movement occupied, an interval so fleeting as scarcely to count at all, he lived through the most disturbing and significant, as it was the most unreal, instant of his whole career. At that moment, the world reeled for him. It was then, only then, that the feeling that he had indeed come into contact with this man before, firmly established itself as the truth : only then that he recognised in this elderly, elegant figure—his own figure ; in the handsome, lined face, rather spoilt by the fleshy pouches sagging beneath the eyes, his own face ; in the hard, stubborn, insensitive old mouth—his own mouth ; in the dead, cold eyes, his own eyes and himself. In those eyes, which matched though they distorted, his own, in those eyes into which he was compelled to stare, so that he could not even make any movement of escape, nor any effort at pretence, was to be seen, in spite of their frigid suavity, a hatred at once intimate and intense. And, during the words that had been spoken, Tristram, too, had felt this same bitter personal antagonism that he read there opposite him. At this very moment, he could have flung himself on this jaunty, old figure, killed him then and there, such was the force of this almost physical enmity. Indeed, the elder man appeared to understand what emotion was at work, for he stepped back suddenly, and put up his hands as though to shield his head. " We shall meet later," he said. And this was the last thing that Tristram remembered.

*　　*　　*　　*　　*

When he came to, he found himself stretched out,

with loosened collar, in the hall of the hotel. Bending over him was the concierge, nonchalant though attentive, but with an unmistakable air of triumph in his shifty, flickering eyes. Tristram could not at first recollect what had happened to him, and inquired. The sniggering little creature, with an air of exaggerated and false respect, replied, " You were asking me for someone, sir, when you fainted. Shall I call a doctor ? " At this, his memory of the events of the last quarter of an hour returned to him, though they seemed an immeasurable distance away. Getting up, he floundered out of the door into the darkness.

That night he made no attempt to sleep, but packed and read until dawn. Quite apart from the feelings aroused in him by so inexplicable an adventure— whether, as it seemed to him, objective, or one of his own mind's making, in which case it was no less alarming—quite apart from his anxiety to leave the place where it had befallen him, he now no longer felt the force of the secret power that had held him in it hitherto. All the difficulty of departing had ceased abruptly in that extraordinary instant of recognition. The magnet no longer exercised its influence. The curious, cumulative lassitude, as well as the expectancy with which it had mingled—sensations which had afflicted him for so long—had now faded out into the natural and healthy colour of his mind.

In the morning he left for Paris. Stations, porters, luggage and shuntings were for once of definite help in soothing his nerves. Soon he felt well, active, alert ;

more rested, too, than for weeks past, though he had spent a quite sleepless night and trailed behind him a long string of days tinged with nightmare and of hours of darkness that had transcended in their agony any he had known. He knew that he was glad to be leaving Granada : yet when he saw all its yellow towers and turrets, and roseate, crumbling walls, shake suddenly, rock and then tremble away from him, as, with a preliminary screech and jolt, the engine wrenched its way along, it was with sadness that he relinquished their beauty. Soon, quieted by the lumbering, hobbledehoy action of the train, so lulling in its very positive reply to the senses, he began to wonder if ever he had really visited the Boabdil Hotel on the previous evening. The material side of his mind, so often honoured with the name of common sense, strongly asserted itself, demanding an explanation. At first he offered it a thousand inadequate ones : but it persevered, and coming to his aid in the only way that was possible, insisted that he should question the validity of his experience. Could he be sure, it urged continually ? Though still profoundly disturbed at what had taken place—or had appeared to take place—he began to see it differently. And during the entire journey, common sense was smoothing out and attempting to falsify the memory wherever such work was possible.

* * * * *

Within the space of a day or two, Tristram was

home in London. He had not warned me that he was arriving, but came straight from the station to see me. We dined together, and after the meal was finished, he described the various moods that had descended on him since my return to England, and the incident or hallucination in which they had culminated.

To confide in anyone offers a wonderful power of release. Indeed, confession, which is the ultimate confidence, becomes a vice. Even condemned murderers must enjoy it. He could now tell me this story, which hitherto he had been compelled to keep to himself. And I am sure that in doing so, he felt that he was dispelling some of the clouds which he had feared were hanging heavily over his reason. While he was speaking, I carefully examined his appearance. He looked extremely well—in spite, according to his account, of a whole month of nervous symptoms, followed by a violent shock and a long and tiring journey. Of course, he possessed all the recuperative power of the extremely nervous type to which he belonged : and the very force of the surprise and dismay he had felt at the time of his adventure had no doubt arrested the process of exhaustion, by providing him with something definite against which to react. Moreover, it had completely driven his love for Ursula out of his head again.

But that which astonished me most in the remarkable story he unfolded was how little, how very little effect, it seemed to have left upon his mind. Notwithstanding his marked tendency toward superstition, he was now able to regard this happening of which he was telling me as a finished, if fantastic occurrence in itself : a thing that was now for ever closed. The presage contained in the few words that had been uttered by the apparition, or whatever it was, the fact that the incident, though singularly ominous, was yet incomplete, escaped him entirely and altogether.

For my part, I was delighted that he should treat the matter in this way, and was, of course, very much on my guard to say nothing which might make him in the least apprehensive. Thus I refrained from giving my own impressions of Granada and its atmosphere, lest doing so should cause him to compare his own love of that city with the dark forebodings that had attacked me during our visit. I joined with him in treating the affair as a grotesque vision. Further, I endeavoured to induce him to think of it as a rich vein of ore from which he could fashion a story.

All the same, it was wiser, perhaps, for him to consult a nerve-specialist. By means of thus confiding in a trained ear, he would rid his mind of any lingering traces of uneasiness that might be hidden far down in it. Without giving my real motives, I contrived to persuade him, and obtained a promise that he would keep the appointment if one was made for him. Accordingly, we went together the next day to see Sir Hector Tavish.

The celebrated doctor treated the story lightly,

affected to believe that no such thing had ever really occurred. Tristram, he said, must remember that he was over-sensitive and imaginative. In a sudden outbreak of nerves, he had asked for his own name at the concierge's desk, and that alone was quite enough to furnish a basis for such a dream. And no doubt it had done so. For a dream it had been. He had fainted, and in his fainting had dreamt. There were many cases within his professional experience of such a kind. The longest, most complicated dream often only occupied a minute or two of actual time. Besides, he added, giving Tristram one of those unexpected, tremendous thumps-on-the-back which it is apparently the prerogative of the great nerve-specialist to deal out to his patients, that sort of thing only happens to poets —a queer lot—think of Shelley's visions—nothing came of them—(By the way, had we seen that bit in *Punch ?*)—nothing—so why fret or worry? Banish such nonsense from the mind—Nothing, absolutely nothing. All the same, it would be better, perhaps, not to drink with his meals, and to take one cold shower-bath—if he had one in the house—every two days : and he might try " Nuttall's Nervese "—Splendid stuff, splendid—worked wonders.

Tristram was much relieved at St. Hector's favourable report on him, and unquestionably ceased to worry. He was so happy to be in London, well again, and able to lead his own sort of life, that the immediate past of his travels no longer existed for him. Even while he was originally telling me of his call at the Hotel Boabdil, I had suspected that I was more interested in his description, than he in the recollection, of it. And after seeing the doctor—except that once he came to request that I should treat the story as told me in confidence—he never, I think, gave a thought to it.

During his lifetime, then, I never mentioned his adventure in Granada to anyone. My lips were sealed. Yet, because his narrative impressed me as one of great interest (for the account of Shelley's similar hallucination had always fascinated me), I noted down the whole of it in my journal, as nearly as possible in his own words. And now, though I write for eventual publication, and to that end piece the story together with the later happenings with which my mind connects it, I only do this that there may be a record of it for other generations. No one now can be pained by the story, and there is much in it that may throw light upon the failure of a great poet—for such undoubtedly he was—a decay as singular and complete as the sudden defection of Rimbaud. So far, indeed, I have been able to draw upon my own impressions, or upon things which he told me : but from this time forth, except for the short and curious swing-back into it a little before his death—a swing-back that constituted a kind of apologetic epilogue to our frindship, and which I will relate when the time comes—Tristram Orlander passed out of my existence.

*   *   *   *   *

Now that I am old and can contemplate his career in its entirety, it is clear to me that the abrupt change which, after his return from Spain, manifested itself in the character and talent, and was translated into the life, of Tristram Orlander, was essentially more odd and unpredictable than anything that ever happened to him, not excluding the incident of which we have been writing : moreover it was a transmutation as absolute as any that results in a fairy story after a mumbled spell or a tap with a magic wand. For example, the tie of friendship that united us, one that had been tested time and time again, and which had at each trial proved more enduring, was in a moment cut. Nor was any explanation offered for this act. All his other friends, practically, found themselves treated in an identical fashion. Many of them never were to see him more, except by chance, or on some public plat-form, where a meeting was unavoidable.

And it must be recalled how much their friendship had meant for him. I do not, by this, refer to the material help which they had given him, to the fact that they had made possible his escape from a long and dangerous illness, but only to remind the reader of how peculiarly dependent he had always been on the admiration, love and applause of his friends. Indeed, it was, as we have seen, the temporary depriva-tion of their companionship which had caused his relapse in Granada. If he were now, as it seemed, in-spired solely by self-interest, his desertion of us became yet more strange. It should surely have bound him to us still faster. Not merely had the pleasantest part of his life consisted in the affection we had given him, but with it he had been able to build up a whole system of life, a mechanism of which he was the pivot. He was so evidently the leader of the only young group of artists and writers existent in England, that since their aims were his aims, their ideas largely dictated by his ideas, he was of intention smashing the thing which he most valued, an instrument which himself had devised and that gave him all he had of power. It was almost as though he now in madness sought to devour his own children. But this rage was not confined to those to whom coincidence of taste and interest allied him. He possessed, outside this circle, a wide scattering of devoted friends : but he threw them all aside, rich or poor, intelligent or stupid. Even his ghosts he now scared and chased away. He had turned his back, it was plain, as resolutely upon his old life as upon his old friends.

When we called, when we telephoned, he was always out. No answer came to our letters. Talking among themselves during the first few weeks, his friends would, for their own sakes, excuse him by saying that he must have fallen into some furtive love-affair, which was taking up all his time and energy. They dared not admit to themselves, so much did his friendship mean, that it might be that some extraordinary alteration of the spirit had taken place within him.

At the time our distress was so acute that it prevented us from seeing the transformation of him as a whole. In perspective, this is easier. The distance enables me a little, though not altogether, to comprehend the nature and extent of this obscure, profound and tragic metamorphosis. That under other circumstances it could have been avoided, I can well believe. But as things were, it was, assuredly, a doom which his proud spirit could not evade. He had reached one of the great turning points of life. His young manhood was now ending, and all the nerve-strain, all the longings and stirrings, usually associated with the sensation of growth, through which he had passed lately, were leading up to something other than a fuller flowering. In the same way that certain hideous physical diseases—acromegaly, for example—sweep down on their victims, spare their lives, but utterly alter, deform and distort their countenances, actually giving them new features, until, in fact, they are no longer recognisable, so had some terrible spiritual scourge attacked him. Moreover, acromegaly has a further sad parallel. Women, when beginning to be afflicted with it, noticing the swelling of limbs that is a symptom, often at first believe that they are going to bear children. So, too, it appeared to Tristram that he was undergoing the pains of spiritual growth, whereas in reality they were only the effects of a bitter and humiliating disorder of the soul.

For the purpose, as he thought, of soothing his

nerves, he had chosen—but, in reality, they had forced him involuntarily to adopt—the material side of life. It had taken him captive. Even if, as he claimed later, he had needed money and a different order of success as a base from which to carry on new operations, yet this idea was but one that had sprung up in him for his own deception.

One ought, of course, to have considered the change in connection with the long illness which had preceded it, and from which one had supposed him to be recovered. But how could anyone have foreseen that it was the prelude to a lifelong mental and spiritual disintegration ? Examining his life as a whole, it is, naturally, quite simple now to link up this process with the numerous little traits that heralded it : traits of which I had noted the existence but at the time missed the significance. And if one had been prepared for a collapse, who, though, could have expected this complete transformation ? For this character had been so defined. We have enumerated many salient outer points of his personality : pride, sensitiveness, enough strength of mind to follow the bent of it without fear, an innate distinction, and great mental fire : a fire, moreover, that kindled others. Now all these had suffered some change : were all still there, but degraded to some low and base variety. Yet it was grief, supposed by moralists to refine, that had been the wand with which this unholy miracle had been accomplished. It was, most certainly, his unhappy love for Ursula, acting upon an uncommon and emotional temperament, which was responsible for this ruin.

Meanwhile, as the weeks had sped by, his friends had thought of another excuse for his silence. They would argue that the cause of it must be that he was working very hard—and they could at any rate still look forward to the results of his labour. We were, even after many months had elapsed without a sign of his existing in as far as we were concerned, prepared to acknowledge that his desertion of us could be justi- fied by its fruit, that in the past it might be that he had sacrificed too much to friendship. But when this work, which we had so eagerly awaited, at last ap- peared, seldom in the world of literature had there been for the admirers of any author so deplorable a humilia- tion.

Brilliant as had been his gifts, one had always recog- nised that it was the inner core of intense personality, radiating through them, that bestowed upon his work its individual strain. (But then is that not invariably true of the artist, as opposed to the great scientist or mathematician?) This is not to suggest for an instant that his books had been marred by manner or man- nerism, but that an impalpable quintessence permeated every word and every line. Now that his character had changed, this beauty was to be withdrawn from the world.

Never was he to write another poem, but instead flowed from him over many years a torrent of muddy fiction, written in that "business-man's prose"—i.e.

prose written for business-men by business-men, and couched in the reasonable language of the office—for which he had so often and loudly proclaimed his contempt in earlier days. Only one quality remained to him intact from his old life, and that was his energy, now successfully harnessed to these books, in which was not a thought, not a phrase of his own, nothing observed with his own eyes or described in his own words.

At first they were enthusiastically received. Some critics rejoiced that Mr. Orlander was "no longer content to cater for a small and rather precious public," that he had at last written a book "of which few would have supposed him to be capable": while quoted everywhere on the cover of the first of these great successes—and a little sinister, it seemed to be, I thought, after his adventure in the Hotel Boabdil—was the sentence, "Mr. Orlander has found himself at last."

But the critics soon wearied of him. The renown he began to enjoy was as changed as himself. The strength of it had died down into a wide and general popularity. In former years, the appearance of a book of his was an event, one eagerly awaited by those who cared for the written word. But now no one of appreciation ever mentioned him, and, in the unfair revulsion of feeling that occurred, his early works of genius were altogether overlooked.

The most widely read of all his books, a series of novels dealing with romantic life in Spain, was issued some five years after our visit. His glamour was now that of a rich and favourite author, hero of the lending-library : which helps to prove that the vulgarity of this second period could not have been assumed. You cannot deceive the ordinary reader. If the common quality of it had not rung true, a million readers would have flung the book down in disgust.

And the life he led was in keeping with the esteem in which he was held. Though he no longer knew us, we could not avoid reading of him, or seeing him, every week. There were yachting-cap photographs of him off the coast of Africa, white-flannel tennis ones of him at his " sumptuous villa near Monte Carlo," nude ones of him bathing at the Lido, flash-light night-club or charity-ball ones of him posed in some rather tipsy group, stern ones of him preparing to cross the Atlantic in an air-liner. There were sermons by him, too, fairly regularly in the Sunday papers, and no species of publicity was omitted. Finally, he was made a knight. Even during the World War of 1953-57, when, as we were always told, " men had minds for sterner things," his celebrity was not allowed to die down. His fame as a writer was used for propaganda purposes in neutral countries, and he could not be photographed often enough visiting the troops, wearing a gas-mask or disguised in various uniforms. When the peace came, he went as a British Delegate to the Brooklyn Conference. Over a stretch of forty or more years, he was one of the darlings of the British Public.

As for his private life, he had married a rich, ambitious, jealous and stupid woman, rather older than himself. I only saw her once. Their lives were spent in seeing people of an equal income and no greater interest. It was rumoured, moreover, that he had "settled down," was faithful to her, and no longer drifted from one love-affair into another.

Eventually, this sad and phenomenal conversion lost its appeal as a topic, even among his friends. The years passed. Any reader of this history who wants to know more of the Sir Tristram Orlander of that period has only to visit the Museum and turn back to the photographs of him, the paragraphs about him, that ran through the newspapers of several decades.

So, it appeared, this was an empty, if walking, shell. But there was to be one more, final flicker of life through it before the fire died down for ever.

*   *   *   *   *

Five years ago, some forty years after our visit to Spain, I met an old friend of mine, and formerly of Tristram's, who told me casually that he had heard tidings of him. He had gone to some dinner-party, and had there encountered a number of people among whom the Orlanders apparently now moved. These opulent, somewhat loud-voiced fellow-guests, rather boasting of their intellectual acquaintance, had declared him to be in a very "queer" and "odd" state at present. Why, he had not written a new novel for nearly six months, and was full of "ideas." Lady Orlander was quite anxious about him. He slept badly, too.

Shortly after this conversation had been related to

me, I received—after so enormous an interval had elapsed—a letter from him. It was a very long one, defensive, pathetic and most depressing, couched in terms of the greatest amiability.

In it he wrote that though, after all these years of silence, it might seen a strange request, he wanted very much to see me again. He referred in most flattering terms to a book of mine which had recently come out, and was good enough to say that it had stirred his imagination more than anything he had read for many years. He added, rather weakly, that seeing people constantly was no real gauge of the affection one felt for them. We were now both of us old men, and surely the time had come for us to meet once more, and that my friendship had always meant much to him : so, would I not dine with him alone at his club one night the following week, and talk over old times ? He often, so often, thought of our young days, but he supposed that all his former friends must dislike him now, on account of his books. Well, they were many of them well-made, he thought : but they must not think that he had deceived himself, or that, on the other hand, it had been a process of decay. They should try to realise that he had over many years deliberately held himself to this unceasing, uncongenial labour, in order to achieve that sufficient foundation of fame and success upon which to build his best work, so that it might have in his lifetime that wider audience, which is so often denied to an author until after he is dead.   Moreover, he had wanted to make enough money for his own comfortable support during the doing of it.   That moment of real achievement, which he had promised himself for so long, was now at hand. He was, if Providence would spare him, preparing his mind for his best work.   And, though it might be that there were only a few years before him—four or five, who knows ?—those years he would devote to giving to literature the best that was in him.   He did not feel old, believed in, was as sure of himself, and of the work he would do, as he had been at eighteen.   Once more he would start in life, once more make a new reputation.   If Verdi, between the ages of eighty-five and ninety-three, had been able to write those two amazing operas, *Falstaff* and *Othello,* so different from any he had composed before, surely it would be easy for him, a much younger man, to make a similar new start ?   Though of past middle-age, he was now setting out on this great pilgrimage he had planned for so long.   During the years that were past, years in which he had sought to build up a material position for himself, it would doubtless have been painful for his old friends to see him.   But surely now, if only in memory of days that were no more, I would accept his invitation ?

Thus we met again.   Because, it must be admitted, of a considerable curiosity, no less than on account of my former affection for him, I went to dine with him.

Since I owed him nothing spiritually, I had been resolved to bring to this meeting a clear and unbiassed eye. Not this determination, nor all my inquisitiveness, had prevented me from rather dreading the occasion. But as soon as I was in his company again, I realised that to be in it was pleasant. Once more I was to find, to my surprise, the old spell of fascination creeping, stealing over me, against my will, indeed. Whatever had happened to him in the meantime, however many talents he had thrown away, however much, even, he might over long years have wasted this one, it was soon evident that the magic of his conversation still remained with him. The jinnee of this magic lamp, which lighted everything it touched, was still his slave. Further it was certainly due to Tristram rather than myself that there was no feeling of awkwardness, and very little—of that which there must always be when two people, at one time intimate friends, meet after a separation that has lasted half-a-lifetime—of pain.

In style, the elderly Sir Tristram Orlander was very trim and prosperous, and, for his age, young-looking, decidedly. The fire, it is true, had died out of his face, nor was there manifested in any expression that tense asceticism, which in other days had been dispelled by the slow, animal smile of mouth and eyes. A sad, dissatisfied look—and one strangely at variance with this present sleekness—had replaced it. Yet in his sleek way, however much one might regret the old carelessness and flame of his appearance as a young man, he was, one had to admit, an undoubtedly handsome and imposing old machine. If he had lost the inward glow that had once permeated every word and movement, there was an outward gloss that parodied it. The charm was still there, even if to those who had known him previously it might seem unpleasantly self-conscious : though the fire no longer flickered within the sheath, yet the exterior was impressive, had in it something of the public monument. The cut of his features, his greying hair, which had a little receded and had thus heightened the temples, his fine, intelligent eyes, his neatly pointed beard, imparted to him an air of rather impersonal distinction : he remained one who, without ever meaning to do so, must inevitably attract the attention of all those round. And, as I looked at him, I realised that the glamour had not, after all, entirely evaporated. / His young self had been the author of books so remarkable that, however much they might for the moment have sunk into oblivion, assuredly they could never die | and even though the thought of him might have lost romance, when you saw him, heard his voice again, it was as though a melancholy spectre of greatness had returned to haunt you.

And during my talk with this ghost of the past, in his present guise of man-of-the-world, it struck me that far from his having become more materialistic since he had sold himself to the world, he had, on the contrary, become more simple : for, because there was nothing on his side of life which he need envy, his covetousness was stretching out in another direction. It was plain that some powerful feeling was once more stirring in his heart and brain, some process of change was once more at work. Memories had started to flower. In fact it was, one realised, that tragic season, St. Martin's **Summer, with its** apparent return to a season long dead, with the same, faint, vague, cruel achings—but now false ones and therefore how much more cruel—with its flowers and sunshine, its birds singing within and without, but now all heralding, if only he realised it, the black annihilation of winter.

At last I understood how emphatically the physical conditions of each age at which he found himself, governed him. His mind obeyed his body : this was the penalty that had been exacted by the acuteness of his senses. It was this same individual blossoming of the senses through the intellect that had given his poems, indeed all the books of his early period, their beauty and freshness, just as, later, it had been responsible for his collapse. There had been no prostitution of his talent, as we had esteemed it, but only a chemical change that had in the end affected his character. The blood, which had, more than his mind, given him his genius, had suffered some modification in its composing, and that which had seemed a deliberate spiritual fraud was but a physical failure. But now again, at this age, some perhaps opposite process was at work.

I watched him. It was, surely, possible to detect in the gathered-up wrinkles above the centre of the forehead, and in the sudden twitchings of the muscles round the mouth, the usual symptoms of great nervous exhaustion. Of course, the writing of these books, however uninteresting and uninspired, must have been a constant strain upon his vitality. Yet in some ways he was calmer. It was evident in talking to him that nothing of the formerly strong mystical side to his character was left. Would it come back, I wondered? He did not now even seem given to superstition : or, at any rate, he allowed no sign of it to escape him. Neither tappings of wood nor other follies need now irritate the onlookers. And one could not help but notice that the life he had led had adapted not only his nature, but also his memory, to its own service. For example, he constantly reverted to our travels together in Spain, spoke of Seville and Granada, and of how much he wanted to go back to those towns : but, as I listened, I became convinced that all recollection of his last night there had left him.—If it were so, I did not like too definitely to remind him of it : and in answer to my tentative directing of the conversation, there came no response, unless it was—and I could not be sure—that far away, down under the eyes, a dim uneasiness struggled to reveal itself. Within him, then, obviously some censorship was at work.

Continually he talked of his old life, asked questions about his friends, as might a pioneer returning home after long years spent in some remote wilderness. And all through the evening ran a note of inquiry about Ursula, whether I had seen, what I had heard, of her. It was, I reflected, much as though we were two reincarnated souls discussing our last worldly sojourn. Of his present life on earth, he told me little—except that, with a fanatic insistence, he ever repeated that the new book which he intended to write would be one that must undoubtedly once more establish his reputation with those who had formerly held his writing in esteem ; with his old friends, too, if they would only read it. For six months, he said, he had been gathering strength for the effort of tackling this work.

We talked on until the early hours of the morning, and when I said good-bye I realised that my old feeling toward him had revived. Owing to the pain I had suffered at his neglect, and the extreme disappointment, and indeed disgust, that his later books had caused me, I had almost persuaded myself that I despised and disliked this man. But now pity mingled with my affection for him. The years had joined together, like the halves of a worm uniting. No gap or cut was there, and our friendship seemed to have continued uninterruptedly : but, from a person of infinite promise, who had exacted the admiration of all who knew him, he had become an object of compassion ! And how careful one must be, I felt, not to allow any trace of this change to be reflected in the manner ; which proved that, in spite of the extraordinary way in which he had behaved for half a lifetime, he was still able to exercise a spell, to make one wish to guard him against the realisation of that which he had lost. It was as though one were talking to an Emperor dethroned through his own folly, talking to him with the deliberate respect which such a position demands from one who was his friend in the days of former greatness. Yet it must not from this comparison be inferred that the evening was in any way coloured with gloom or tragedy : it was not. His personality was still vivid enough to carry one across any such impression. We parted in the mutual knowledge, I think, of an unusual inner contentment, and with the promise of many meetings in the near future. But I was never to see Tristram Orlander again.

* * * * *

Upon his friends of the last forty years or so, I imagine that he had been able to make little effect. With them, the spell would not act completely. They knew that he was a very popular, very rich, and therefore very great, author and accordingly listened to his stories, laughed at his jokes. But it was impossible that one used to so different an audience, however much his sensibility might have coarsened, should not miss the old, magnetic sensation of accord between artist and audience which is ever the reward of the great executant. After the evening we spent together, it may be that he understood that though any aura of romance, which had formerly emanated from him, was now ex-

tinguished, that though he had so altered (or he may
have softened it to himself by pretending that it was
merely because he was so much older) as no longer to
be capable of producing, even on the instruments specially attuned to him, those effects which formerly had
been his, yet he was able still to exercise a spell of
personal fascination upon persons who were respon-
sive. And this may have made him anxious to resuscitate other old friendships. Also, it must be remembered
that, whether this was due, as I believed, to the age
which he had now reached, or was the result of the
tremendous, and as one discovered later, unsuccessful
effort he was making to return to the Tristram
Orlander of his first books, some ferment was undoubtedly at work within him.

He devoted more time than ever to his new novel.
But the ideas would not form themselves, the words
would not come. Instead, memories of early days
besieged him, would leave him no peace, were far
more luminous and substantial than the recollection
of his middle years or than the facts of the present.
Was it the beginning of old age, he wondered ? But
within him, the mysterious stirrings and promptings,
hopes and fears, that he felt at this stage, the return
of the fever of youth, as it seemed to him, gainsaid
it—besides, he did not feel in the least old. So
perpetually, however, was his mind, though it had
grown hard and defined in substance and outline,
congested with the projections of events past and over

long ago, that he had been forced to send me that singular letter, full of the mingled boastings and timidity born of remorse : and now the same processes —to which was added his consciousness that I had made some response to him—impelled him to write to Ursula.

With those to whom one's life has been intimately knitted, there is, after a break, no middle course. Either one encounters them quite by chance and despite every effort each day, cannot look out of a window or walk out of a door without beholding them there, directly in front of one : or else one is destined never to see them again, is left puzzled as to how it is, that though, before the quarrel, one constantly met them by accident—as often as by appointment—now it seems that they have been wafted to another world. Thus during the immense interval of years that had elapsed between her marriage and the receiving of this letter from him, Ursula had never once set eyes on Tristram. On the other hand, though she had never been a close friend of mine, I had at no period lost touch with her, and had witnessed many phases of her life.

Her husband, to whom apparently she had grown devoted, she had governed absolutely : while, able always to attract, sway, and often, where she wished it, to dominate, she exercised on English life for many years a marked and widespread influence. In days when the owners of hereditary wealth were bent solely on their own pleasure, when to make use of the privileges which had been handed on to them, or to adopt any definite standard, was apt to be regarded as " priggish " or " stuck-up " ; when, in consequence, all round them the class to which by birth they belonged, and which up till this moment had for many centuries held and wielded the power in England, was now sinking down, uneducated, helpless, inert and each day poorer, Lord and Lady Drayling had built up for themselves a position of very real political authority. In precisely the same manner that, as a girl, everything she did was used to obtain a finer, fuller interpretation of life—every picture at which she had looked, every book which she had read, never an end in itself, but only a means to it—so during her married life, she had brought toward this one object everything that she and her husband possessed, innate or acquired, inherited or traditional. And this combination of purpose with background had become so exceptional in those days that its effect was further enhanced.

Many supposed that such a career, especially for one who had always been so much alive, must have been dull, must have seemed dreary to herself. But she, too, had changed. It was difficult for them at first to perceive within this wise, tall, witty, beautiful but apparently most conventional woman, the outgrown contour of Lady Ursula Rypton, once so widely abhorred for erratic and original conduct. They did not comprehend that she was guided by her own quite definite principles, her own high sense of esthetics in life, and had always been well aware that for her the whole essence and secret of existence was to be discovered in contrast : nor could they understand that in the true original, eccentric behaviour is commonly an outburst of youthful energy, and that originality is to be looked for rather in mind than in conduct. Thus, those who had previously abused her for her difference from others, now railed at her seeming conformity. Yet no one was ever found to challenge her loveliness, and it flowered on to astonish a later generation.

In the long period of her married life, then, she had reigned supreme. But now her children were in their turn married, her husband was dead, her sway shattered. To all this, which for her spelt the demolition of so much that she had constructed through the years with infinite toil and artistry, she made no demur. The conception of the design which each one must weave for himself, that had so largely inspired her life, now helped her to face old age, with its inevitable melancholy, and served even to deprive the thought of death of some of its horror. Or was it merely, she used to wonder, that she was tired ? But, looking back over the pattern she had woven, she was satisfied : up to this point, it was, indeed, an exquisite one : and, since the breaking off is inherent in any design that is once started, one must be prepared for it. And it was important that this should be accomplished well, smoothly, beautifully. And now a great physical change swept over her. Up till these last months she had remained preternaturally young; the transparent graces of youth yet dwelt in her when she was already approaching the gates of old age. But, all at once, it seemed as though, acknowledging that every design must end, and that hers demanded an old age of the proper kind, she had dwindled into an old woman. Though still beautiful, it was with the guttering, abstract beauty of the ancient. And, more, it must be owned, for esthetic than for ethical reasons, she had gone to live very quietly in the country, devoting herself to such things as gardens and good works : for to her there was something insanely ugly and brutally stupid in the mad, painted carnival of age that proceeded in the great cities. Thus, the London which for so long she had decorated knew her no more.

I conjectured that, despite her undoubtedly genuine love for her husband, and though Lady Drayling had never seen Tristram since her marriage, she had spent much time in thinking of him. He had been so much part of the texture and substance of her early life. His friendship was bound up with her young days : his love for her had terminated them. Furthermore, he was the only man who had ever shaken her being to its foundation. Her love for her husband had been of another order : it had been an attachment, a practical, affectionate, comfortable, protective family affair. Nor, I think, in just reading and hearing of Tristram Orlander, had she at all divined the transformation of him that had taken place. That he had never seen her, that she had never received a letter or message from him, was entirely explained, she thought, by his formerly overwhelming passion for her. Her own behaviour had been excused by necessity, but it had been cruel—must have appeared cruel—she knew : and in her mind an infinite pity was united to her original fondness for him. Concerning the decay of his work, though at one time she would have been the first to remark and deplore it, now that for so long she had turned her mind away from art and literature towards politics, she had lost her ability to judge it. After all, life was the art that mattered, she considered—in this very different, had she but known it, from the real artist, who is always aware that he is set apart, hedged off from life by a barrier invisible, except to himself ; so that he must observe and go on observing.—It was a pity, she thought, if, as she had heard it said, he had never fulfilled his promise : but he was, in any case, famous—and fame she could appraise and appreciate. He had married, she had been told, a rich, ugly woman. Obviously, then, he had never again fallen in love : and this, it must be admitted, counted with her as something in his favour.

When, therefore, Lady Drayling once more received a letter from Tristram Orlander after so many and such overflowing years, she instantly recognised the handwriting on the envelope, and before she could open it, her heart had broken out into a winged fluttering, as of a bird trying to escape, that surprised and somewhat shamed her. She read his note with a pleasure that she had never expected to feel again, and determined, as he suggested, to go up to London and have luncheon with him. To herself, she made excuses : she said that an old rhythm had come back to the design, that a theme had returned which would help to complete its beauty. But, though she both dreaded and looked forward to it, the idea of seeing him again certainly lifted the restaurant at which they were to meet on to a quite different plane in her mind from that which it had hitherto occupied.

Tristram, for his part, was awaiting the day with an extreme impatience. It came : and he was sitting for what seemed endless hours in the over-decorated little room—spun, it seemed, out of white and green sugar—which led into the dining-room. Thence sounded an immense chattering, and through the glass doors he could watch the people, and the silent, prestidigitation of hurrying young waiters, all of them moving, as it were, automatically to the same inaudible music : for the needs of their customers demanded this beat of time. But Tristram was not long allowed to observe this scene in peace, for the directors and headwaiters, too mindful of their famous client, worried him with their unnecessary attentions and false smiles.

As he sat there, this placid, prosperous, good-looking elderly man, no one could have gauged his emotions. The most varying storms were driving his spirit this way and that every moment. Now he was saying how right she had been to reject so worthless a suitor, now blaming her bitterly, laying upon her the whole responsibility of his subsequent life. It was she who had made him sell himself (for in these curious, crucial days, inexplicable even to himself, there were even times when he could bear to admit the truth). She had been answerable for the whole thing. And then, again, the wind veered. A new, faked, manufactured love for her, that very closely mimicked the old one, rose up in him, and he did not challenge its authenticity. After all, it had been his fault, not hers. He acknowledged it. Through these timeless minutes, he pictured her continually—he saw again her eyes (how well he remembered that unfaltering, almost unseeing, blue gaze of the shadowy eyes), her mouth, her hair, the movements of her long hands. He recalled them, as if it had been but yesterday that he had left her. Alas, she, too, would have altered, he supposed.

People kept on coming in. Each moment the door revolved with that peculiar sound—feeling, perhaps, more than sound—of pressure : the same that one experiences when going through a long tunnel. He wondered why for so many years he had hated this usual prelude to restaurant or hotel : it was not that it irritated him, he definitely hated it, was made uneasy by it. (There must be some reason for this, and for a moment some dim memory stirred at the back of his mind.) Yet now it should be the herald of good news. At each warning revolution he looked up. Young and old were ground through this mill. Would she never come, he wondered? An old woman with grey hair was now being whirled through it. His eyes followed her absently. As she turned round in search of her friends he thought how much she put him in mind of someone—who was it, he questioned himself idly? He was not paying much attention to her, for he was absorbed in waiting for Ursula. But there was something, he decided, a little remarkable about the face; an air of command and conviction, of kindness and certainty—a rather unusual combination in a woman. She must have been beautiful, too. He could deduce it from the hollows of the sunken old eyes, the darkness of those hollows that set off the curious, faded glare of the eyes, from the straight features, the resolute set of the head upon the wrinkled neck—he knew now whom she recalled to him—old Lady St. Donat.— Well, she must have been dead a long time.—How singular, he reflected, and how typical of the delusive way in which life works, that he should be made to recollect her, for the first time in so many years, upon the very day that he was waiting here for her daughter: it was like thinking of someone as you walked along— the only time you had thought of him for a long period —and then turning a corner to come upon him suddenly; a common experience, if a queer one. He wondered if she seemed to resemble Lady St. Donat merely because he knew that he was going to see her daughter,

and whether thus it was the habitual working of the
subconscious mind, or if the likeness was in fact actual,
and the whole minute incident part of a general pattern
imposed from outside.   For an instant these specula-
tions interested him more than the person who had
suggested them : he forgot to observe the old woman
or to watch the door.   But she had been looking at him
attentively for several seconds, and this once more compelled his eye.   Yes, she must have been really lovely
—in her day.

It was at this moment that she was sure, and as she
walked towards him a light that was truly beautiful
glowed in her pale, lined face.   He understood.   It
was Ursula.   His emotion changed again.   He had
been cheated, he felt : a stranger had been foisted upon
him.   Was this the woman to whom he had sacrificed
his life (for, in his sudden rage, he thus dignified the
spiritual bankruptcy that had overtaken him, forgetting
that but a few minutes before he had owned to himself
that it was his own doing ?)   Was this the woman
who had broken and cast away his genius, yet the very
thought of whom had brought back that unaccustomed
fire in his elderly being ?

They sat down together at their table, rather incongruous, perhaps, among the horde of young and
noisy who surrounded them.   But no one watching
them—this beautiful, stern, resigned old woman into
which time had struck the once tempestuous, lovely
girl, and this celebrated, well-groomed business-novelist

into which the once romantic, ardent and even then famous young poet, had been transmuted—could have formed the slightest idea of what hopes each had built on this meeting : and even themselves could not have analysed or defined these vague and sanguine expectations. They were talking calmly and ordinarily of the things which ordinary people talk about, yet which interest nobody. She, certainly, looked much older than he did. Further, his impression, before he had recognised her, was a correct one ; for with every day that had dwindled into the past, she had relapsed more and more into the shadow and effigy of her mother. As a girl, there had been very little resemblance between them ; perhaps there was a " family look," that was all. So many people, however, even the most intensely personal, as the blood chills and grows stagnant in their old veins, cease to be individual, and show themselves as but one more coin minted by their race. With the years, then, she too had become much less a person, much more daughter and mother, offspring and progenitress. Living so much in public, it might be, had taken away something, and in its stead had substituted that spectral impersonality, which, in its most developed form, is to be seen in the Royal Families of Europe : a quality that, at the best, converts them into so many worthy, hardworking and efficient machines for saying the right, if obvious, word, and accompanying it with the appropriate gesture. In these august homes, the aptitude for universal average representation is often of necessity encouraged at an early age : but fortunately, with most people, the loss, or rather weakening, of individuality is so gradual a process, that, when it is complete, they seldom have the strength left them to discover it. Certainly Lady Drayling had never found it out, or, at least, had never regarded it in that way. Inevitably the looks, the tricks and mannerisms even, that had always provoked her in her mother, had stolen down on her, adopted her, irretrievably smuggled herself away under them. Nevertheless, to-day her old self had to some extent returned to her, was merely weighed down and smeared over by these accumulations of acquired traits and inherited characteristics. Yet probably this was the only occasion upon which they had been noticed and identified.

When Tristram looked at her, his heart grew dead ; for in these few hours he was able to understand again in the sense that poets understand. He saw that she who had once definitely represented an ideal—youth, daring and freedom—was now old, tired, and if measured only by the standard of those among whom he had latterly made his life, stiff and formal. He tried to overcome the petrifaction, essayed to melt this superficial outer-hardness in which she was imprisoned—if, indeed, there was anyone inside—with the warmth of his conversation. But he could not rescue her. The charm upon which he had relied, for it had worked with myself only a few nights before, to-day was out of order. He could only talk of banal things in a com-

monplace fashion. On and on he chattered—politics
—people—weather, himself listening to nothing he
said. Saddened and angry as he was at this transformation, which, after all, he might have foreseen : albeit,
also, his nerves were goaded by the tricks she now displayed, those idiosyncrasies of movement, speech and
intonation he had so frequently observed in her mother
(he was surprised how well he remembered these, but
recalled that, as a matter of fact, Ursula and he had
so often together deplored and ridiculed them), there
was, yet, springing up in him a new feeling towards
her ; one of passionate, pitying sympathy. The whole
of his being, moreover, was still in ferment, full of
vague longings and achings, the old, almost forgotten
symptoms of growth and development.

As for her sensations—at first she thought herself content. The design was so nearly complete.—For if, by
its own nature, it could never, she realised, be finished,
was like a story which the author can never hope to
conclude, but only to stop working at—it was, nevertheless, a beautiful and perfect object to leave, to hand
on. The artist, though, was satiated, weary, worn
down : but even her presence here to-day, she flattered
herself, was but one more effort for her art. And yet—
was it, she wondered ? Certainly at the sight of him
she had experienced an emotion, so long unaroused
that it had nearly died away from her memory. But
she was altered, she knew it—somehow or other she felt
empty and expected all others—except, perhaps, this one

man—to be in the same condition. Perhaps as he talked, she, too, may have suffered disillusionment, the final one. A faint sadness, a fatigued wisdom, the dying grey fire of her eyes, the deep, unalterable, harsh music of her voice—these were now all that she had to give him—all that remained. But there was also— and she had overlooked it—the past. She could give him the past.

Through his anger and sympathy, it was continually borne in on him that he must pretend to be pleased, pretend to be happy. But as he examined her, he could not imagine how she had cast so enduring a spell upon him : and even while this astonished him, he felt its influence. Not for anything in the world could he have been induced to betray his feelings, to say any- thing which might bring a look of pain to that face he had scarcely recognised. Besides—he recollected sud- denly—it would spoil her design, to the making of which he had been sacrificed in the first instance. For her it would be like having to restitch a piece of tap- estry. At any rate, he supposed angrily, the last, long decades, for the bleakness of which she was respon- sible, had sufficiently enured him to suffering : they had accustomed him to dreadful situations, at least had taught him how to play them. (But, he said to himself, how ridiculous was this planning and exalta- tion of life : like her mother, again, with her silly imaginary landscapes full of idealised but familiar buildings, huddled together.)

It was for this woman he had ruined his life! He thought of the books, which as a young man he had written : of those others which he might have created, had he not chosen instead to be successful.—But, alas, however bad his later work had been—yes, bad : he owned it—there was the further distress of knowing that he could not altogether lay the blame upon her. After all it was not the want of material success that had prompted her to refuse him. She would have consented to marry neither a poor poet, however distinguished, nor a mediocre author, however rich. Actually his failure in love, although it had appeared cruel and insupportable at the time, could now, in perspective, become in itself a solace : for Tristram was aware that if she had not loved him, she would never have married Drayling. It was precisely his success as a lover that had shattered his hopes. It was obvious, however, he thought, that her former love was deep in oblivion, decently covered over with conventional memories so that no ghost, even, of anything real should return to haunt her. Himself, while still he felt it, began almost to doubt whether it could ever have been. All the expressions of it had ceased to exist with the personality itself. The tones of the voice, they were still there at times : but all the movements he had so loved, all the individual turns of speech, even, all the things that had for so many years tormented him (for he had succeeded in persuading himself that never a day had passed by without his thinking of her, whereas in truth he had been wholly occupied in turning out his books, and happy, at any rate superficially, in their enormous sales and wide recognition) were now either overlaid by inherited tricks, gone altogether, or had faded merely into so many affectations of an old, sad woman.

All this time over him pressed the icy surface of small talk, through which he could not break, however much he struggled.   There must be the sound of conversation, he knew, else she would feel that something was amiss.   And so he talked mechanically, talked on, acting the part that he thought she was expecting of him—and she was disappointed, profoundly, horribly disappointed.   For she was beginning to know, perceive and understand.   The tendrils, almost atrophied by long disuse, were gently starting to grope their way again towards the light.   Her heart ached for the elderly, courteous gentleman with the self-conscious charm that he had become.   Here, from someone who, when last she had seen him, had been incapable of doing or saying a dull or usual thing—incapable of it to a degree that had often been embarrassing, even to one as little subject to such an emotion as had been her young self—she found someone who made the same remarks, paid the same compliments, as every other man of his age that she knew : except that she could see that all the while, though outwardly attentive, he was inwardly away—" not at home."   This condition, she surmised, must be habitual with him.   He had been obliged probably, she imagined, to find this safe hiding-place within his own body, where he could never be disturbed or discovered. Well, she hoped for little enough from anyone now—but from him she had at the least expected himself.

During the first part of the luncheon, while he had forged an exterior, while he had talked politics or food, weather or old friends—not listening, indeed, to anything he was saying and welcoming every interruption from the waiters—and as, in order not to let her see his real feeling and thus sadden her, he was forced to adopt a sort of wistful, tender, old-man air, he had been sorrowful as well as angry. But now an intense, an unexpected, fury welled up within him. He did not understand its nature, could not at that moment perceive that the old feeling, with all its fervour, had at last returned, and was flowing in this new channel. If his fear of wounding her, or of frightening her, had not restrained him, he would have liked to get up and leave, to dash things upon the floor, or, at moments, actually to hurl them at this corpse opposite, if only to see how she would respond to such treatment—but then he could not be quite certain that the corpse might not yet see and feel in a dim recess of her being. Her young self, even, might, for aught he knew, be hovering near her in the air, and he must not give it pain.

It seemed as though they had been sitting there for hours, dull and inanimate. His fury rose still higher. And then suddenly, quite suddenly, something wonderful happened. The heat of this suppressed intensity made itself felt, burnt through the ice, and was thereby transformed. The charm worked and the years rolled back.

While the waiters, impatient to get away, pecked at their table, this elderly, this strangely enchanted couple sat on, regardless of their surroundings, for a whole hour : an hour in which there was an entire life of love's undercurrents. This for them amazing afternoon deepened outside its winter gloom, but within each of them the inner light shone radiantly. They had walked for a lifetime among the flowers that never fade, to bird-song that never dies throughout an endless spring. Yet when they parted, she left contented : whereas he went away more uneasy, more saddened, and with many curious sensations flaming within him, reborn of youth : reborn after the days he now so cursed. The tree was beginning to bear blossom once more, but just before the first frost was due. But as he looked back down the years, and saw how, as a young man, he had thrown away his gifts, deliberately betrayed himself, a great hatred for that other, younger self entered into him.

It was only a few days after this meeting that I saw Lady Drayling and she told me of it. At last she had seen him again—but only yesterday she had received another letter from him. He was ill, and had been ordered abroad for a change. It was nothing much, she hoped. He had seemed very well, though, of course, after so many years, it was difficult to tell. No doubt, with such a busy life, he was tired.

When I returned home, I found waiting for me a letter—but this time one typewritten by his secretary —to the same effect. But such information was hardly necessary, for soon every newspaper in England proclaimed the " Serious Illness of Famous Novelist, Creator of Spanish Vogue," and published little paragraphs describing his yachts, villas, dogs, clothes and parties.

And now the manner of his end will be here described, as I am sure it came to him. The facts upon which this structure is built up are already so generally known that, if this account of his death appears at first sight a little more singular than the one almost equally curious which everyone acknowledges and accepts as the truth, it must, however, be remembered that those happenings which render it so, are the very ones for which I can vouch of my own experience or as confided in me by himself during his earlier years. Thus the whole affair, when properly examined, seems to me to resolve itself into an almost Euclidian problem. Certain premises are granted, from which it is seen that if various lines are prolonged, they will intersect one another at a particular angle : while, when this is effected, its result is to prove the premises correct.

*   *   *   *   *

Tristram had been sleeping very badly during the last few months. This was unusual, for his nerves were much quieter, stronger than when he was a young man. But then he had fretted greatly and for many weeks over the book that he had mentioned to me at dinner, and had hinted at in his letter of invitation. He had made a strenuous and prolonged effort to write it, but with no success. It would not be written. The idea of it sulked in corners of his mind with an obstinacy which only an author can imagine. Want of sleep, combined with this failure, and, surely, above all, with his age—for even if he did not realise it, he was no longer fit for such struggles—now produced a breakdown. The doctors did not consider it very serious, but, since he was an elderly man, thought it better to take no risks : and, though his health had been really remarkably good for many years past, ordered him to stop all work and go abroad. Rest, change of air, and change of scene, they said, was what he needed. And this time, fortunately, he could afford to obey their commands. He was to receive no letters, and they advised, very tactfully advised, Lady Orlander not to accompany him—let him go alone, taking his own car, with his valet and chauffeur to look after him.

Almost before he set off, he was better. It really seemed unnecessary for him to go at all. But he looked forward eagerly to the tour which he had planned. He was to drive through France and Spain to Morocco—he was extremely anxious to visit Spain once more. But in no place, the doctors told him, was he to stay more than two or three days—because fatigue, of the order that arises from constant travelling, was precisely what he needed. It was March by now, and he decided first to follow the Mediterranean coast of France, through Perpignan and such places up to Port Bou, and from there to continue along the same coast as far as Barcelona and Valencia. He would visit Murcia and the date groves of Elche, and thence would proceed via Granada, Malaga and Seville to Gibraltar, where he was to take a boat for Tangiers.

The prospect of staying at Granada (I am more or less certain of it from his conversation at dinner that night) pleased him. He felt not the faintest anxiety or apprehension. Of what had taken place in his mind concerning that incident at the Hotel Boabdil, by what means this deep and terrible mark had been smoothed out or erased, I am not aware. Some special inner censorship, it had seemed to me, had been at work : but through these long years the dispersal of such feverish and painful memories may equally well have been due to the customary action of the machine, that winnows all the impressions with which the mind is stored, and only leaves us, for our deception, the light but delusive residue of happiness and joy : a deposit of events on occasion of a pleasant melancholy, but never menacing or tragic, and one which seems, however small, by its vibration and lightness to fill a lifetime. In the same way that a serious illness is afterward recalled with difficulty, its more painful phases obliterated from the memory altogether, so it may have been that about Granada Tristram at this time could remember little but its extreme beauty and that it had completed his return to health.

Moreover, most people find, as they grow older, that to go back to a place they have known in days past, and which is for ever thus illumined by the rays of all the bright suns that have died, gives them more pleasure than to visit for the first time some new place. For, however interesting and lovely this is said to be, they will be forced to create it for themselves out of a now depleted store of energy. It is, admittedly, the quality of a conservative mind, similar to that which prompts in so many people who have seldom read a book, the intolerable refrain that "whenever a new book comes out, I read an old one." Further, even when the impression, which can never afterward be recovered, of your first visit is shattered by your second entry into a town, even when you perceive that the groves have been cut down, the streams drained, the wild flowers tidied away, the palaces rebuilt by the yard, there remains something fascinating in the game of fitting the new on to the old impression. The process has the charm of a jigsaw puzzle, needs something of the X-ray-like eye of the expert who can detect the outlines of Raphael's hand beneath the flashy daubing of an apparently nineteenth-century picture offered for auction in a sale-room. So, you conclude, where the town-hall now stands, was formerly the site of that cavern, with the bathing pool in front of it in which you used to swim.   The identification that ensues, if it proves to be correct, is its own reward, almost ample enough to compensate you for the destruction that has been wrought.

It was, therefore, not without a certain pleasant excitement that Tristram left France and northern Spain behind him and drew near the places he had known. How little the country had altered ! Even the weather seemed unchanged : the same magic Andalusian spring, with never a cloud or whip of rain.   And in this landscape, which he had almost forgotten among the golden deserts of the fashionable gambling and watering resorts that he had frequented for so long, he once more found peace, was healed.   Certainly, he felt, on his return he would be able to write that book which had worried and eluded him for months.   His mind went back continually, and with a sense of great comfort, to those distant days, when once before he had found health here.   An almost sentimental feeling for this countryside seized on him, a consciousness that it possessed for himself a special and hidden significance which could not be described or defined.

Often he would stop his rushing car, get out, and would walk through the mirror-smooth air, where nothing stirred.   He would pass under the shadow of bare, golden hills, on which, ever and again, stood the rusty-pink and orange ruins of Saracen castles, outlined against the quivering blue of the sky or drenched in an unimaginable flood of light ; or, again, he would tread the border of vast, undulating plains, half-heath, half-garden, on which grew a tangle of tough, dark, squat vegetation, dwarf palm-trees and aromatic plants, so that, at each crackling footstep he took, a new scent was exhaled, while the pink, white, and mauve paper faces of the rock-roses were already beginning to sprinkle this sombre mass as though with confetti. Then, going back to his machine, he would be whirled down leagues of ribbon-like road, half a mile of dust extending behind him as the golden mantle of a very material glory. Mountains and clouds would float nearer, trees and little houses dash past him. The car would slow down, perhaps, to pass through a village, consisting always of a broad street of white, one-storeyed pavilions, crowned with flashing tiles and majolica flowerpots. Under this burning sun, these white houses looked as cool as the foam of distant breakers, or assuming in their whiteness a thousand variations of pale colour, became diaphanous and insubstantial as a mirage, denied conclusively with their defiant cleanliness the whispered insinuations of Spanish dirt. Or now they would emerge into open, agricultural country, would glide by isolated, golden farms, round which the peasants laboured slowly in droves of ten or twenty, closely followed, parodied even, by an equal or perhaps greater number of tall, match-legged storks, grotesque black-and-white figures, always accompanying, busy and useless in their striped garb as so many clowns at a circus, eternally and clumsily eager to help.

How strange it was, he reflected, that the peasants laboured here to-day in exactly the same way as they had worked forty—or, indeed, it was to be supposed, two hundred—years ago. Everywhere else in Europe, the machine had long ago ousted the hand in farming. But Spain had not changed in the least. His own circumstances, however, were very different from what they had been on his last visit. And as he was whirled comfortably along in his own car—and without his wife, whose presence had begun latterly to weigh upon him—he began to congratulate himself mildly on the alteration in his fortunes. Even if his literary reputation had suffered in recent years, how very much more pleasant in some ways was this journey than his first one in Spain. He was older, it was true, and more friendless—that came, of course, of being older—but at any rate he had now his own servants to wait upon him and no longer was himself forced to throw his few possessions into a torn suit-case. Everywhere the directors of the hotels made special efforts for his comfort : and he was followed—and rather enjoyed it—by the respectful, ox-eyed attention of the American tourists, ever on the alert for yesterday's best-seller. There was no doubt—and all this brought it home to him—that he was a very famous man. Indeed, just as in my younger days our transatlantic visitors were willing to cross the world in order to see for themselves the places described or lived in by Mr. Robert Hichens, so now would they undertake special " Orlander

Tours" of Spain. That my fellow-countrymen did not participate in these literary orgies to the same extent, was doubtless due more to a greater poverty than to superior taste. It was thus rather in the guise of a prince travelling incognito among his subjects, that Tristram returned to Granada. But, really, he did not wish to think of his books at this moment. He preferred to live again in his early days. It was extraordinary how this country affected him, he thought. And it was with a curious, steady mounting of interest and excitement, as though Granada—rather than Fez or Marrakesh, neither of which cities he had ever seen —was the climax of his journey, that he approached this city which he had so much loved.

Now he was in the lion-coloured plain, now at the gates again. How well he remembered it ! It was just the same. The life of the town had perhaps filled out a little : the shell no longer seemed so much too large. There were a few more public buildings to parody the old. Now he was passing the port-flushed face of the eighteenth-century barracks, its façade set with the absurd giant-figures of uniformed halberdiers in niches. Now he was in the main street. The gypsy-women, even more brightly clothed than forty years before, were swinging their way lithely along the pavements. He noticed that the muleteers still wore their braided coats, and could hear them giving their hoarse, invocative screams. Now the car was turning up the steep narrow street that led to the wood. The shop windows were still full of sham oriental antiques, and of those photographs of American and English spinsters, who thus posed for a moment, and with no Sheik or Vizier to command them, had yet contrived to gain an eternity of harem-life. Now it had snorted under the first Moorish arch, and was dashing up through the wood, the tall trees only just breaking into their green and gothic tracery : while below them, under the coiling serpents of the ivy, by the side of the shimmering and singing waters, the purple flags echoed the shadows in a stronger tone. Even above the panting of the car he could detect other sounds, the rushing of the waters, and birds cutting for themselves their crystal cages. This, he remembered, seeing through the trees to terraces and paths, was where that Frenchwoman and her child used to beg. Well, she must certainly be dead by now, and the sickly, whining boy as well probably, poor miserable creatures. The only thing left of them in the living world, he supposed, was their impression in the minds of the few people sensitive enough to dislike them. But why had he feared them, he wondered ? For just in this second a fleeting memory of fear crept somewhere at the back of his mind. And while he was thinking of these things, the car suddenly pulled up in front of the Hotel Boabdil. (Apparently it was still the only good—or, rather, expensive—hotel in the town.) He had only just time to look up, and notice at one side a fresh litter of smaller and more dumpy domes—as though the older and bigger ones had given birth to this yet more degraded and deformed progeny —before the door swung round, and a regiment of porters, dressed apparently for wrestling, rushed out from their ambush as though to storm the car, swarming over it and leaping up to attack its roof, seizing the bags and coats, wrenching, even, out of his grasp the little dispatch-box he was holding.

He entered, to find that the interior had been entirely remodelled. It was quite extraordinary, though, he said to himself, how nowadays hotels can be turned completely inside out, after this fashion, and at the same time remain unaltered and inalterable, with every peculiarity of atmosphere intact. For example ; the levels had all been changed. Here you stepped down where before you stepped up, everything had been completely rebuilt—but nothing was different—so that it was impossible to imagine for what purpose, except that of spending the company's money, these alterations had been carried out. Here were still the ice-cold marble or tiled walls, the mosaic floors, and the ceilings, dripping with red stalactites like threatening, blood-stained knives, the silvered radiators, which in their stiff attitude and chirruping resembled so many gigantic grasshoppers, the pictures, the chairs that like sensitive plants destroyed themselves at your touch or even at your approach, the stained glass, more raucous yet, the oriental lamps, well-shaded but swinging giddily in the multicoloured but stagnant upper air of the overheated rooms—all were the same, but different,

brought "up-to-date," although identical. By this
time the interior of the hotel, had it been allowed to
remain, as we had seen it some forty years before,
would have gained a semi-historical, period interest,
that could be gently ridiculed though never removed.
But this method of constantly replacing one nightmare
by another permitted nothing to live long enough to
add any outside quality to its innate hideousness.

Pondering on such esthetic problems, Sir Tristram
Orlander was conducted to the lift, and then ushered
up to his private suite. It was in the new part of the
hotel, under the knot of little domes. He noticed,
with a momentary feeling of irritation, that the number
on the door was 12 (A)—an insult to the intelligence of
even the most superstitious, an obvious pretence,
equivalent to calling an undertaker a "mortician."
But, since he nowadays affected to despise superstitions,
he did not like to complain or to change his room, as
he would have done in former days. It soon ceased to
worry him, however.

While his valet unpacked, set out neatly his books,
photographs, writing equipment and the few personal
belongings with which he always travelled, he wandered about his rooms. The sitting-room was a handsome, inevitably Moorish affair, decorated with too
many stalactites and hanging lamps, but very comfortable. He had often seen it before, he felt, was
almost at home in it, so familiar did it seem—it was,
of course, exactly like the private rooms in every

modern Spanish hotel. He noted, placed on a low, oriental table, a Tauchnitz edition of his Spanish novels, specially bound for the hotel in pseudo-saracenic covers. Moreover a management indebted to him for many visitors had presented him with a huge bouquet of flowers, tied together with ribbons in the Spanish national colours.

It was with a sense of satisfaction, then, that he surveyed the rooms, and mentally compared them with the one bare, cold little room (he could see it now) which he had occupied during his first stay in Granada. Of course the inn had been pretty, very pretty : and this hotel was hideous. But after all there was a great deal to be said for comfort. And, really, could any place with such an outlook be called ugly ? He walked up to one of the tall windows, divided in the middle by a slender column, so as to get the full detail of it. The breadth of the view was overpowering. The entire valley lay revealed, with the nearer towers and belfries rising clustered round the foot of the hill, like the spires and turrets of golden bell-flowers in a garden. As he stood there, it seemed as though the springtide of the year was rushing up to meet him. The huge tawny plain, in this season crossed, chequered and diapered with every pattern and tone of green in dots and stripes, squares and circles, now shone beyond the city, while in the distance thousands of blossoming fruit-trees rolled their delicate globes of light colour over this vast, level lawn away toward the horizon, or from the foreground waved at him their innocent pink-and-white banners. The whole scene was vibrant, changed every minute, and even as he looked, there came a new life to it, for the windows of the city turned to glowing armour off which rebounded the hot lances aimed at them by the late-afternoon sun.

And Tristram felt this life flowing over him, renewing him. It was as though all this surge of spring was focused upon himself, and every ray of light and colour was renewing the dead fibres of his soul. But, albeit the feelings that he experienced seemed to him those of his youth, there was nevertheless a change, a change in their direction. For the melancholy, vague longings that had beset him before his illness had been transformed into hope and confidence ; which, while now he associated them with his young days, had never really existed in that troubled, restless, if occasionally exultant, period.

He turned round to look at his sitting-room again : and decided that he liked it. But then he felt so well at present that everything pleased him. He looked forward, almost, to opening the letter from his wife—whose letters usually profoundly bored him—which he saw lying on the table—the only one, thank heavens, for he was allowed no other correspondence. Evidently he had only needed a rest. Already a month's travelling had built up his nerves, had made him feel better than for years past. Indeed, his nerves, he thought, were in splendid order again. He felt sure of himself and his abilities. Not for forty years or more had he been conscious of this power and energy. Indeed, much as he was enjoying this sense of comfort, solitude and change, he wondered whether he ought not to return at once, so as to begin his book. He almost wished that it was possible. He knew he could write it now, was sure he could. After all, even if the doctors had forbidden it, he could work a little on his travels. But not at Granada, for though he knew it, remembered it so well, he must see everything again. This evening, however, he was feeling somewhat tired after the long day and so much fresh air. He walked to the window. It would be dark soon, for through the arches he could see flaming primeval dragons drifting across the city, trailing their fiery scales near the towers and domes, while, behind, their passage was reflected in the dulled, slanting white mirrors of the snow.

He would not go out, he decided. He would have dinner up in his sitting-room, and then after reading a little, would go to bed, rather early. He knew the place so well, that even if he did want to see it all again, there was no point in hurrying out that very evening. There were three whole days in front of him, in which he could do as he liked.

When dinner came, the food proved to be good but cosmopolitan : very different from the enormous Spanish meals that used to be given him in the *fonda*. (He wondered whether it still existed ? The proprietress must certainly be dead by now.) But as he drank a glass of brandy after dinner, he gradually became aware that his mood had changed, his contentment had vanished—he could not quite make out why. And then he realised that it was because he did not after all like his room—there was something about it which he did not care for. In fact, he disliked the whole hotel. For his own soothing, he said to himself that no doubt it was the sudden return of his old inclination toward superstition that had put him against it. Well, it was ridiculous—but so was 12 (A), as a number for a room. Of course, the superstitious were generally regarded with such scorn by those who did not share their weakness, their intelligence was so derided by the practical-minded, that doubtless it was imagined that such a deviation from the ordinary run of numerals would escape their notice, or that, if detected, its purpose would not be apparent to them.

He went to his bedroom, but this now pleased him no more than his sitting-room. Such an aversion as this one which he had formed for his rooms is well calculated to keep the person who entertains it awake for long hours. But on the contrary, he soon fell asleep, and slept through the night till the sun was sending its golden showers in at his windows. Immediately on waking, however,—albeit he forgot it later —he realised that his sleep had been restless and troubled, though unbroken : that it had been full of dreams, crammed with incidents he could not now remember, acted by personages whom he could not now recall. But, at the time, these dreams had seemed to be possessed of sequence and meaning for him.

What a lovely day it was ! One window faced on to the distant sierras, and from them there flew in with a quivering of white, dove-like wings, a little flower-scented wind. He breakfasted, dressed slowly, went downstairs, and was before long walking through the light-dappled woods to the Alhambra hill. He remarked, again, how little anything had changed, and yet how different it was. Taste having veered once more, the palace of Charles V had now been as much spoilt as its neighbour. It had been given a glass roof to protect it, the windows were glazed also, and the circular court, with every weed scraped away, resembled a derelict concert-hall. No longer was any seeding flower allowed to aid its precise beauty with an un-looked-for though natural contrast, nor was the song of any leaping bird permitted to rouse winged echoes in the damp, mossy caverns of its corridors. Instead, the place was dry and tidy, filled with a doddering army of guardians, whose chief delight it was to waste endless minutes in their punching and tearing of tickets, a manœuvre they executed as if they were engaged in creating out of this flat paper some miracle of cutting-out, some marvellous likeness of man or animal. Tristram thought of how often he had rested here, finding a refuge from the heat, or watching the stern, sculptural face of the blind man, as he sang his sad, loud but quavering music. He walked out, and turned his steps toward the Alhambra.

Here, on the other hand, he found a change for the better. Time had softened the earlier restorations : the hardness of the incised tiles had crumbled a little, while on this day, ideal for it, the water trilled, rippled, gurgled, bubbled and dripped from every tank, cistern, fountain, basin and jet to cool the golden honeycombed grottos, hung with stalactites, that surrounded the gardens. These, replanted many years ago now, had grown up : there were tall cypresses, and the clipped hedges of rosemary, box and myrtle were broad and robust. In the quartered beds the blue and white irises were in flower, and over the blossoms droned the bees in their gold-striped uniforms ; the bees, that fantastic communist association, which, it seemed, must be responsible for the mathematical loveliness of this fabulous hive. Never in the many days he had spent here had this palace looked more beautiful. He thought, for a minute, of that strange night when we had broken in upon its quiet and haunted mystery, when the water lay jade-green under the moonlight, and the domed pavilions were lofty, subterranean caverns, the gloom of them only occasionally deepened where an icy dagger of light stabbed them high up in the darkness. And it seemed to him now, as he wandered through the courts and alleys, that he had recaptured much of the zest of those days.

The whole morning he remained here, and then

walked back to luncheon. The hall of the hotel had, of course, been remodelled countless times, but he noticed that the concierge's booth—which he remembered so vividly—was still there, albeit fitted with ever so many more mechanical devices for creating noise and disorder. As he looked at this ludicrous Moorish hut, he quite expected to see, bobbing up from under the ledge, that malicious, meagre head and trunk of long ago, with its silly, if reptilian, quick sideways flicker of the eye. But the face that greeted him to-day from this well-known frame was quite otherwise : intelligent, if pale and rather weak-looking. It was an appearance which must certainly fail to arouse any such feeling of animosity as the other one had stirred up in him ; a head, moreover, that could be trusted to arrange things, undedicated to the god of Muddle. Yet as the porter looked at him, with the steady, inquiring gaze of the good hotel servant, Tristram was sure that he had seen him before—before and under different circumstances. The rather plaintive intonation of the voice, speaking such accurate and copious French, surely he had heard that before, too, somewhere ? But the identification, lurking at the back of his mind, escaped him—and the feeling passed away. No doubt it was the long journey—nevertheless, all through this last golden afternoon the impression returned vaguely at intervals, fluttered underneath all his thinking, and would not be caught.

He did not move from the plateau, for the day was

so well suited to it that he was loth to drive down below. He had seen the Cathedral so often, and there were still two more days here in which to revisit the various sights of the town. The few narrow streets at the back of the Alhambra were invitingly cool, and he strolled down them, for he wanted to find the *fonda* in which he had stayed : and again he wondered whether it was possible that the fat and charming proprietress could still be alive ? By this time she must surely have been removed out of that pungent cloud which her cooking ever created for her, so that her majesty could be seen through it amid the sunset glow of stoves and fires but dimly, like a goddess on the dark but roseate ceiling of some eighteenth-century Italian palace : but might she not, perhaps, be found spending a peaceful old age in her garden of white irises, and looking away with faded eyes toward the flashing white wings of the mountains ? However, he could not find it. The inn must have disappeared— but then it was over forty years ago. He gave up searching for it, and, instead, visited the gardens of the Generalife, sheltered by those high, golden downs, for which he had formerly felt such a repulsion.

The evening was drawing on. Once more he waited to see the sunset from the terrace, and then, as dusk came seeping up from the valleys, he retraced his steps through the wood to the hotel. He meant to rest on his bed for an hour or so before dressing for dinner. It had been rather a hard day, notwithstanding its leisureliness. But arrived in his sitting-room, he changed his mind. Despite its oriental absurdity, it looked so comfortable that he decided to sit down in an armchair and read. After telling his valet that he would ring when he wanted him, and would probably dress at about eight o'clock, he searched for books. Buried under the resplendent pile of his Spanish novels, lay— he had overlooked it hitherto—" Ring Down " ; one of his earliest and best books. And, because many years had passed since he had even glanced at it, because he had so lately been engaged in trying to return to this identical vein, he began to read it, though inwardly rather dreading the comparison which it must evoke in his mind. Yet as he read on, this novel caused him more pleasure than bitterness, while at the same time, he experienced a sense of utter disassociation from it. He could admit freely that there were qualities in it not to be found in his later work ; but he wondered how he had ever mastered this particular vein and subject, how and under what conditions he had written this remarkable book, for none of the labours of its composition remained with him. How curious it was, the way in which once a book appeared, clothed and printed, the author felt so little responsibility for his offspring !

It was the first time a book of his had ever enthralled him. It absorbed his interest until he was conscious of nothing else. Certainly there filtered to him through it nothing of the dislike for this room that had disturbed him during the previous evening. Precisely how long he sat there, I do not know. He had read—but one remembers how swift a reader he was—some one hundred and twenty pages, when he was startled out of this other existence that himself had inspired, out of moving through this other world of which himself had been the creating god, by a loud knock at the door. So actual was his participation in this other life, that it was as though the abrupt rapping called him back from a great distance. Indeed, his physical response to it was quicker than his mental one, for his heart gave an automatic leap and bump at the sound, as if in fright, and he heard his voice—although it seemed a long way off—shout, " Come in." The pseudo-oriental lights in the room were softly veiled ; but a single shade had somehow become tilted to one side, and its lamp threw down an intense beam of hot light upon the door.

It was thrown open, and the concierge entered, saying, " The gentleman to see you, sir." But it was the porter, his head thus illumined from above, rather than this unexpected visitor, who first held Tristram's attention. With a sensation of nausea, as though an invisible but iron fist had hit him in the diaphragm, at last he grasped the fluttering memory, or association, that had been eluding him all the afternoon. Of course it was ! He had been sure from the beginning that he had seen this face before, and now he recognised it. It was that of the whining, piteous child, whom many years ago he had seen so often walking in the wood, hand in hand with its villainous, black-mantilla'd French mother. However, the concierge, unconcerned and grave, appeared quite ignorant of the effect he was making. But, masked by this surprise, a much deadlier one was in waiting. The porter retired, and the stranger advanced into his place. It was only now, really, that Tristram began to puzzle over his visitor. Up till then his mind had been concerned, to the exclusion of everything else, with the identity of the concierge. But who could be coming to see him at this hour, and in this place? Who could it be? He looked up, and saw standing there a tall, young figure, his gold hair shining under the light, the narrowing, upward-slanting and deep blue eyes fixed upon his and flashing out a whole fire of contempt and hatred; a tall young figure, every line instinct with beauty, pride and genius. The prosperous, famous, elderly man sat there not stirring, without a movement, though the book he had been reading fell from his hand with a clatter down upon the floor; sat there, gazing at this apparition. What actually took place, who will ever know? But certainly into those moments was concentrated a lifetime of terror and mystery, and of a growing materialism that had been shattered at a blow. The past came toward him, as might a charging bull, in one overwhelming rush. And it was in that familiar welter of years and deeds that Tristram Orlander went down; went down, perhaps, too, in circumstances which he, in his young days, would have been the only writer to understand and appreciate.

*   *   *   *   *

There are many who believe that Sir Tristram Orlander was murdered. Others maintain that, however inexplicable and suspicious were the several incidents relating to his death, it was yet due to natural causes.

The story of it, as I have built it up, is mosaiced of many things. The first intimation I received of what had happened was to open a paper one day, and there read his obituary.* The protracted proceedings of the inquest, which subsequently filled the news for many days, I followed very carefully, and found that it was possible for me to interpret, in the light of the things which I already knew, several of the curious details which were then revealed and which to others must have then appeared incomprehensible.

No one disputes that a young stranger was shown up to room No. 12 (A). That is beyond question. Some suspicion, it is true, might have fallen upon the porter, but for the fortunate accident that two or three people saw the young man enter the hall. Indeed, he was of so striking an appearance that their descriptions of him were far more definite, particular, and concurrent than is usual with witnesses. Moreover, on their way to the room, the concierge and the stranger he was conducting passed Tristram's valet, who saw them both go into his master's room. He offered to lead the stranger in,

* Reprinted on page 306.

but the concierge insisted on doing it. As he came out, the porter talked to the valet for several minutes. Both of them had been struck by the likeness between the famous novelist and his visitor. The valet, who was devoted to Tristram and had been in his service for many years, wondered who it could be, as he was sure that his master was not expecting any callers. The concierge told him at the time, and afterward repeated on oath, that when asked for his name, the young man replied, " Same name—Tristram Orlander—*Mr*. Tristram Orlander, though. He's expecting me, I believe."

Thus, it was not surprising, when this fact transpired, that the conviction grew up and flourished everywhere that Sir Tristram had been murdered by an illegitimate son : a rumour that caused needless pain to his widow. But actually this belief was in any case quite opposite to that of the doctors : for expert medical opinion was, on the whole, satisfied that the dead man did not meet his end through violence, the discoloured patches on his neck, which somewhat resembled the marks produced by strangulation, being due, not to the pressure of human fingers, but to the character of the stroke or apoplexy which had seized on him.

Nevertheless, it was queer, people said, that the stranger, if guiltless, had never come forward to prove his innocence. Search was everywhere made for him, a stranger, an Englishman of remarkable appearance, in Spain. The description of him was so circumstantial

and minute that surely even the Spanish police could
hardly—for there had been no time for him to escape
—have failed to detain him had he existed. But during
these endless proceedings, all the time, my thoughts
went back to the spring when Tristram first visited
Granada—his theories there, and his dreams. I remembered so well his saying that the question, once formed,
received its answer, in events as much as in words.
And as, day by day, I followed the evidence, I was even
more struck by the likenesses than by the discrepancies
between this and the earlier encounter there, which he
had related to me (indeed the very existence of such
discrepancies as there were, was, according to his
theory, an essential part of any such occurrence) until
I began to believe that I held the key to this mystery.
Thus, when, for instance, I learned, through reading
the Spanish papers, that the concierge—a smudged
photograph of whom was inset—would be remembered
as a small boy by all visitors to Granada in former
days, since he and his mother, a Frenchwoman now
dead, had been well-known figures there, always to be
seen walking through the Alhambra wood, my belief
deepened into certainty. I remembered the dream, as
Tristram had told it me. I looked it up in my journal.
So the details piled themselves up, one on the top of
another.

In occurrences of this kind* there is little use in
discussing " probability." It is best dismissed from
the mind, kept for things more rational. To me there

seems nothing more strange in the story my late friend told me, and in its sequel, than in the fact, visible to all, that for a lifetime a man is dogged by his own shadow. Indeed, of two individuals, the man who cast no shadow would be the one who inspired fear in us.

THE END

EXTRACT FROM GOETHE'S MEMOIRS, ETC.

Notwithstanding the anxiety and extreme affliction I felt, I could not withstand the desire of seeing Frederica once more : it was a cruel day to us, and its circumstances will never be effaced from my memory. When I had mounted my horse and offered my hand for the last time, I saw tears swimming in her eyes, and my heart suffered as much as hers. I proceeded along a path that leads to Drusenheim, when a strange vision, which must have been a presentiment, suddenly disturbed my mind. *I thought I saw my own image advancing towards me on horseback* in the same road. The figure wore a grey coat with gold lace, such as I had never worn. I awoke from this dream, and the vision disappeared. It is singular enough that eight years after, as I was going to see Frederica once more, *I found myself in the same road, dressed as I had dreamed, and wearing such a coat,* accidentally and without having chosen it.

From the Story of San Michele by Axel Munthe.

One day he (de Maupassant) told me that while he was sitting at his writing-table hard at work on his new novel he had been greatly surprised to see a stranger enter his study notwithstanding the severe vigilance of his valet. The stranger had sat down opposite him at the writing-table and began to dictate to him what he was about to write. He was just going to ring for François to have him turned out when he saw to his horror that the stranger was himself.

" It is with deep regret that we have to announce the death of Sir Tristram Orlander, famous novelist and man of letters. This tragic event took place last evening under mysterious circumstances, of which the details are not yet fully disclosed, in a hotel in Granada, where he was staying in search of health and rest. That certain things connected with Sir Tristram's death should be suspicious, will undoubtedly serve only to deepen the sorrow which the whole nation will experience at news of the loss it has sustained and to render yet more heartfelt the sympathy which it will offer without stint to a grieving widow. Lady Orlander, who was warned by telegram, left London late last night for Spain.

" Tristram Wellesley Orlander was born in Ireland on October the 18th, 1894, the only offspring of his parents, who died while he was still a boy. He was the last of an ancient stock, long noted in the annals of Irish history for the distinguished record of their political and military service. At school, it is unnecessary to say, he was singled out by his enthusiasm for all games, and thus rapidly became a favourite with boys and masters. Educated like his forebears at Eton, seldom had there dwelt in those ancient courts of culture a more popular boy, and when he passed on to

Oxford he left behind him a void which it was difficult to fill. Leaving Oxford at the outbreak of the Little World War in 1914, he was, to his chagrin, as he was wont to relate in after years, condemned as unfit for military service, and assigned to a post in his native country. He returned to London on duty in 1917. Already he had struck out for himself. The qualities that had so often served him on football-field and cricket-pitch, again asserted themselves, and when peace came, as eventually it did come, finding the Army already forbidden to him as a career by his health, and that politics no longer attracted him, he was already laying the foundations of a very remarkable literary career.

" But his life was not easy. His earlier writings were marred by a morbid and eccentric tone, the influence no doubt of that literary coterie in which he found himself. His poems especially—though they gave him fame and popularity in certain rather precious circles, where, indeed, they still enjoy an artificial esteem—were particularly disappointing in this respect, and contrived to prejudice their writer in the eyes of the great public. And though the critics were not deceived by these youthful lapses and always watched the young author's career with interest, there were few who guessed at that time the extent to which Tristram Orlander would make good.

" There is something, it may be said, appropriate, if tragic, in Destiny's choosing of this great novelist's death place, for it was in Spain, and more particularly in Andalusia that Tristram Orlander found himself. His first Spanish novel was published in 1929, and it is safe to say that never with one book did any writer make such a host of friends. The other volumes of 'The Spanish Saga,' as it is called, thereafter appeared successively at rapid intervals, and created a vogue which has never died. Indeed, it will be recalled by many that at the meeting of the International Hotel-keepers' Union in London in 1958, Sir Tristram was requested to take the Chair, for it was stated that his books had done more to popularise Spain than all the cheap tickets ever issued or exhibitions ever held.

"The nation, however, will mourn in Sir Tristram Orlander, not only a great writer, but a great public figure. His interests were extremely varied, his good deeds innumerable. Wherever the English tongue was spoken, he was looked up to, and his name was revered. He was created a Knight of the British Empire for his services to literature in 1948, while he later obtained a further high honour by being created a Knight of the Royal Elizabethan Order for his services during the late Great War (1953-57). In 1958 he attended the Brooklyn Peace Conference as the official Peace Delegate representing English Literature. There he entertained largly and made countless friends. A number of academic distinctions, both foreign and British, were conferred on him in later years.

"Sir Tristram, who dies without issue, married in

June, 1937, Mary, daughter of the late Robert Grosse-
heimer, the famous tobacco-king and philanthropist."

A correspondent writes, " While the Nation honours
the dead, and mourns in Tristram Orlander one of her
chiefs, we, his friends, undergo a sensation of irre-
parable loss. And yet we hesitate thus arrogantly to
proclaim ourselves his friends, when there was such a
mighty host of them, known and unknown to him. All
his readers, I think, were his friends, and all dumb
animals, all little winged things. He was a man every
Englishman must like, for, though in his earlier years
he had been associated with writers of a different
calibre, there was nothing of affectation about this Englishman . . . . for though he was Irish, he was English
too. A man of singular charm, he made friends wherever he went, whether it was on his yacht to Deau-
ville, on the Riviera, or in the desert, and with his
passing many feel that a light has passed out of their
lives. A. W."